AN IMPERIAL GAMBIT

WARDENS OF ISSALIA, BOOK THREE

JEFFREY L. KOHANEK

FALLBRANDT PRESS

ISBN: 978-1-949382-04-4

PUBLISHED BY JEFFREY L. KOHANEK and FALLBRANDT PRESS

www.JeffreyLKohanek.com

BOOKS BY JEFFREY L. KOHANEK

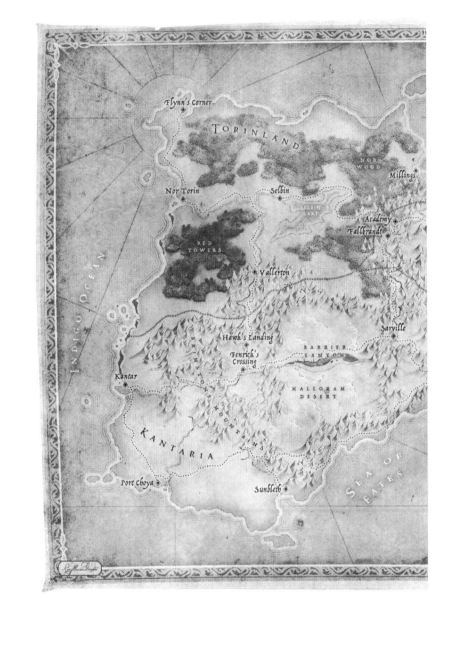

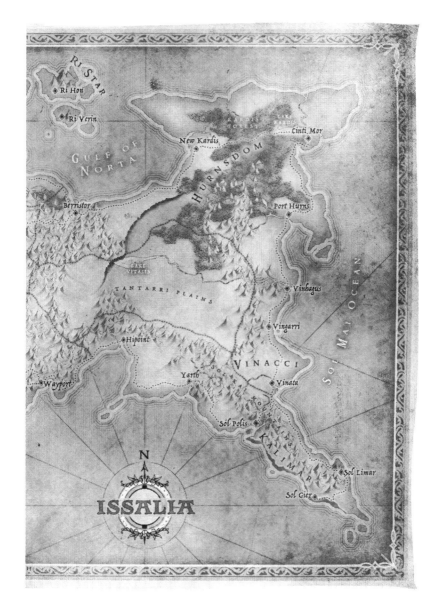

JOURNAL ENTRY

The game is afoot – a game like no other. The world is my Ratio Bellicus board. The game pieces are real people with hopes and dreams and lives they believe they control. I know the truth of it – a truth my peers don't even acknowledge.

While my enemy hides their pieces from me, I know the hand that moves them. In that knowledge, I have an advantage. My opponent's motivation remains clear and they all believe in that clarity. They see Chaos as evil. I see it as a tool, not so different from a knife. A knife can carve beauty from wood, slice an apple, or stab someone through the heart. How the tool is used defines its purpose. Magic is no different.

To my opponent, my hand remains hidden – my game pieces and their abilities unknown to them. Within this subterfuge, I study and consider, and I scheme. I shift a game piece here and move another there. The game pieces used are as important as the schemes guiding them.

My prodigy and her counterpart now dwell inside enemy headquarters, feeding from a well of misguided trust as they prepare for an act of betrayal. Sometimes, piercing your opponent's heart actually becomes the knife's purpose.

There may soon come a time where I become an active participant rather than simply the hand that directs others. When the time comes, my enemy

Journal Entry

best beware that I am well versed in knives and betrayal. Beware the hidden assassin, for a successful Imperial Gambit hinges on the placement of such a game piece.

From the journals of Master Espion, Delvin Garber

PROLOGUE

Six Years Ago

With a meaty fist gripping the back of his shirt, Ikonis stumbled to one knee and splashed down in the narrow ditch. He pinched his nose at the revolting smell and began to gag. The guard lifted Iko to his feet and chuckled. The men surrounding the nearby fire laughed with him.

"You'd think growing up in this dump would've taught you to step over the runoff from the jakes," the man said aloud, stirring another round of laughter.

"Good one, Scully," one of the guards sitting beside the fire remarked.

Jerking the back of Iko's tunic, Scully hurried him past the fire. Iko grimaced, knowing that his leg would now stink until he could clean it. *Scant chance of that happening tonight,* he thought.

As the firelight faded behind them, the darkness rushed in. Clouds above masked the stars and left the canyon darker than normal – so dark that Iko found himself imagining things in the darkness. Evil things. Things that could kill as quick as thought. Yet, he thanked Issal for the darkness. It improved his chances of surviving the night. More than any other night, this one would determine the path of his life – if a path even remained come morning.

With a hand pressed against his back, Scully guided Iko so fast that he had to rush his steps to avoid falling face first. In the darkness, he focused on the ground a stride ahead to avoid any other missteps.

A building materialized, the pale walls flickering dimly from the distant fire. When Iko reached the door, Scully pulled him aside. The guard's keys jingled as he fumbled for the right one. A moment later, the key slid into the lock and it clicked. With a *bang*, the guard shoved the door open, and pale blue light bled from the interior. He spun Iko around and used a key to unlock the shackles about the boy's wrists. Iko felt warm breath on his neck when Scully leaned close.

"Remember exactly what I told you," Scully whispered before shoving Iko in.

Stumbling forward, Iko caught himself by the foot of a bed, narrowly avoiding falling. He stood and turned toward the open door.

The guard bellowed. "In the future, don't drink so much water. I don't enjoy these late night latrine runs. Next time, I might make you wait until morning." Scully's gaze swept across the prisoners in the bunkhouse, forty-eight in total, and he bellowed. "Get to bed, you scum! We have a long day in the mines tomorrow." He laughed as he pulled the door closed and locked it.

Iko turned to find his mother in the middle of the room, standing beside Kardan. The others began to gather around the pair as they always had. Iko strode down the aisle, the waiting crowd splitting to create a path for him. At the center, surrounded by adults ranging from thirty summers to beyond sixty, thirteen-year-old Iko found all eyes on him.

"What did Sculdin say?" His mother asked.

"Tonight's the night. After the fire has died down and the guards are asleep." Iko dug into the waistline of his tattered trousers, lifting his prize high for everyone to see. "I have a copy of the bunkhouse key. Once all is quiet, I am to climb out the east window. Scully said that the bars have been pried loose. We should be able to knock them free so I can squeeze through. Once outside, I am to unlock the doors, but everyone is to remain in the bunkhouse until the signal."

"Very good, Ikonis," she crooned while rubbing his dark, unkempt hair. "What exactly is the signal?"

Iko shrugged. "I'm not sure, mother. He said we would know when it came. Once we hear it, we must take the guards down quickly."

His mother gave him a tight smile and a nod before she turned toward the people clustered around them. "You heard Ikonis. I suggest you get some rest, but be ready for the call. When it comes, we will have a small window to act. Everything hinges on tonight."

The bunkhouse was dark, lit only by a waning glowlamp in the corner. Iko stood on his bed, peering out the window. Conversation among the guards had ended hours earlier, along with the glow of the fire, which had faded to orange embers. Shadows slipped past, eclipsing the light as a pair of guards walked toward the wall.

"It is time, Iko," his mother whispered.

He turned toward her and climbed off the bed to stare into her dark eyes, now at the same height as his own. Given another year, he would be taller than his mother and perhaps as tall as his father one day. He hoped to live that long. Tonight, his future balanced on a blade, threatening to fall in either direction – death or freedom. *Odd,* he thought. *Both choices are a form of freedom.* Either way, he would never work in the mines again.

Iko gripped the key in his fist. "I'm ready, Mother."

"I believe in you, Ikonis. May Issal watch over you."

With a deep breath, he crossed the room to the window where Kardan waited.

"Give me a moment." Kardan turned and gripped one of the thick iron rods that barred the window. "The bars are loose, as the man said."

Kardan's biceps bulged as he began applying pressure. Despite an age approaching fifty summers, the former master paladin retained his strength, hardened by more than a decade of laboring in the mines. The first bar snapped off and Kardan dropped it on the empty bed beside him. After pulling two more bars free, Kardan strained against the third, but it would not budge.

"I think I can fit," Iko said.

The man appraised Iko with narrowed eyes before nodding. "Come here. I'll lift you."

Iko moved closer and Kardan lifted him, flipping him around so his calloused feet fit through the bars first.

"You stink, boy," Kardan whispered.

"Sorry," Iko said as the man fed him through the window. "I slipped in the latrine ditch."

When his hips were through, Iko lowered his legs toward the ground while Kardan supported him. Iko then lifted his arms over his head to make himself narrow. Even then, Kardan had to push against Iko's head to squeeze him through. Suddenly freed, Iko fell to his feet and landed on his rear in the sand, his fist still clenching their key to freedom.

He stood and snuck along the building before peeking around the front. Although Iko knew that guards patrolled the top of the wall, he couldn't see them in the darkness – the same darkness that would mask his own movement.

Hugging the wall, Iko crept to the door and slid the key into the lock. With a turn and some pressure, it clicked. He immediately snuck back around the corner and – remaining on his toes for stealthy foot-steps – ran to the next building.

With the second door unlocked, he moved to the third. Far from the fire, the darkness held firm, his surroundings nothing but shadows and gloom. Anyone, or anything, could be right beside him and Iko wouldn't know it. Thoughts of monsters or demons or some-thing even worse began to creep into his head and sent his pulse pounding. He stopped with his back against the wall of the third bunkhouse and waited for his nerves to calm. When he was about to move to the fourth building, a rustling sound arose from ahead. Terror seized him, clenched a firm grip around his throat, and held his breath captive.

Footsteps came from behind the fourth building, and shadows shifted in the darkness. Two guards strolled across the yard, their silhouettes barely visible. The guards walked right past Iko, close enough for him to catch a whiff of their unwashed bodies.

"What's that smell?" one man asked. "Did you soil yourself?"

Iko almost gasped when he realized that they smelled the soiled leg of his trousers.

The other man snorted. "Not me. I thought it was you."

They were past him now.

"You should try standing downwind from yourself. You're no flower, you know."

"How am I supposed to stand downwind from myself?"

"I dunno."

"Yeah. Next time, think before you say something so stupid."

Their voices faded in the distance. Iko released his breath and found himself panting, his heart racing. *If I had not stopped, I would have run right into them.*

He shook his head to clear it. *Focus,* he told himself as he padded toward the last building. When he reached it, he put his back to the wall and peered around the corner. Darkness...until light abruptly flared from behind him.

Iko spun around as an explosion of green flame blasted the prison wall apart. Despite the wall standing hundreds of feet away, the force of the blast washed over him – a deep thump followed by a wave of heat that made him cover his face. He lowered his arm to find a cloud of smoke and dust, swirling to reveal a massive gap in the wall – a gap filled with orange flames. Scattered burning debris lay throughout the compound.

The door to the first bunkhouse opened, and prisoners poured from the building. Kardan and his mother ran to the nearest bunkhouse and opened the door as Iko realized he had yet to unlock the fourth building. He scrambled to the door, inserted the key, twisted, and threw the door open.

"We are taking the prison!" Iko screamed. "Come out and fight for your freedom!"

The people inside sat up from their beds and stared toward Iko with wide eyes and gaping mouths. In seconds, those expressions morphed into something Iko had never before seen on those faces, not in the entire thirteen years he had spent with them: hope. They scrambled out of bed and barreled toward the door.

Iko turned and ran ahead of the mob, joining the others as they poured from the bunkhouses. All of a sudden, a man in front of Iko lurched, spun about, and fell with an arrow in his chest. The woman to his right stumbled to her knees, choking on the arrow in her throat. Iko's gaze went to the wall, and he found guards upon it, loosing arrows toward the crowd.

The door to the guard barracks opened and armed men emerged. The mob hit them in a flash. Prisoners died, but they greatly outnumbered the guards. Swords from the dead guards appeared in prisoners' hands. Arrows struck more prisoners – in the arm, in the shoulder, in the head. Iko then spotted another guard atop the wall. The new guard raised a bow and fired, taking out the nearest bowman. It was Sculdin.

Sculdin ran along the wall and shot again, taking out another bowman. Before he could kill the third, the man noticed Sculdin, turned, and fired, the arrow striking Sculdin in the shoulder. Sculdin's bow fell from the wall and a knife appeared in his other hand. He threw it, the blade spinning until it struck the last bowman in the forehead. Iko turned away as the guard fell from the ramparts.

Eight more guards rushed out the door at the far end of the guard barracks. Among them was the one Iko feared the most: the arcanist.

The arcanist's eyes glowed bright red – a sign of his dark magic coming to bear. A rune drawn on the hand of a guard beside the arcanist flared with a crimson hue, glowing, pulsing…fading.

The guard stumbled and then righted himself. A grin appeared on his face. Twisted. Evil. Although the guard stood a hundred feet away, Iko found himself backing up. The guard leaped, and Iko's jaw dropped. When the man landed in front of Iko, he swept his sword in a wide arc – the blade's motion seeming as if it had cut through nothing but air. The four prisoners standing before the guard fell, their bodies cleaved in two.

Iko blinked and wiped the blood splatter from his face. He backed away, panting as the man advanced, the guard's face darkened by shadow as the fires burned behind him. The man's blade lifted high, and Iko knew he would die. A shove drove him sideways as the blade fell, the sword taking the arm off the man who had pushed Iko aside.

The Chaos-charged guard lifted his face toward the sky and released a mighty, frightening roar. He then leaped impossibly high, landed among another cluster of prisoners, and tore through them as if they were paper. A burst forward and the ensorcelled guard's shield struck a prisoner hard enough that he flew into another cluster of prisoners, taking ten down with him, their bodies broken. Another lunge and a sweep of the sword sent body parts spinning through the air. The man was a demon possessed – a killing machine.

Iko saw a sword at his feet. Gritting his teeth, he picked up the heavy blade, and he ran. He would stop this man powered by evil magic. He would see the end of Chaos.

With all his might, Iko lifted the sword before him as he charged the magic-enhanced guard from behind. When it struck, the tip bit into the man's back, and Iko stumbled to his knees. The man staggered forward and then swept a deadly backstroke, the sword sailing over Iko's head. The guard looked down, their eyes meeting, the man's rage sliding away. He lowered his sword, and the rage in his eyes cooled. Iko had not recognized him in the dark, but the Chaos-charged man was Burns – a guard he knew well, a guard he had hated for years.

"I'm sorry about your father, Ikonis," Burns said. "Tell him for me, for you are about to join him."

The man raised his sword and chopped down. Iko closed his eyes and heard a scream that was not his own. He opened them to find Burns holding the stump of his wrist. A blade flashed and struck the guard's neck, taking his head off clean. The guard's body collapsed, and Iko turned to find Kardan standing over him with a sword in his hand.

Their eyes met and Kardan gave Iko a nod. "For your father."

Caught up in the emotion and death surrounding him, tears blurred Iko's eyes. He wiped them away to find Kardan's hand extended toward him. With Kardan's help, Iko stood and surveyed the situation. Dozens lay dead, but far more still stood. Only prisoners remained. Or rather, only the liberated remained.

His mother was kneeling on the ground beside Tom Gambo. The man had lost an arm and was bleeding profusely. The blood flow stopped, the stump healing before Iko's eyes. His mother removed her hand from Gambo's forehead and stood.

Her gaze surveyed the surviving prisoners as they gathered. Kardan shifted to stand beside her.

Gripping Kardan's hand and holding it high, Iko's mother bellowed. "While the price was steep, we are free!"

A weak cheer rose up.

"This is not the end, it is merely a beginning." Varius spun about as she addressed the people surrounding her. "When the sun rises, we will be away. In our possession, we have enough food to complete our journey to Yarth, where we will begin to rebuild. The gold cache from this mine will secure what is required. The flash powder reserves we take will enable us to create weapons to combat Chaos. A new future has begun this night, a future with the Hand founding a new Empire – an Empire free of Chaos."

Another cheer arose, this one deafening.

As the freed people fell quiet, Iko's mother began visiting other wounded, healing those she could, blessing those she could not. The dead were gathered and thrown into the guardhouse, which was set on fire. It burned hot and lingered for hours.

It was a long night – a night of horrors, a night of hope, a night of change.

When the sun rose, it was a special day – the first day of Iko's life beyond the prison walls. He found himself on a wagon full of barrels and black rock that sparkled in the sunlight. Kardan was on one side of him, his mother on the other. When Kardan snapped the reins, the horses pulled the wagon across the compound yard and through the open gate. A half-dozen other wagons followed close behind, trailed by sixty-two people on foot.

As the destroyed prison wall faded from view, Iko found himself with a future to think on, something around which he could shape his life. In that moment, the first time he could actually consider such things, he found clarity. His goal was simple, yet daunting – build a better future as defined by his past. For his father, he would see the end of Chaos.

1

UNNECESSARY RISK

Curan coaxed Gorgant to a stop, the stallion stirring briefly before he settled.

"Easy, boy," Curan crooned as he slid to the ground.

There was a half-filled water trough and a stack of hay beside it, both welcome sights. In a hushed tone, he addressed the horse, which shifted his ears toward him.

"I prefer a bed tonight, so you must remain out here. Last night beneath that pine offered little sleep, and I could do without the needles for an evening." Curan's hand ran down the stallion's neck in a strong, smooth stroke. "Eat. Drink your fill. Do not stray. More importantly, bite anyone who comes near you. You are a Tantarri steed. They should fear you rather than they think they might profit from you."

Curan knew that Outlanders paid significant sums for Tantarri stock, as they should if people were allowed to purchase something so majestic. An odd thought. Yet, Tantarri horses were the fastest, the most intelligent – the best horses in Issalia. He eyed Gorgant's lines, the fall of his dark mane from his ears to his withers, the rippling muscles beneath the horse's grey coat. Horses were beautiful creatures, yet few could equal Gorgant's majesty. Curan was proud that the horse had chosen him as a worthy rider. When his stomach grumbled, Curan patted the horse and turned his attention toward the inn.

The Horned Frog was of wooden construction, similar to the other buildings in Sarville. Having two stories made the inn stand out from the other structures along the road – structures covered in shadow although the sky above remained bright blue.

The mid-afternoon sun hid beyond the tall peak to the west, leaving only the mountaintops to the east in direct sunlight. Clusters of deep green pines stood out amidst the red, orange, and yellow of leaf-trees covering the valley hillsides. Soon, few leaves would remain – the final resistance in the face of the coming winter.

A small village in the heart of the Skyspike Mountains, Sarville had a population measured in the dozens at best. In fact, Curan had seen only two people during his fifteen-mile approach from the mountain pass, both working in the fields just south of town. He closed his eyes and listened. Rather than hearing the sounds of a city, the rush of the river behind the inn filled the air, joined only by the chirping of birds perched in the tall pine across the road. Still dominated by nature, Sarville seemed a peaceful, lonely slice of humanity.

Despite his aversion to Outlanders, Curan forced himself up the steps to the covered porch, pushed the door open, and stepped inside, careful to duck as he passed through the doorway. Shadows lingered in the room, cast by the light coming through the windows at the front. The center of the room stood open but for a single post with a dormant glowlamp mounted on it. Tables lined three of the walls, and an open stairwell ran along the fourth wall. Beneath the stairwell, a lonely broom leaned in the corner, beside a door that appeared to lead to the kitchen. Quiet conversation came from the only occupied table. Four men, woodsmen of some sort, sat behind empty plates and spoke in hushed tones.

Curan crossed the room and chose an open table along the far wall. He shed his travel cloak and hung it over his chair before sitting so he faced the front door.

A young woman walked past him and placed mugs before the men seated beside the front window. She had brown hair, blue eyes, and a voluptuous figure framed by a cream-colored tunic, a tight brown vest that forced her chest to bulge, and a brown skirt that flowed around her ankles as she walked. In her early twenties, the woman was just a few years older than Curan. She collected the empty plates in one arm, spoke with the men for a moment, and disappeared into the kitchen. Moments later, she reappeared and stopped beside Curan's table.

Her gaze swept over him before settling on his face. "You're a big one. I bet you can eat your share."

Speaking to strangers – to Outlanders – still made Curan uncomfortable. However, his new life would require it so he forced the words out.

"I would like some food. Food and a bed."

She nodded. "I have roasted crowster and potatoes."

"That sounds wonderful."

"I'm assuming you can pay for it?" Her hand rested on her hip, her brow arched as she waited on his response.

Curan removed the coin purse from his belt and pulled out a gold piece. He held it toward her. "Will this cover it?"

The idea of exchanging coins for food was a foreign concept. He had seen his father do it during their trips to Nor Torin, but the last outing was three years past. Worse, he had never paid attention as to which coin had been used. When her eyes widened, Curan knew he had made a mistake.

"Well…" She smiled. "That'll get you as much food as you wish, along with a bed. Ale, too."

She reached for the coin with greed in her eyes. With reluctance, he let the woman take it, her fist clamping around it before she stuffed it into the neckline of her dress.

"My name is Mandy." She shifted closer, smoothed her skirt with one hand, and twirled her long brown hair with the other. "You're a fine looking young man. Perhaps you would enjoy some company as well?" The look she gave him – the half-masted eyelids, the knowing smile – he had seen it before from the girls in Mondomi, the ones who saw sex as a game. Swallowing hard, his gaze shifted toward the table.

"Um…not tonight. Just the food and a bed, please."

"Alright. If you're sure…" Her tone taunted him, as if he were passing on the chance of a lifetime. "Let me know if you change your mind."

She slipped away, off toward the door beneath the stairs.

When Curan looked up, he found the men at the occupied table staring in his direction. All four had runes marking their foreheads, three of them identical to the others while the fourth had one of a different sort. Curan didn't know what the runes represented, only that they were a relic of the past – a lingering reminder of the Empire that once ruled Issalia. The glares directed toward Curan made him wary, and his gaze flicked to the front door, far across the room. When his focus returned to the men, he found them huddled in conversation with one leaning over the table.

The kitchen door opened, and Mandy appeared with a mug in her fist. She sauntered to Curan's table and placed the ale before him. "Drink up. You'll need your energy." Her smile wreaked of innuendo.

"I...I didn't order this."

"Nonsense. You've been traveling, and you need to drink something." She pointed toward the tankard as foam ran down the side. "Besides, I'll feel guilty if you don't drink it."

"All right." Curan lifted the mug and took a drink, the cool bubbles rolling down his throat. The ale lacked the sweet aroma that accompanied Tantarri pumpkin ale, but it was still refreshing. "Thank you."

She smiled and glided toward the kitchen, her hips swaying overtly as his eyes followed. When she disappeared, he turned and found the four men approaching. Two were oversized, burly men with thick beards – one black, the other brown. A third man stood tall, with a lean frame. The fourth was shorter than the rest, sporting a shorn scalp and a brown goatee, his leather vest revealing well-muscled arms. The short man addressed Curan.

"Hey, boy. What's with the body art?" The man gestured toward the ink on Curan's arms, which depicted intertwined runes and images. "You one of those Tantarri?"

Curan's eyes narrowed as he considered his response. "Perhaps I am one of those Tantarri. Why should that matter?"

The man grimaced as his eyes shifted toward Curan's hair. Unlike the rest of his people, Curan's hair was light brown, his eyes blue. Thanks to his father, he was unlike his people in numerous ways.

"We folk in the Greenway don't care much for those who don't follow Issal. If you're one of those heathen Tantarri, you've found your way into the wrong village."

Curan sighed. He knew where the conversation would lead.

"Listen. I've been riding for the past two days. I'm exhausted. I just wish to eat and get a good night's sleep." He reached his long, muscled arm out and patted the short man's shoulder. "I'll be happy to buy you each an ale if you will let me be."

One of the burly men snorted while his tall companion blinked at the idea. The short one sneered with his response.

"We don't want your ale, *boy*. We want you out of Sarville. But first, leave your coin purse on the table."

Inhaling with long, slow breath while sporting a contemplative expression, Curan lifted his coin purse in one hand, showing it to the short man as he stood. Rising to his full height of six and a half feet, Curan clenched his fist around the coin purse. The short man stared at it with a furrowed brow. In a flash, Curan's fist burst forward, smashed into the man's nose, and sent him staggering backward into his companions. Curan spun toward the kitchen door, tossed his coin purse on the table, and grabbed the broom, holding it before him as he turned toward his foes.

The two burly men stood their companion upright while the short man held his hand to his face and blinked the tears from his eyes. When he pulled his hand away, he glared at his crimson streaked fingers – evidence of the blood running from his nose.

"You're going to get it, now," the man sneered.

The four men separated, one burly man shifting to each side of Curan while the tall and short one stood in front of him. There was only one way out of the situation, so Curan gave himself to his training: when confronted by a superior force, attack first to eliminate a coordinated attack by your opponents.

With a thrust, Curan drove the broom handle into the black-bearded man's stomach, which elicited a grunt. He then feinted toward the tall man, who leaped backward, and smashed the broomstick across the scalp of his shortest opponent. The stick broke in half, sending a spray of splinters in the air as the short man staggered to one knee. The big brown-bearded man to Curan's right came at him with a meaty fist. Curan ducked beneath the blow and drove the splintered end of the broomstick into the man's thigh.

"Argh!" the man cried out as he stumbled backward.

Sensing movement behind him, Curan bent and thrust his foot backward, driving his heel into black beard's stomach. He spun, following with a roundhouse punch. His fist struck the bent-over man's temple and sent him careening to his hands and knees.

The tall one's fist flashed toward Curan's face, and Curan dodged just enough to receive a glancing blow across his cheek and ear. Raising his arm to block the next punch, Curan grabbed the tall man's tunic and pulled backward with all his might as he dropped to the floor. The man's head smashed into the kitchen door with enough force that it cracked the frame...and his head. He collapsed to the floor, bloody and unconscious.

Seated on the floor, Curan found the short man coming at him with a fist cocked back for a massive punch. Curan dodged to the side and the punch missed, instead striking the doorframe. Staggering backward, the man held his broken hand by the wrist while howling in pain. Before the short man could escape his range, Curan scissored his legs – one high, one low – with the man's leg between them, sending him crashing to the floor.

Curan stood and scrambled past his downed opponents to create space. With his hands ready to fight, he surveyed the room.

The brown-bearded man had his tunic off, exposing a hair-covered, overweight torso. The man yanked the broken broomstick from his leg, his face in a grimace as blood welled up from the wound. He wrapped his tunic about the leg and began to tie it off.

Near the door, the tall man lay unconscious, blood tracking across his forehead and pooling on the floor. The short man sat beside the tall one, his blood-covered face scowling at Curan while he held his wrist. His hand was swollen, the skin torn open, fingers bent into a useless claw.

The black-bearded man sat on the floor with one arm on Curan's chair, his other hand holding his head. Based on the distant look in his eyes, he was in no shape to fight.

Curan shifted toward the table to gather his cloak and coin purse. The kitchen door swung open as the barmaid emerged with a plate of food. She paused to stare down at the four men before glancing toward Curan.

He gave her an apologetic look. "I'm sorry about the mess. I'll just take the food with me. Keep the gold."

A cool mountain breeze blew from the north and pushed Curan's hood back, exposing his face to the gray skies above. He had worn his hood up the entire day in hope of avoiding any additional trouble. The fight in Sarville was not something he relished – an unnecessary risk with nothing to gain. Recalling the inn left him longing for the bed he had purchased for the night – a night he had, instead, spent sleeping poorly on the forest floor a few miles outside of town.

Waking with the breaking dawn, Curan had taken the road north, along the valley that many called The Greenway. Tall snowcapped peaks watched over him during the journey. The snow would undoubtedly extend throughout the valley once it was in the grasp of winter.

Curan decided not to stop and eat when he reached Fallbrandt, nor did he speak to any who had passed him. With his hood down and a grim expression that warned others away, he continued through town with only his destination in mind, eager to reach it before the gray sky drew dark.

Moving at a fast trot along the forest road, Fallbrandt was soon miles behind him. He came to a large clearing, surrounded by forest with a tree-lined road splitting the center. After a brief glance toward the military academy to the east, Curan focused on the sprawling structure ahead, its form appearing more clearly as the trees beside the road fell away.

The complex consisted of blocky buildings at the center and long wings that extended toward the mountains to the east and west. It was the largest structure Curan had ever seen – even bigger than the castle in Nor Torin. Regardless, the monolithic building looming over the rear of the complex is what demanded his attention. *I was sure father was exaggerating when he described it, but he may have been understating, instead.*

With the nudge of Curan's knee, Gorgant turned down the road encircling the eastern side of the fabled Fallbrandt Academy of Magic and Engineering. The horse continued past the circular tower that terminated the eastern wing and past a building that Curan assumed was the arena. He recalled stories of his father's days at the academy, before the new military school even existed. Curan's father remained somewhat of a legend at the school, the only novice to defeat all other paladin trainees and win the vaunted Arena Challenge. Even if he had not made a name for himself in the Arena, his father's exploits on the battlefield would have rectified the situation. Curan wondered if his new role would offer the same opportunity. Further, he hoped that he might live up to such expectations.

When Gorgant cleared the arena, the full majesty of the Arcane Ward came into view. An ominous gray tower, twelve stories tall and windowless, the Ward was unlike any building Curan had ever seen. Something about the structure made it seem as if it were imposing its will upon the valley, demanding everyone's attention, yet threatening anyone who dare approach it. Rather than an exaggeration, his father's description of the Ward actually paled to seeing it in reality.

The gravel road led Curan to a cobblestone courtyard nestled between the school, the tower, and the thirty-foot-tall wall connecting them. Two guards stood beside the arched black doors that led to the tower, watching him warily. Another stood beside the black gates to the training yard behind it, holding a spiked halberd with a massive blade. Curan frowned at it, wondering how the weight of the blade didn't force it to tip away from the man's grip.

Squeezing his heels, Curan drew Gorgant to a stop. He slid to the ground and put his hand on Gorgant's neck, the stallion shadowing him as he approached the guard beside the gate.

"This area is forbidden," said a guard in the black and gold armor.

"Yes. I am aware," Curan replied. "I have been invited here by Master Hedgewick."

"Do you have papers?"

"No."

The guard grimaced. "How do you expect me to let you in?"

"Send someone to find Hedgewick. He knows me."

"And, your name is?"

"I am Curan DeSanus. My father is Cameron DeSanus – my mother, Head Clanswoman of the Tantarri. I am here to become a warden."

2
POTENTIAL

Cassilyn Talenz sat upon a pillow, her legs crossed, her palms facing up while her wrists rested on her knees. Although her eyes were open, she remained locked in a state of meditation. The skill was something unique to Cassie – an ability to divide her mind such that she had an awareness of her surroundings while maintaining her connection with Order. Before her brother left the Ward, Cassie had discovered a new Chaos rune while conducting this waking trance. In the weeks that had passed since Brandt left, her attempts to repeat the process and discover another rune had yielded nothing but frustration.

From her dimly lit corner of the Atrium, Cassie watched Curan, ICON's newest recruit, training under a Power augmentation. Tall and muscular, the Tantarri cut an impressive figure in his black training vest and tight brown breeches. He took two steps and leaped impossibly high to land upon a fourth-story platform with a *thud*.

Even though it was late morning, the overcast autumn sky offered limited light and made it difficult to see him among the twisting construction of beams, poles, and ropes that formed the Jungle. Movement caught her attention when Curan appeared at the far end of the platform. He then jumped off, flipped once, and dropped to the stone floor, his knees bending to a squat as he landed. With a burst, he launched himself forward, and swung his wooden sword at a practice dummy standing a hundred feet away.

Made from thick bundles of hay, bound with rope and cloth, the ten-foot-tall dummy weighed almost five hundred pounds. The teen's magic-enhanced strength made it appear far, far lighter. When the sword struck the dummy, a spray of loose straw blasted from each end and sent the dummy spinning through the air. If not for the Elastic augmentation infused in the wooden sword, it certainly would have shattered upon impact. The dummy crashed to the floor twenty feet away and continued tumbling until it struck a wall.

Curan leaped, spinning with a roundhouse kick that struck another dummy. This one sailed in a different direction, spinning end-over-end. The calm of Cassie's meditation fell away, replaced by alarm.

With widened eyes, she screeched and rolled off the pillow as the tumbling dummy hit the floor, bounced, struck the pillow, and continued past her. The dummy passed so close that loose straw scraped her trailing hand before it collided into the wall with a deep *thump*.

Lying on her stomach, Cassie stared at the dummy as it teetered and fell on its side. She turned toward Curan and found him cringing, his blue eyes apologetic.

"Sorry," he said as he walked toward her. "I was imagining it as a battle with dozens of enemies surrounding me." He glanced backward, toward the other scattered dummies littering the floor. "I guess I became caught up in the moment." He stopped two strides away, towering over her. "Are you all right?"

Rising to her hands and knees before standing, Cassie dusted herself off. "Yes. I'm fine, but you almost had to call a healer for me." Her gaze landed on the dummy that had nearly crushed her. It appeared beaten, dead. "I don't even want to think of how much that would have hurt."

His brow furrowed. "Couldn't you just heal yourself?"

"No. I can only heal others."

He appeared doubtful. "This is true?"

She shrugged. "I connect with my patient's source of Order, their life force, and use it to repair their injuries. I can't do the same with my own source of Order. That's just the way it works."

After a moment of consideration, he nodded. "Thank you. This is valuable to know."

In some ways, Curan reminded her of Chuli. Both were quiet, reserved, and extremely polite. And, yet, Curan struck an imposing image, matching his father in height but had not yet fully grown into his body. His eyes, deep blue and alert, continuously measuring the people around him.

"You have been here for over a week," Cassie spoke in a friendly tone, "but I know little about you other than you don't seem to talk much."

He shrugged.

"Yet, you are always listening, filing facts away." She said it as a statement of fact.

"I guess."

"You remind me of your father."

His eyes brightened. "You know him?"

"Of course," Cassie smiled, recalling how Cam used to pick her up and spin her over his head when she was little. At the time, it seemed as if she were soaring over the city. "He and my parents have been close friends for many years."

"You met him in Kantar? At the castle?"

"Yes, I would sometimes see your father at the castle, my home. Cameron would come visit Kantar every year or two. He often shared stories of you and your sister. It was clear to me, even when I was young, that he missed you whenever he was away."

Cassie examined Curan more closely. The teen bore the same physique as his father, well over six-feet tall with broad shoulders to match. His darker skin, combined with brown hair and blue eyes, made it difficult to discern his origin. If not for the body art on his arms, it would be difficult to identify Curan as Tantarri.

Her gaze then fell on the markings outlined on his right bicep. She had first thought the image was inked there as a matter of convenience, which was true. However, the symbol was more than just a Power rune. Curan's bearing and personality reminded Cassie of his father. Behind his quiet exterior, Curan was carved from reliable integrity. Power was not a toy to him. It was a tool used to defend others – a means of expressing compassion toward those who could not defend themselves.

Still, the symbol on his arm made it possible to perform an augmentation instantly when needed. After consideration, Cassie decided that a Power rune permanently marking a wildcat was a stroke of genius. In fact, it was something she wished for all wildcats. She wondered if ICON's leaders would agree.

"I last saw Cam two years ago," Cassie said as she began crossing the room with Curan at her side. "He spoke highly of you. I could see his pride when he described the skills you had developed. Your father said that you would become a strong defender of your people, so I'm surprised your parents agreed to let you join us. Not only will they miss their son, but your people will miss your skill as a warrior. Sending you here was a sacrifice. As a warden, you fight not just for the Tantarri, but for all citizens across Issalia."

Cassie then noticed Delvin standing on his balcony, watching her and Curan as they crossed the Atrium. He gave her a nod, turned and faded from view. *How long had he been watching? What is that man up to, now?*

Curan spoke as they continued across the room. "When Chuli came to us, my mother wished to deny the request that I come to Fallbrandt. I was eager and argued for it. I love my people, but I yearn to make a difference.

"I have been training as a warrior since I was eight summers, learning all I could from my father and from the other leaders. They tell me my potential is great, yet I remained untested outside of a sparring circle. Unless war comes to Tantarri lands, something I never wish to see, I would live my entire life with that potential unfulfilled."

When Curan stopped in the middle of the room, Cassie did as well.

His eyes were downcast while he spoke. "Despite my eagerness and attempts to convince her, my mother would not relent. Her attitude was fierce, and her stance firmly against my leaving. Despite this, my father's quiet way has an effect on my mother...always has. He merely moved close, took her hand in his, and asked her *Would you deny our son the right to fulfill his purpose?"*

Curan's lips turned up with the hint of smile. "With a fierceness that would make anyone else flinch, mother stared into his eyes. I watched closely, fearing my chance would pass me by. And then, she rested her head against his shoulder and hugged him. My mother is not always in the right, but she would never admit it aloud. I know her manner well. The hug was her way of relenting. My father and I had won."

"I'm glad to have you here." Cassie gave him a friendly smile.

The door opened and Everson entered the room, joined by the sound of whirring with each step he took. Of average height and build, the dark-haired gadgeteer appeared unremarkable until you saw the mechanical legs that allowed him to walk. Even without that invention, Cassie knew the teen's mind was far from unremarkable. Quite the opposite, actually.

Flashing a smile, Everson called out, "Cassie! I'm glad I found you."

"Hello, Ev," she replied. "I was watching Curan train while under a Power augmentation. I thought it best to stick around in case he somehow injured himself."

Curan snorted at the comment.

"Did you eat yet?" Everson asked.

Cassie shook her head. "No. I was planning to grab lunch when we were finished here."

"Perfect. I'll eat with you, and…if you aren't occupied for the afternoon, I could use your help with some enchanting."

Cassie resisted the urge to frown. "What about Rena?"

"Henrick has her working on his submergible experiment."

"His what?"

"Never mind. Can you do it?" Everson's eyes were pleading. "Ivy and I requested Nindlerod, Hedgewick, and Firellus to witness the trial late this afternoon, but there are a number of late modifications that require an augmentation."

Cassie stared into Everson's forlorn eyes, grasping for an excuse before her conscience gathered momentum. *Too late. You've lost, Cassie.* She sighed.

"Fine. We can eat, and then I'll meet you in the Forge." Cassie turned toward Curan. "It's been an hour. Your augmentation should soon be wearing off." A quick survey of the room revealed over a dozen of the heavy sparring dummies, all lying on their sides, scattered like leaves stirred by a gust of wind. "You had better begin stacking the dummies beside the wall. If you wait much longer, they will feel far heavier...perhaps too heavy for even you to manage on your own."

Curan strode toward the nearest dummy. "Good idea. I'll clean up and meet you in the dining hall."

Cassie sat alone, her inner-self floating in the ether. She held tight to her own source of Order while gathering latent Order from her surroundings. Once collected and channeled by her will, Order encased the Chaos inside the wooden strip, capturing it. With the raging storm of Chaos symbols sealed within the harmony of Order, she opened her eyes and examined her handiwork.

The knobbed wooden strip that wrapped about half of the wheel appeared no different than it had before the Infusion. She pressed a finger into it. When she lifted the finger, a dimple appeared briefly before filling as if it had never existed. The result was identical to her prior attempts on the other wheels.

"How are you faring?" A voice came from behind her.

Cassie turned to find Everson approaching. "I just finished the last one."

His eyebrows rose in surprise. "You did both strips? On every wheel?"

She wiped the sweat from her brow and nodded. "Yes. It's harder than it appears. The concentration and effort required to gather Order outside a living thing is not trivial."

"Other arcanists have said the same thing, but I didn't expect you to finish so soon. You're faster than Rena and much faster than Deirdre."

Everson's statement rekindled something Master Wykatt had said to Cassie and her brother just weeks prior. *Considering the strength your parents possess with magic, you two may be just scratching the surface of your full potential.* Cassie was determined to discover where her potential might lead.

"Well, if you have nothing else for me, I should go practice my meditation."

A girl with a slender build, straight black hair, and a pale complexion sidled up beside Everson. "Don't you want to see us test it?" Ivy asked.

Cassie turned toward the machine and considered the idea.

Steam-powered carriages were a rarity, but this one was unique beyond anything normal. At first glance, it appeared similar to the steam carriage her parents used back in Kantar. The visible modifications were understated, but the result might be amazing.

With her curiosity piqued, Cassie nodded in response. "Yes. I would like to see it."

"Perfect," Everson said before turning toward Ivy. "By now, Nindlerod should be finished teaching class at the academy. Gather the other gadgeteers so they can help push this thing outside while I assemble the masters."

"Everson…" Ivy's tone was one of warning.

"Oops. Sorry." With an exaggeratedly serious expression, he took her hand. "My dear. would you grace me with a favor? I would greatly appreciate it if you could gather a few others and push our creation outside. Please?"

Ivy rolled her eyes. "Sometimes, you remind me of your sister. Yes. I'll see you outside in a bit."

While Everson walked away, Cassie noted how Ivy's gaze followed him. The look in her eyes said it all.

"You love him."

Ivy blinked and turned toward Cassie. "What?"

"You and Everson are always together. I see the way you look at him."

Ivy blushed, her eyes flicking toward Everson as he exited the room. "I am very fond of him."

"Does he know?"

"Yes. I think so. We have been…seeing each other lately…spending time together outside the Forge."

Cassie smiled and gripped the girl's hand. "That's wonderful, Ivy. How does he feel about you?"

With her large, dark eyes downcast, Ivy shrugged. "I'm not sure. I...I'm just happy to be with him for now, so I don't ask."

"Have you kissed him?"

Ivy's blush deepened by two shades, but she grinned when her eyes lifted to look at Cassie.

"You have." Cassie nodded. "Good. Keep kissing him. That should help to reel him in if he is unsure. And if that doesn't work, there are other things you can try..."

Ivy gasped. "Cassilyn!"

Cassie laughed. "I'm just saying..."

"No. No need to say more." Ivy glanced toward the door Everson had passed through, her expression becoming contemplative. "I don't know what the future holds for us, but as long as I'm with Everson, I'm happy." Her lips pulled up in a devilish smirk. "We'll see. Perhaps kissing is not the end of it."

3

DANGER

A gust of north wind whistled through the gap between the stable and the Ward. Everson Gulagas secured the top button of his coat, cinching his collar to keep the next blast from sneaking in. He watched two old men, both leaning on canes while they walked beside a third man who was in his middle years. Canes had once been Everson's friend...his only means of walking. He glanced down at his legs, sealed in metal that housed actuators, pumps, and a powerful energy source – his greatest invention powered by an amazing discovery. *No. I don't miss my canes one bit.*

Everson watched the three masters as they approached the appointed position along the inside of the western wall. Beyond the men, a portion of the wall was noticeably lighter in tone than the rest – evidence of a recent repair. Everson found himself wishing he had seen the incident, but only Cassie and Brandt had been present when the animated boulder smashed through the wall. Regardless, Cassie's discovery of the Speed rune was the type of thing that fueled Everson's inspiration. *I must discover other applications for that rune,* he thought. *Increasing the speed of an animate, living thing, is amazing, but there must be other ways to use such an augmentation.*

Ivy stood beside him, grasping her collar with both hands to keep the wind at bay. When Everson slipped his arm around her, she leaned toward him, huddling close for warmth. The heat of her body pressed against him stirred his blood. A twist of his head put his face in her long, dark hair, the scent reminding him of a blooming garden. Beyond Ivy, Cassie shifted impatiently, her cloak held tight, her hood up, her brown curls mostly hidden.

When Everson looked north again, masters Nindlerod, Firellus, and Hedgewick had come to a stop. Their backs faced the recently repaired section of the wall. Master Hedgewick waved, and Everson used his free hand to wave back. With the road open and the men ready to witness the trial run, he turned to Ivy.

"It's time." An eagerness tempered by anxiety fluttered in his stomach. "Let's climb aboard and see what this thing can do."

He reluctantly removed his arm from about Ivy and opened the door to the steam carriage. Ivy put her hand on his shoulder as he helped her climb aboard.

Everson turned to Cassie. "Come on. Let's not make them wait."

Cassie green eyes widened in alarm. "What?" She stared at the steam carriage as if it were a mechanical beast, ready to eat her. "I'm to ride with you?"

He grinned. "Sure. Why not? There is enough room."

"Is it…safe?" Her eyes shifted from Everson, to the carriage, and back.

"Trust me. I know what I am doing. Since when are you afraid of danger, anyway?"

"You might be confusing me with my brother," Cassie said before stepping close to the machine. "Still, a little excitement might be just the thing I need." Her voice carried a tone of resignation, as if she were talking herself into the act.

Cassie climbed in, followed by Everson, his Chaos-powered legs expelling a puff of compressed air as he stepped into the interior of the metal contraption.

Everson pulled the door closed with a clang and secured it. Turning, he found Ivy and Cassie already seated. He climbed past the front seat to stand in the driver's position, his back against the panel that ran from floor to ceiling and divided the driver's position from the main cabin. Through the window above the converted boiler, he saw the road before him and the masters waiting in the distance. He gripped both drive levers and spoke over his shoulder.

"The structural changes, combined with Chaos conduction, should make this thing much faster than a standard steam carriage. I suggest you hold on and remain seated."

Without waiting for a response, Everson pushed both drive levers forward. A squeal arose from the two Chaos-conduction chambers, the rear wheels began to spin, and the machine began to hop, stirring a cloud of dust. Suddenly, it blasted forward, pinning Everson to the panel behind him. At an alarming rate, the carriage sped down the road and raced past the three spectators. Everson's eyes grew wide when the north wall, which had been a mile away when the ride began, drew close. He scrambled for the drive levers and pulled them back to neutral. His hands then gripped both brakes, but when he pulled, one lever stuck in place. With the right side braking and the other rolling freely, the carriage spun about and continued spinning.

Screams arose from all three passengers as the world twirled past them repeatedly and the wall drew closer and closer. They reached the bend in the road with only fifty feet of long grass between them and the wall. Everson held tight, fearing a massive collision. Still spinning, the wheels caught a rut and the carriage tipped sideways. Everson stumbled and fell to one mechanical knee. The carriage hung up, teetering while Everson's breath caught in his throat. Creaking arose from the machine as it swayed back and forth, threatening to tip on its side...and then it dropped back on its wheels. The force of the fall sent Everson sprawling onto his back and his head smacked against the interior wall. He blinked at the pain in his head, his hand going to the sore spot as his breathing calmed.

Everson rolled to his stomach, climbed to his feet, and peeked out the window. The carriage had stopped a few strides short of the wall. A glance down the road revealed a cloud of settling dust, stirred from the gravel. He shifted, peeked into the cabin, and found his passengers holding each other, their eyes round with fear as they panted for air.

He gave them a weak grin. "See. I know what I'm doing."

Cassie released Ivy and blurted at Everson, "You almost killed us!"

"Well, I wouldn't go that far."

She stood and poked finger at him. "What if we had hit the wall?

Going that fast, we would have been flattened!" Moving to the door, she gripped the handle and threw it open. "First, Curan almost crushes me with a practice dummy, and now you practically drive me into a wall at a ridiculous speed. What else can happen today?"

Cassie abruptly stopped in the doorway, her face relaxing as she stared into space. Everson turned toward Ivy, who shrugged. When his gaze returned to Cassie, he found her nodding to no one and surmised that Brandt was contacting her over their telepathic connection.

"It's my brother." Cassie turned toward Everson. "He's with Quinn. They are meeting later tonight to send a full report. He says it's important."

The corridor was eerily silent, but it was late and that was to be expected. Everson glanced back at Cassie before knocking, the rap of his knuckles on the door echoing down the hallway. The tap of approaching footsteps came from beyond the door. It opened to reveal Master Hedgewick, who gave them an affable smile. The man pushed his rectangular spectacles up and moved aside to allow them to enter.

A glowlamp on the wall, another on the desk, and a third at the center of a long table provided the only light. At one end of the briefing room, the desk stood empty save for the lamp and some notes. The table at the other side of the room was another story.

Every ICON leader was present. Nindlerod sat on one side of the table, the old man nodding with a grin when Everson faced him. Beside the engineering master was Firellus, who, like Nindlerod, rested his cane across his lap. Firellus stared back with his beady dark eyes, a gaze that tended to make Everson squirm. Headmaster Ackerson was there, seated between Firellus and Master Alridge, the academy's expert on arcane arts. Captain Goren had even come from the Torreco Academy of Combat Training to join the meeting. Seated beside Goren was Kwai-Lan, the Ward's combat master.

Last was Delvin Garber with his arms behind his head, leaning back in his chair. As usual, his expression featured the hint of a satisfied smirk – as if he knew secrets unknown to others. *Perhaps he does.* While Everson was unsure if Delvin had a title, he certainly held importance inside ICON. Delvin was Quinn's mentor, as he was for the other espions. He also spent more time away from the Ward than in it, but nobody ever seemed to know where the man was when away.

Hedgewick gestured toward the table as he took a seat. "Come. Sit. We have been waiting for you."

With only two empty chairs remaining, both at the near end of the table, Cassie claimed one and Everson the other. With all eyes turned toward him, Everson fidgeted, his gaze flicking from one face to another. His armpits grew damp, his stomach sour. He glanced toward Cassie and willed her to say something...anything. Thank Issal, she did.

"I informed my brother that we are ready. He and Quinn are together, alone..." she frowned. "They are in Sol Polis, at the citadel. In an abandoned tower. He says it's a safe place for them to talk."

Hearing this news struck a chord inside Everson, his concern for Quinn drowning his insecurity. "Empire headquarters?" he blurted. "How is *that* safe?"

"Hush, Everson," Firellus said. "It is time to listen. We need information."

With a nod and a deep exhale, Everson fell quiet.

"Brandt is relaying Quinn's story." Cassie said as she closed her eyes. "After arriving in Sol Polis, she joined the castle staff as a handmaid for a magistrate. She was able to...manipulate the situation and soon became the handmaid for Archon Varius. In that position, she discovered that the Empire is developing weapons using something called *flash powder,* among which are the flash cannons that fired at Admiral Tenzi's ship."

The leaders seated at the table nodded at this information.

"That makes sense," Delvin said.

Hedgewick leaned closer. "Who is behind this? Certainly, it requires a scholar to refine something so dangerous into a weapon."

Cassie opened her eyes and looked around the table. "Does the name *Jarlish* mean anything?"

Hedgewick gasped. "Karl Jarlish?"

The man's face twisted to a grimace, and he pounded his fist against the table. The suddenness of Hedgewick's reaction – so out of character – startled Everson. Judging by the way Cassie jumped in her seat, it startled her as well.

"That filthy scum," Hedgewick grit his teeth as he spoke. "How could he take my discoveries...my creations...and turn them against us?"

Nindlerod leaned forward and put his hand over Hedgewick's fist. "Easy, Benny. Let us hear them out and follow logic to our next step. Getting carried away with emotion will only lead to bad decisions."

Hedgewick's shoulders slumped as the anger bled from him. He nodded to the old engineering instructor. "Of course, Pherran." He turned toward Cassie. "I apologize for the outburst. Please. Continue."

Cassie closed her eyes, and the room fell silent. A moment later, she continued her tale.

"This Jarlish was later tasked by Varius with developing smaller weapons – something a soldier could carry into battle. Quinn fears what it might mean if we engage in war with the Empire.

"Quinn's role as Varius' handmaid was going well until..." Cassie's eyes opened in a start. "Wyck showed up."

Delvin sat forward, his eyes narrowed. "Wyck? He's no espion." He glared at Firellus. "Why was that knucklehead there?"

Firellus shook his head. "I don't know. I sent Wyck to Cinti Mor under the guise of a simple soldier. I used connections to get him a position as a guard at the citadel. My directions were simple – guard Prelate Dorlan and to listen for information coming from Sol Polis."

With her eyes again closed, Cassie continued. "Apparently, an act of heroism while at Cinti Mor earned Wyck a promotion to Sol Polis. While there...he attacked Archon Varius in her personal chambers. When Quinn tried to talk him out of it, he attacked her, instead. They fought, and...Wyck died."

Goren slapped the table, causing Everson to jump in his seat again.

"Why would she protect an enemy leader?" The military captain demanded. "Worse, how could she justify killing a fellow soldier? A fellow warden?"

Cassie grimaced. "You people keep interrupting me. Do you want to hear the report or not?"

The scowl remained on Goren's face, but he sat back in his chair and crossed his thick arms. Yet, he remained quiet.

"The day before Wyck attacked Varius, Quinn overheard the Archon arguing with General Kardan. The general wanted to attack Kantaria and push their forces north to capture Fallbrandt before winter. Varius was against it and urged him to wait. She was the one person stopping the council, and the general, from going to war against the west. Quinn feared what would happen if Wyck killed her.

"Brandt arrived in Sol Polis the day after Wyck died. He also is at the citadel, working undercover. When Quinn discovered..." Cassie gasped. "King Dalwin is alive!"

"Pretencia?" Nindlerod exclaimed.

"How? Where is he?" Hedgewick demanded.

"Quinn discovered the king locked in a dungeon cell. She and Brandt freed the king and sent him off to Wayport on Admiral Tenzi's ship. He should arrive there in a day or two."

Hedgewick glanced around the table. "Well, that is..."

"Wait!" Cassie interjected, "There is more."

Everyone turned toward her and listened.

"The failed assassination had unexpected results. After Quinn killed Wyck and saved the Archon's life, Varius made Quinn...her personal guard. The new position offers Quinn better access to information than when she was a handmaid." Cassie's eyes flashed open. "Oh, my."

"What?" Everson asked, unable to restrain himself. "What is it?"

When Cassie's gaze met Everson's, he saw the concern in her eyes. "The attempt on the Archon's life also altered her stance. The Empire is now preparing for war. Quinn doesn't know where or when, but they will strike...and it will happen soon."

4

THE FIRST TILE

The tower was dark, the room dimly lit by a small chunk of glowstone. Broken furniture and debris from the collapsed ceiling covered the floor. Three stories above the Sol Polis citadel grounds, the room was high enough to be buffeted by the steady sea breeze – a wind that whistled through broken windows. The sound was eerie, a plaintiff wail, as if the tower mourned for its old self – tall, majestic, and full of life. Despite the risk of injury from the building collapsing upon them, Quinn and Brandt chose the tower as it was among the few places in the citadel where they could meet in secret.

Seated on a fallen block of stone, Quinn told her story while Brandt relayed it to his sister and ICON's leaders, hundreds of miles away. During the exchange, Brandt leaned against a broken tabletop – a dust-covered relic lying at an odd angle atop a pile of rubble. With her tale recited, Quinn fell silent and waited for Brandt to finish the conversation with his sister. His ability to communicate with Cassie still amazed Quinn and left her wondering what it would be like to have such a skill. *How do you turn it on and off? Is the other person always listening? Can they overhear your thoughts?* She gasped. *Does Cassie always know what Brandt is doing? What he is feeling?* The thought left Quinn blushing. She considered asking him but feared the response. The truth might be worse than not knowing. However…

Brandt's eyes opened to reveal a sparkling intensity despite the dim lighting. Quinn set her curiosity aside and focused on the mission.

"Did Cassie have anything to say in return?"

"Nothing we couldn't have determined ourselves," he shrugged. "Delvin said we are to remain in position and gather more information. They want us to discover more about the Empire's plans. With war coming soon, the kingdoms must prepare. They plan to notify the western rulers so nobody is caught off guard."

Quinn sighed. "I expected as much. While I can make no promises, I will do my best."

He stood and moved closer, resting his hands on her shoulders.

"Just remember, I am here and will help in any way I can."

She gave him a small smile. "I know. I wish it were that easy..."

When Quinn rose to her feet, he slipped in closer, his hands shifting to the small of her back. She put her hands against his chest, intending to push him away, but her desire overcame her resistance. Their lips met, and Quinn felt Brandt's heart beating in time with hers, thumping loud enough to drown out the whistling wind. After swimming for some unknown time in the rush of their connection, she opened her eyes and resurfaced. Her lips fell away, and she gently pushed him back.

"We must go." Quinn turned toward the door. "Varius is meeting with Kardan and the Council tomorrow morning. She expects me to guard the door. As it is, I'll have little more than six hours sleep."

"Sleep is a good idea. I must wake even before you, before sunrise." Brandt frowned. "Life as a steward is even more boring than I had feared."

A smirk tugged on Quinn's lips. "Is the little prince unhappy with his new role?"

"Ugh." He wore a pained expression. "Not you, too. I'm not that bad, am I?"

"At complaining? Actually, you have proven quite deft at it. If you continue, you may surpass Jonah one day."

He glared at her. "Are you messing with me?"

She patted his cheek. "Of course I am."

Turning toward the door, Quinn eased it open. A deep groan from years of neglect came from the hinges, the noise growing louder the wider she opened it.

"Remember the loose stairs," she whispered as she began her descent down the spiral staircase.

Quinn paced before the door to the council chambers. Tarvick and Berd stood guard outside the door, neither moving. They hardly even blinked. When Quinn stopped before them, the guards stared into space, refusing eye contact. Quinn's mouth turned in a frown. She had tried to mend the bridge between her and the guards, but they wouldn't have it. She even considered approaching Sculdin about it until she realized he was likely the source of the distaste they displayed toward her. After all, she had killed their new star soldier. Never mind that the man had tried to assassinate their Archon.

Beyond the door, Varius, Kardan, and the eight council members were discussing war. Quinn ached to be in the room with them, to know what they planned. Since nobody, not even Kardan, was allowed to enter the room armed, Varius perceived herself safe and had assigned Quinn to wait in the main hall. Outside of poisoning, Varius had little to fear from the council members, not with Kardan beside her.

Redirecting her attention toward the floor, Quinn resumed pacing. By the time she spun on her heel a second time, the door opened and council members emerged. The men – ranging from their early fifties to seventy years of age – walked past as if Quinn didn't exist. A few spoke to each other in hushed tones. The others remained silent, making no sound other than the swishing of their white cloaks, trimmed in blue, and their retreating footsteps on the tiled floor.

A moment later, the door opened again. Kardan moved to the side and held it while Varius walked past him. The Archon's white, floor-length dress and golden cloak were a stark contrast to the general's dark blue uniform, also trimmed in gold. Kardan was tall and imposing with broad shoulders, standing a full head taller than Varius. Quinn wondered why the woman even bothered with another guard when Kardan was beside her.

"Come along," Varius said as she passed Quinn and headed toward the stairwell.

With Kardan in the lead and Quinn in the rear, the trio climbed to the fifth story and stopped outside Kardan's office. Opening the door, he stood aside and waited for Quinn to enter.

The curtains along the far wall were drawn and sunlight streamed through the window, providing ample light to the familiar room. A quick survey revealed chairs beside a table with maps laid out on it, shelves along one wall filled with books and charts, and Kardan's desk, the papers upon it aligned and orderly.

"The room is clear," Quinn said, turning toward the door.

Varius entered with Kardan trailing and closing the door behind him.

"Today's meeting went better than expected," Kardan said as he walked toward his desk.

"Yes. The Council members are odd," Varius agreed. "They balk or bicker over the most mundane, inconsequential subject, and then they surprise you by aligning decisively on a major initiative with thousands of lives in the balance."

Kardan circled behind his desk and took a seat. "While I require time to prepare our resources, at least we have a plan in place. It's now up to my team to execute it."

"A few variables remain in play, Leo." The Archon pulled a chair from beside the table, turned it toward his desk, and sat with her hands resting on her knees.

"Your son."

"Yes. He should return soon. The news he carries might dictate our next move." She crossed her legs, her fingers tapping the chair arm while she stared toward the window.

What is she thinking? Quinn wondered.

Kardan leaned forward, resting his elbows on the desk. "War is a mistress of many faces. Strategy and preparation can place an outnumbered army in a position of strength. The element of surprise or superior weapons can do the same." He picked up a sheet of paper and stared at it. "And yet, history has shown victory to favor the greater force. Our new weapons bolster our chances, but I would prefer to field more..."

A knock startled Quinn. The conversation had held her in rapt attention while she leaned against the door. She turned and opened it to find Ydith standing in the hall beside a balding man in his fifties. His skin was tan, his face rugged. The stump at his left shoulder drew Quinn's focus to it. Her gaze then lowered to the sword at his hip.

"I have a report for General Kardan," the man said.

Quinn's brow furrowed. "And, your name is…"

"His name is Gambo," Kardan said, rising from his chair. "Tom Gambo."

Seeing Kardan approaching, Quinn stepped aside. Gambo entered the room and Kardan embraced him, clapping him on the back.

"It's good to see you, Tom. You look a bit worn."

"Yes. I've spent the past five months in the saddle." The man bowed his head toward Varius. "Archon, I am ready to report."

Varius did not stand, but she did nod and reply, "Please do. I pray you have good news."

Gambo ran his hand through his graying hair, or what remained of it. He appeared weary. "The good and the bad depend on your expectations. The gold you gave me is gone, and more was promised. In the end, the added soldiers are going to cost you."

"Fine," Varius said. "Gold is something we can spare."

Kardan sat behind his desk. "The report, Tom. Let's hear it."

The man nodded. "As we planned, I made my journey directly for Nor Torin. When I arrived, I met with some old acquaintances and put the word out – I had gold and was seeking swords to join me. The result was better than expected. From Nor Torin alone, I yielded four hundred fighters. We left the city to head east. I put a trusted man in charge and rode ahead. We worked our way across Torinland, around the Gulf of Norta, and across Hurnsdom to the coast before we turned south. By that time, my force was approaching three thousand strong. They should arrive at the rendezvous point inside a week."

"Three thousand soldiers?" Kardan grinned. "Combined with our current force, that brings our numbers close to twelve thousand. I doubt Kantaria and Torinland can combine to match that, unless they press ordinary citizens into service."

Varius added, "That leaves the Tantarri, and their numbers have always been few. They will add another five hundred warriors at best."

Kardan nodded. "Yes. The numbers now make sense. We will increase the supply lines immediately to feed our expanded army."

Varius stood and circled the desk to stare out the window. "We are at the brink, Leo. Once the first tile falls, the others will follow. The moment marking the end of Chaos is approaching."

5

KNIFE OF DESPAIR

Cassie wrapped her cloak tight about herself, but the wind was persistent – a gust finding its way past the barrier and giving her a chill. As usual, the wind was far stronger atop the Ward tower than on the ground, far below.

A blanket of gray covered the sky, dark to the west as it threatened to snow. White caps already covered the peaks in that direction – a reminder of the storm from a week earlier. When her gaze slid toward the base of the mountains, she found the colors of autumn now faded – the trees having shed their leaves in preparation of winter's impending embrace. Spending the winter at the Ward was a concept Cassie had yet to fully comprehend. The mild days of winter in Kantar were likely nothing like a winter in this mountain valley. *Something tells me my wait to play in the snow won't be long now.*

"I'm ready," Everson said, drawing Cassie from her reverie.

She turned and found him standing beside the modified catapult. A round wooden disk, slightly larger than a person's head, waited in each launch bucket. The rune on the face of the first disk began to glow while Rena released the stored Chaos she had gathered. When Everson pulled the lever, the disk shot toward the eastern horizon and burst into flames. The rune on the next disk flared before it launched and became a ball of fire arcing through the sky. When the symbol on the third disk glowed red, it chased the others, bursting in flame and burning out before it could land.

"I'm done," Rena said, gasping from the effort. "I couldn't hold it any longer."

"You did fine, Rena," Everson said. "Splitting your charge into three augmentations is impressive."

"Yes. I'm improving," she huffed with a nod. "When I first arrived, I couldn't even charge a second disk."

"That is why we train – to hone our skills." Everson pulled another lever and the Chaos Conduction engine sparked to life, cranking the catapult arms back down into launch position.

Cassie watched Rena closely. The girl's emerald eyes, auburn hair, and button nose painted a pretty picture, but Cassie sensed a sadness beneath the surface that made Rena's smiles seem hollow. The two girls were roommates, but they each may have well lived alone since Rena spent most of her time away from the apartment or locked in her bedroom. While Cassie knew that Rena, Torney, Everson, and Quinn had grown up together in Cinti Mor, she knew little else of the girl outside her role as a Warden. For all her smiles and hellos, Rena's expression grew somber when she thought nobody was watching. It had grown worse of late – ever since Torney had left on his mission with Jonah, Chuli, and Thiron. Rena's melancholy became even more apparent when she was around Everson.

With new disks placed in position, Everson turned toward Cassie. "Are you ready?"

Cassie took a deep breath and blew the air out through pursed lips. She closed her eyes and reached for Chaos. As if drawing another breath, she absorbed the surrounding energy and opened her eyes. Despite the pressure inside her, she used a controlled release to feed some of the energy into the rune on the first disk. Everson launched it and she focused on the next Heat rune. When it began to glow, the disk sailed after the first. The storm inside Cassie raged and she fought to restrain it, releasing half of what remained. Cassie feared that her head might explode while she waited for the third disk to launch. The moment the fourth disk came into view, she channeled the remaining energy into the Heat rune. When launched, the disk chased the others, bursting into a fireball that streaked across the sky before burning out in a puff of black smoke. As the wind carried the smoke southward, a wave of exhaustion washed over Cassie, causing her to stagger. Her breath came in gasps, her body feeling numb and empty.

"You did it, Cassie! All four disks." Everson turned toward her. "I'm sure Alridge would be proud."

Cassie nodded weakly. "Thank you, Everson. Can we go back inside? I'm freezing."

"Yes." He waved for them to take the lead. "Let's go. We can take the lift down."

The trio took the ladder down to the twelfth floor and boarded Everson's Chaos-powered lift. With the pull of a lever, it began a steady descent, the interior of the Atrium sliding past as the lift went down. They stopped at the fifth floor, and Cassie climbed off, saying goodbye to Rena and Everson who planned to take the lift to the bottom before heading to the Forge.

Cassie entered the corridor and found Headmaster Ackerson waiting by her door. Her brow furrowed as she wondered about the cause behind his visit. He turned toward her and she stopped, a chill raking over her when she saw the look in his eyes.

"Cassilyn," the headmaster said in a solemn tone. "I need you to come with me."

"What?" Worry began to churn inside her. *Is it Brandt?* She suddenly feared attempting to reach him, afraid of how she might react if he didn't respond. "Where are we going?"

"Come along," he said as he walked past her. "The others are waiting."

The headmaster descended to the third level and led Cassie to the debriefing room, her mind clouded with worry the entire time. He opened the door and moved aside while she entered. With only two open seats, ICON's leaders were, again, all present. The anxiety inside her grew worse and her hand went to her stomach as she felt like she might vomit.

"Please. Take a seat, Cassie." Ackerson closed the door and circled around the table.

Still unsure of the reason for the meeting, Cassie sat beside Ackerson and clasped shaking hands before resting them on the table.

"A messenger arrived today," Ackerson said. "The message he carried contained grave news – news you all must know.

"Eight days ago, there was an attack in Kantar. General Budakis was found dead in his bed – murdered."

Cassie gasped. *No, not Gunther.* She had known Gunther Budakis her entire life. Despite his often gruff exterior, she knew he had a heart of gold.

"Several guards were slain in the process, but that isn't the worst of it." Ackerson's expression was frighteningly grim. "The assailant carried an explosive device. When triggered, the blast destroyed much of the palace's top floor."

Unable to restrain herself, Cassie cried out, "What about my parents? Are they all right?"

Ackerson's eyes met Cassie's for a moment. Within them, she saw a sadness that left her terrified to hear his response. His gaze lowered, and he took a deep breath before replying.

"I'm afraid that King Brock and Prince Broland were killed in the explosion."

A knife of despair struck, piercing Cassie's heart. Her hand went to her chest. Shaking her head, she gasped for air. *It can't be true. It just can't be true.* The room blurred through the tears obscuring her vision. After a few ragged breaths, she choked out a response.

"My mother." She wiped her eyes with the back of her hand. "What of my mother?"

"The messenger left Kantar six days past," Ackerson said. "At that time, Queen Ashland was alive, but remained in a coma. Her wounds had been healed, but she had suffered severe damage to her head, and the healers are unsure if she will ever wake."

— ✦ —

Faint starlight from the Atrium skylights filtered through the gap in the curtain. That light is where Cassie focused her attention while she lay in bed. Awake. For hours.

She had considered contacting Brandt to share the heart-breaking news, but she couldn't bring herself to do it. *How can I do that to him?*

How can I repeat something so horrible when I don't believe it myself? It can't be true, can it?

She had made a conscious effort to shield her pain away from her bond with Brandt, to keep him unaware of how she felt. It was a subtle skill – one she guessed Brandt had not yet developed. If he had, he would have masked his feelings far better than he had – especially when he was with Quinn. More than once, Cassie had found herself blushing at her exposure to his interactions with the girl.

*He is happy to be with her. I don't want to ruin it with...*she couldn't even bear to mentally repeat the news. *I must sleep. But...how can I sleep when my mind is such a cluttered mess?*

To calm herself, Cassie sought meditation. She found her center, Order at the core of her being. She held it to herself and willed her healing abilities to repair her sundered heart. Of course, that was not possible. Still, in her core, there was a sense of peace. The pale blue aura of Order surrounded her, drew her in deeper, pulled her toward it and the solace it offered.

Then, she sensed something beyond it, as if Order were a gateway rather than a destination. Extending herself, Cassie slid through and found a ghostly version of herself floating in a void. Bubbles, both near and distant, surrounded her. Looking backward, the blue glow of her inner self remained. Tentatively, she reached for the nearest bubble. Rather than pop, the wall bent to her pressure, yet it was soft enough that her hand slid inside. She put her other hand against the bubble and it, too, slipped through the wall. Confused, she withdrew her hands and frowned at them. They were transparent like the rest of her, but still intact. Curiosity took hold, and she pushed her face against the bubble. Her head slipped through the surface and reality shifted.

Cassie found herself standing in a room – a bedroom she had never seen before. She held her hands up to inspect them, her gaze shifting toward her body. Her appearance was normal – flesh and bone and fully clothed.

Rena sat on the floor beside a bed, playing with two dolls. The girl appeared years younger than the Rena Cassie knew. When Rena looked up at her, she smiled.

"Hi, Cassie. Have you come to play?"

Cassie decided she had somehow fallen asleep and was in a strange dream. Rather than fight it, she played along. She *did* need the sleep.

"Yes, I'll play with you."

Cassie sat on the floor with her legs crossed and Rena facing her. Rena held a doll toward Cassie, who accepted it and turned it toward her. The doll's mouth had been sewn shut.

"What happened to her mouth?" Cassie asked.

"Father likes it that way."

"Why?"

Rena shrugged, looking at her own doll, its mouth also sewn together. "It's best if she can't talk."

"I don't understand."

Rena leaned close, her voice a whisper. "If she can't talk, she can't tell secrets."

A sound came from the room beyond the bedroom door – the sound of a door opening, heavy boots entering.

"Rena, I'm home," a man's voice said.

Rena's eyes grew wide. "We can't let him find you. You must hide!"

"What? Why?" Cassie was confused as the dream became increasingly more odd.

"Please, Cassie. Just trust me. Get under the bed. Please." Rena was frantic, and tears streaked her face.

Unnerved, Cassie rolled under the bed a moment before the door opened.

"Is someone in here?" he asked.

"No," Rena shook her head emphatically. "I was only talking to my dolls."

"Don't lie to me, Rena." The man's voice carried a threat that gave Cassie chills. "Remember what happens if you lie."

"I wouldn't lie to you, Father."

From her position, Cassie saw the man's legs, his heavy work boots. Three quick steps into the room and his hand appeared, gripping Rena's arm and lifting her.

"You are full of lies, Rena," he growled. "I'll teach you not to lie to me."

The room darkened and fear emanated from Rena...raw, uncontrolled terror, as the man dragged Rena out the door.

It's only a dream, Cassie told herself. She recalled how she had come to this dream from her room in the Ward. The Ward made her think of her magic. Chaos magic. She slid out from beneath the bed and spotted a pen in an inkwell on the girl's desk. Using it, she drew a rune on her hand and summoned Chaos. With the Chaos channeled into the rune, it began to glow, filling Cassie with Power. Her vision grew spotty. She staggered as the Power took hold, her vision clearing.

She darted to the door, tore it off the hinges, and ran into the next room.

It was a dungeon.

The room was two hundred feet long and half the width. The ceiling was so high that Cassie couldn't see it. Instruments of torture filled the space – tables with clamps and pulleys, tubs of water with ropes hanging above them, a cage filled with rats, clamps, vices, and other oddities Cassie couldn't name.

A naked woman was hanging over the center of the room with ropes about her wrists and ankles. Her eyes were missing. Her mouth sewn shut. The sight made Cassie gag.

Rena's scream came from the far end of the room. Cassie spotted the girl, her arm in the grip of a man who stood ten feet tall. Gritting her teeth in defiance, Cassie leaped across the room in two giant steps. She then challenged the man whose back was facing her.

"Let her go!"

The man turned around and Cassie gasped. With long, greasy black hair that dangled to his shoulders, he had skin that was pale, eyes glowing red, and black talons on the ends of his fingers. The sight triggered Cassie's memory, recalling descriptions in books she had read. This wasn't a man. It was a banshee.

The monster smiled, the expression lacking any semblance of humor.

"So, you *were* lying to me, Rena."

"Please, Father," Rena begged. "Don't hurt her. She's my friend."

"Friends corrupt you. They convince you to share secrets that are never to be shared. It's why we moved from Cinti Mor."

Cassie sought the raw power in her body and gathered her courage. She would face this monster. After all, it was only a dream.

"Let her go!" Cassie screeched in defiance. "If you want to hurt someone, try me."

With a sneer, the monster tossed Rena aside. The girl tumbled into the corner and then curled up in a ball.

The banshee launched itself toward Cassie, swinging a massive, five-foot long arm toward her. Leaping in the air, the beast's talons swept beneath Cassie's feet as she sailed over it. She landed behind the monster and kicked at the side of its knee with her heel. A nasty crunch came from the joint and the monster howled in pain. It swept a long arm in an attempt to backhand her, but Cassie ducked beneath it. She then grabbed its wrist and thrust her palm into its elbow. A terrible crunch sounded when the joint imploded, bending the beast's arm in reverse.

Darting through the gap in its legs, Cassie ran to the nearest table and lifted it. She spun about and launched the table into the monster. The table struck the banshee in the face and the monster flew backward while table pieces scattered across the room. When the monster landed, it slid across the floor and struck the wall. Covered in blood, the banshee did not move.

Cassie ran to Rena and knelt before her.

"Are you hurt?"

Rena uncovered her eyes, gawking in wonder. "You beat him?"

"Yes."

"Is he alive?"

When Cassie looked at him next, she saw a man, not a monster – his arm broken, his leg twisted. The man had a bloodied gash across his forehead, but his chest still rose and fell.

"He's just a man," Cassie said. "He still lives."

"Good." Rena said.

"You don't wish him dead?"

"No. He does…things that are wrong…evil. And yet, he is still my father." Rena looked Cassie in the eye. "How did you do it? How did you stand up to him?"

"I used Chaos, Rena. You can do the same thing."

Rena's eyes grew round in realization. "You're right. I can do magic and…he is just a man."

The room seemed to morph, bend, shrink, and suddenly, the bubble popped. Cassie found herself in the void, surrounded by bubbles. Turning, she found the blue light of Order and moved toward it, willing herself through it and, then, she opened her eyes.

Pale twilight now filtered through the gap in Cassie's curtains. She sat upright and rubbed her eyes. It was nearly morning, but she was exhausted, as if she had not slept at all. Sliding out of bed, she grabbed her robe and wrapped it around herself. As she exited her room, Rena emerged from hers. The two girls stared at one another.

"I had the weirdest dream," Cassie said. "You were in it, but you were younger and playing with dolls that had their mouths sewn shut."

Rena's hand covered her mouth, her eyes blinking in surprise. "You were there? You were really there?"

"What?"

Rena moved closer and whispered. "My father." She turned away in shame. "You know…his secret…my secret?"

"It was real?" Cassie blinked, her mind racing. "I guess I do…but it's horrible. Oh, Rena. It's not your fault. I'm so, so sorry."

Rena embraced Cassie, rested her head on Cassie's shoulder, and began to sob uncontrollably. Cassie held Rena tight, caressing the girl's hair and telling her it would be all right. In the back of Cassie's mind, she realized what had happened. *I have done it. I visited another person's dream. I wonder if I can do it again.*

6

A NEW ORDER

A scowl crossed Tenzi's face when she entered the captain's cabin on the Razor. The cabin had been her home on the sea for years, and it would be again once it was repaired.

Sunlight leaked through the patchwork boards that covered the hole in the back of the room. Her old bed still lay on the floor, broken and shattered. The cabin door was noticeably absent, destroyed in the same attack that had rendered the six-foot hole in the wall. She should thank Issal that she had not been hurt, but the bitter taste of defeat lingered and would likely remain until she delivered retribution.

"Captain," Parker's voice came from behind her. "We approach the harbor. Do you wish to take the helm?"

With one last survey of the room, Tenzi released a sigh. "I will pilot the ship." She eyed his tall, lean frame, his brown hair aglow with the sunlight behind him. "Thank you for thinking of me. I know...I haven't been the best company of late."

He smiled. "You know how I feel about you. I know you better than anyone, so I understand how deeply it irks you to see your ship damaged."

She gripped his hand and stared into his dark eyes. "At least...at least you were not killed. That would render damage I could never repair."

Parker stepped into the shadowed doorway, his palm cupping her cheek before his fingers slid into her hair. He bent forward, their lips meeting, the kiss lingering. Heat smoldered inside Tenzi, a spark come to life. Their lips parted, and he stared into her eyes.

"You are forever the captain of my heart," he said softly.

"I had better be." Tenzi grinned. "Now, let's get this vessel docked."

"Aye, Captain." Smiling back at her, he moved aside to allow her past.

When she emerged into the sunlight, the gusting wind forced her to pull her wide-brimmed hat down. A look toward the harbor revealed the ship's position.

Tenzi's gaze swept over a bay highlighted in bright turquoise – a beautiful contrast to the cerulean blue sea surrounding the ship. A wide river emptied into the bay a short distance from the docks of a walled city. Trade vessels were moored along the two primary piers, busy as dockworkers loaded and unloaded cargo. Seeing it was time to prepare for landing, Tenzi cupped her hands to her mouth and shouted.

"Up the masts! Tend the lines! Make ready for port!"

She turned, climbed the stairs to the quarterdeck, and found a tall, thin man at the helm. A dark goatee framed his chin, and a gold ring dangled from one nostril. "Thank you, Joely. I'll take it from here."

The man nodded and stepped aside as Tenzi gripped the wheel. The smoldering fire kindled by Parker's kiss began to burn hotter as she reconnected with the ship, feeling the force of the wind in the sails above, the draw on the rudder below, and the rush of the waves against the hull. Despite twenty-six years on the sea, sailing remained her passion – a life she loved more than anything. Save, perhaps, Parker.

The pale walls of Wayport hugged the coast, beyond the long docks that stretched into the bay. Built upon a shallow slope, rooftops throughout the city appeared above the walls, none higher than the citadel, which was tucked in the city's corner. The tall citadel wall stood only strides from the sea to the south and the river to the east.

Gulls flew past and dove into the water as they hunted the fish swimming in the ship's forward wake. A cloud briefly eclipsed the sun and continued northeast, carried by a cool sea breeze. Tenzi smiled to see the wind coming from the southwest. *Thank Issal. This city is stifling without that breeze.*

The ship crested the breakers and slid into calmer waters. Tenzi called for the upper topgallant sails to furl, followed by the topgallant sails. She turned the wheel and the ship slowed as it headed toward an open slip at the end of the western pier. A narrow-bodied cutter sailed past and Tenzi tipped her hat to the opposing ship's captain, the man wearing a bright red rag over his scalp, his dark blue tunic loosened to expose his chest. *Deiter has always thought too much of himself.*

Moving at half-speed, she directed the ship toward the pier and called for the mainsails to drop. The crew – fifteen men and Shashi, whom Tenzi considered tougher than the men – performed their tasks with efficiency and without prompting. Sails were bound. Lines were pulled tight and secured to cleats. Men made ready at the rail with coils of rope in hand, pier posts in focus.

When a collision with the pier seemed imminent, Tenzi cranked the wheel and brought her about. The bow came within an arm's length of the dock and slid past harmlessly. Loops were tossed to the thick pier posts. As the slack lessened, the ropes grew taught, straining for a long moment before the ship settled.

Tenzi descended the quarterdeck stairs and crossed the deck to find Dalwin Pretencia climbing the stairs that led to the crew and guest cabins. The king had changed much, particularly during the journey. He was now clean-shaven, as Tenzi had grown used to over the years, his shaggy beard nothing but a memory. The twisted nest of hair he had sported when boarding the ship was gone – his long, gray-streaked, black bangs were greased back without one hair astray. Whatever he used to hold his hair in place shone in the sunlight and made it appear wet. Tenzi had known Pretencia a long time. Yet, she had seen more smiles on his face over the past few days than she had during the prior nineteen years.

"Well done, Admiral," Dalwin said with a grin.

Tenzi winced. "Stop calling me that. The Kalimar Navy is gone, and this ship is all that remains. I am now simply a captain."

The thin man arched a brow. "Captain Red Viper?"

Tenzi rolled her eyes. "That name is even worse. Please, not while we are on shore and absolutely not while the Razor still needs these repairs. There is a risk that someone might recognize the ship because of the hole. I tried to have it repaired when we were last in Wayport, but Delvin appeared and forced us to leave before the repairs were complete."

Pretencia nodded knowingly. "When you brought young Talenz to Sol Polis."

For a king, he has an annoyingly loose tongue. Rather than try to silence him again, Tenzi changed the subject. "If you are ready, we should head to the citadel."

"Yes. Let's be off. The sooner we notify Chadwick, the better." He cupped his hands to his mouth and yelled, "Master Thanes!"

Parker turned from his conversation with Shashi and strolled toward them. "What is it, sir?"

"We wish to be off to the citadel…and to consume a hot meal while we are there."

Longing reflected in Pretencia's eyes. Tenzi understood. Food on her ship left much to be desired. Worse, whatever he had eaten during his last weeks in Sol Polis had to have been pitiful at best.

"Hex," Tenzi called out, the big man's shaved head turning toward her. "Arm yourself. You're coming with us." When Hex stalked off, Tenzi turned to Pretencia. "Let's be off."

Shashi pushed the boarding plank beyond the rail, the far end bouncing off the dock before settling. With the plank in place, Tenzi descended, using the boards nailed across the plank to keep from slipping. She then crossed her arms and stood on the pier, waiting for the others to join her. As often happened when she had a quiet moment, Tenzi found her gaze drawn to the water.

The varying aqua and deeper blue colors of Wayport Bay was a sight that never grew old. She cherished the soothing rhythm of the surf, the soaring gulls in the distance, the whisper of the breeze – it was a symphony of nature at her favorite port. In the distance, she spotted a ship coming from the west, its course set for Wayport. She wondered if it had originated at Sunbleth, the nearest port in that direction, or if it came from somewhere more distant, such as Port Choya, Kantar, or even Nor Torin.

When she turned toward her own ship, she found Pretencia carefully descending the plank, followed by Parker, his bow slung over one shoulder, quiver over the other. Hex – armed with a longsword – came last.

Led by Tenzi, they walked the length of the pier and crossed the open yards of the warehouses that lined the shoreline. Uphill, they went, directly toward the south gate and into the city.

Tenzi found herself thankful that the weather had turned, the stifling humidity of summer now gone and the temperature moderate enough that she was comfortable in her loose tunic and black vest. Her other vest, the red one, remained on the ship – an article she only wore when at sea since it was a mark of her secret identity. She wondered when she might next find the opportunity to become Red Viper. The thought drew a smile. Surprisingly, she had discovered a pirate's life to her liking.

The group turned east, following the street that led to the citadel. As she passed clusters of people and weaved through the oncoming foot traffic, Tenzi considered what she should tell Chadwick. She had always found the duke affable, and most often, reasonable. Illiri was another story. The duchess was pretentious and thought far too highly of herself. While Tenzi had to admit the duchess was pretty, she believed that most men – at least the men she respected – would balk at Illiri's self-centered personality. It left her wondering how Chadwick suffered the woman. *Perhaps I would understand if I were a man.*

At the end of the street, they reached a guarded gate standing between two tall, rectangular towers. The citadel wall extended from each tower, running north and south. Without pausing, Tenzi approached two guards she didn't recognize.

"Good afternoon. I'm Captain Tenzi Thanes, requesting an escort to the citadel. We need to meet with Duke Chadwick."

The female guard glowered at Tenzi, while her male companion's jaw locked tight. After a moment, the female guard replied, "I've heard the name, but how do I know you are who you claim to be?"

Tenzi glared at her. "Do I match the description?"

"You do, but many women might do the same with a simple change of clothing."

Tenzi sighed. "Fine. Just escort us to the citadel. Someone there will know me."

The female guard returned the glare and then turned her attention toward Tenzi's companions. "You are armed. No weapons allowed inside."

Fighting her urge to sigh again, Tenzi said, "That is why I am requesting an escort. We keep our weapons, at least until we reach the castle, and you follow us to make sure we don't cause trouble."

Glancing toward her companion, the woman said, "Wait here. Let nobody pass until I return."

She waved Tenzi and her companions forward but waited until they all passed through the gate before following from the rear. Heading toward the palace, Tenzi crossed an open plaza, toward a wide set of stairs standing two stories tall. Climbing the stairs, Tenzi led the procession across the top landing and approached the main entrance. A guard who stood outside the door nodded toward the female escort as the others entered the building.

The receiving hall was spacious with a domed ceiling three stories up and a pale marble tiled floor below. In the middle of the room, she found a cluster of guards surrounding a familiar face.

Captain Sharene, who stood as tall as the men encircling her, finished issuing commands and the guards dispersed. When the captain noticed Tenzi and the others, she crossed the room, accompanied by a tall male guard.

"Well, if it isn't my favorite admiral."

Tenzi snorted. "I'm not sure I consider that a compliment, Sharene. How many other admirals do you know?"

"I admit, none. I'll give you the benefit of the doubt, regardless." She stopped and addressed the female guard who had escorted them from the gate. "What is this about, Aruna?"

"Captain," Aruna bowed her head. "This group requested an escort...and to remain armed. They wish to see the Duke."

Sharene arched her brow. "Armed? You know we must disarm you before you see Chadwick."

"Yes, of course," Tenzi agreed. "Is he busy? And what's with all the security?"

The captain of the guard glanced toward the door across the hall. Four armed guards stood beside the doors, two with swords, two with crossbows.

"The Duke has increased his guard of late. Why, I do not know." Sharene's tone made it clear that she would speak no further on the issue. "He is currently in court, issuing a dispatch. Once the messenger comes out, you can see him." She glared at Tenzi. "Assuming you have surrendered your weapons."

While she felt naked when unarmed, Tenzi assumed they would be in little danger based on the number of guards present.

"Do it." Tenzi said as she pulled daggers from the sheaths strapped to her thighs and held them, hilt first, toward Sharene.

The woman accepted the blades with narrowed eyes. "I know you, Tenzi. Give me the others."

Allowing a smirk, Tenzi pulled knives from the sleeves of her tunic and from both boots.

Sharene accepted them. "And the one from your back..."

Tenzi's smiled twisted to a frown as she drew a knife from the small of her back, hidden beneath her vest. When she turned, she found that Hex had surrendered his sword, Parker his bow and quiver.

With an armful of weapons, the man turned and walked toward an open door to one side of the hall.

"I recognize Parker," Sharene said as she handed the seven knives to a guard. "Who are the other two?"

Tenzi gestured toward Hex. "The big man is with me for protection." She gestured toward Pretencia. "This gentleman is my guest...an old acquaintance with a story that Chadwick will wish to hear."

The woman scowled at Pretencia, her eyes measuring him. The door to the courtroom opened and a man emerged.

Sharene turned toward Tenzi. "Come along, then."

They crossed the room, the guards parting as Sharene approached the doors. She opened one and held it while Tenzi and her companions entered.

Light streamed through tall, arched windows that faced the bay on one side, inland on the other. A tree stood just outside one of the bayside windows, nestled between the castle and the tall wall surrounding the citadel. Inside the room, rows of benches faced a dais at the front. Although the room could seat hundreds, it stood empty save for two guards stationed beside the dais and the two people seated upon it.

Chadwick was as Tenzi remembered – middle-aged, with flowing brown locks and a matching goatee. Dressed in a silver-trimmed midnight blue doublet with lace at the collar and at the wrists, he appeared nearly as vain as his wife. Illiri sat beside him, wearing a dark red dress that exposed her shoulders, the revealing neckline making her sizable chest impossible to ignore. The woman's black hair was piled atop her head with stray curls dangling at the sides. Illiri's outfit, her thickly applied makeup, and her dark lipstick gave Tenzi the impression of an expensive escort rather than a duchess. *Perhaps, that description is more accurate anyway.*

With Sharene in the lead, the small procession strolled the length of the carpeted aisle that split the benches. Chadwick was leaning toward Illiri, listening as the duchess spoke quietly in his ear. When Sharene stopped five strides from the dais and the others settled beside her, Chadwick's eyes grew wide.

"Dalwin?"

Pretencia walked past Sharene and gave Chadwick a nod. "Thank you for seeing us, Duke, Duchess."

Illiri's white face paled further. "How did you escape?"

Tenzi frowned. "Escape?" *I thought everyone believed him dead.*

The duchess briefly grimaced at her husband, the expression fleeting. "Yes. Escape...death from the attack on Sol Polis."

"Varius," Pretencia's face twisted after saying the name, "thought I might be of value at some point. Rather than execute me, she imprisoned me in my own dungeon and allowed the world to believe me dead."

Chadwick asked, "How did you escape your cell?"

"Two enterprising young people came to my rescue, freed me from my cell, and brought me to Admiral Thanes." Pretencia gave Tenzi a nod. "We left Sol Polis in the dark of night and sailed directly for Wayport. We landed today and came directly to your court.

"Although King Brock is not here," Pretencia dipped his head in deference, "I appeal to you as the local ruler. I formally seek asylum in Kantaria until I can find a way to reclaim Kalimar."

Chadwick's eyes flicked about the room nervously. He sat back with his chin in his hand, his brow furrowed while his fingers worked as if he were trying to rub the goatee off his face. He turned toward

Illiri, his face still in deep contemplation. Tenzi heard a door open and turned to find a guard waving for Sharene.

The captain of the guard bowed toward the duke. "Please, excuse me, Your Grace."

While Sharene walked toward the exit, Tenzi turned to address the man on the dais.

"Duke Chadwick, I think it best if King Dalwin remains here while we send word to King Brock. I could take him to Kantaria, but the sea has become quite dangerous." Tenzi held her hands out, palms up in appeal. "The Empire has a weapon that can destroy a ship...sink it with one blow. If they are aware of the king's escape, they may come after us. My ship was known to have been docked at Sol Polis, and it presents a risk – a risk we dare not ignore."

Chadwick turned toward Illiri again. Tenzi's brow furrowed, having seen it before. *She holds the helm, not Chadwick.* After a long and silent moment, the duchess nodded.

The duke turned toward Pretencia. "King Dalwin, we would be honored to have you remain at Wayport as our guest. For..."

The door burst open, drawing everyone's attention. Tenzi turned as Sharene strode down the aisle, her face like stone. Behind her was a young man, tall with black hair, amber eyes, and broad shoulders. His clothing was fine enough for presentation at the palace, yet lacked the frivolity of the Duke's outfit. Eight armed guards trailed the young man.

When they reached the front, Sharene stood to the side, and the young man walked past Tenzi to stand before the dais. The guards fanned out behind Tenzi the others, the outer two each raising a loaded crossbow, aimed at the young man. When the remaining guards drew their swords, Tenzi turned toward the newcomer in curiosity. *Who is this? Why do they perceive him as such a threat?*

"Duke Chadwick, Duchess Illiri," the young man bowed his head.

"Um...Master Kony," Chadwick stammered. "What brings you to our court?"

"I just arrived from Kantaria and came to the palace, straight away," Kony said. "I am here to inform you that King Brock and Prince Broland are dead. The queen may join them, for she remained in a coma when I departed."

Tenzi gasped and glanced at Parker, who stared at Kony with a furrowed brow and pain in his eyes. Brock had been Parker's friend even before Tenzi met Parker – and that was twenty years ago.

Chadwick and Illiri locked eyes for a long moment. He leaned forward and addressed Kony. "You know this for sure? The king and prince are dead?"

"Yes. You see, I was there when the incident occurred."

The duke sat back, his fingers tapping the arm of his chair.

Kony turned and eyed Pretencia. "I believe it is time for you to commit, Chadwick." He turned back toward the Duke. "After all, we cannot have a rogue king roaming free, can we?"

Chadwick's eyes flicked from Kony, to Pretencia, to Tenzi, to the guards. He kneaded his hands and squirmed in his seat.

"Oh, for Issal's sake," Illiri swore. "It is time to be a man, Chadwick. Arrest them and let us be done with this charade."

With a nod toward his wife, Chadwick said, "You're right, Illiri." He turned toward Kony. "Ikonis, please join us on the dais. I do not wish you to get hurt."

As the young man climbed upon the dais, Tenzi's and Parker's eyes locked. He nodded, and she knew what she must do.

"Dalwin Pretencia," Chadwick announced, "I am formally placing you and your companions under arrest. Any who resist or attempt to flee will be killed."

Pretencia's face grew red, his cheeks shaking as he sneered, "You cannot do this, Chadwick. I'll not be locked in a cell again."

"Would you prefer death, Your Majesty?" Contempt dripped from Illiri's tone. "A new order has risen. One that already claimed your kingdom, and will now add Kantaria to its lands. Chadwick and I will govern all of Kantaria now that Brock no longer stands in our way."

"You heard the duke," Sharene said to the guards. "Put them in shackles."

Tenzi lifted her hands and held them behind her head in surrender. Moving carefully, she slid a hand beneath her hair and gripped the hilt of the blade that hid in her vest, between her shoulder blades. With one fluid motion, she spun, launched the blade toward a guard who held a crossbow, and ducked low. The dagger struck him in the throat and he pulled the trigger, sending a bolt over Tenzi and striking the opposite bowman in the shoulder. Tenzi raced toward the second bowman as he staggered. She dropped to her hip, slid across the marble tiles, and stole the crossbow from the guard's grip as she glided through his legs. Rising to her feet, she shot a bolt toward the window as she leaped. The window shattered when the bolt struck, and she flew through the opening while glass rained down. Dropping the crossbow, she wrapped her arms around a tree limb to catch herself. When she looked down, Tenzi found herself dangling two stories above the ground.

"Get her!" Illiri shrieked from within the room.

Tenzi looked back at the broken window as guards rushed toward her. She rapidly walked her hands along the branch, toward the tree trunk. With a jerk, the branch bent and bounced with added weight. A backward peek revealed a guard hanging by one hand and trying to get a grip with the other. He grabbed a smaller branch that snapped, and he fell with a cry.

When her feet were able to reach another branch, Tenzi shifted to it, scrambled to the trunk, and began to climb upward. Once she was well above the wall, she worked toward it with her feet on one branch, her hands holding the one above it. More shouts came from the broken window, joined by shouts below as guards poured out a door into the garden below.

She neared the wall, the branch supporting her feet hanging a stride from it and a few feet above it. The wall was two feet thick, the drop beyond exceeding fifty feet to the river. A *twang* sounded and the leaves before Tenzi's face scattered in a burst when a crossbow bolt flew past. Glancing backward, she found another bowman running toward the window. With a prayer on her lips, Tenzi jumped off the branch, pushed off the wall with one foot, and launched herself beyond it. As she plummeted toward the river, she prayed that the water would be deep enough, or her escape meant nothing.

7

WITHIN THE VOID

Cassie kept her cloak wrapped tight about her to fend of the cold. Snow beneath her boots crunched with each step. Another set of footprints dotted the road, heading in the other direction. Snow had begun to gather in those tracks – tracks Cassie had made less than an hour earlier.

She stopped and listened. Somehow, the world seemed quieter during the snowfall, as if everything had stopped to stare in wonder. Again, her gaze shifted toward the gray blanket overhead. Softly falling snowflakes settled on her cheek, her forehead, her eye, each melting within moments of contact. She opened her mouth to the sky and waited. While snow did collect and melt on her tongue, the moisture was a pittance. *It would take forever to quench my thirst this way.* With a sigh, she lowered her head, pulled the hood up, and continued back to the Ward.

Weeks prior, she had anticipated the first snowfall, expecting a wondrous experience. Unfortunately, recent events had consumed her joy and left her hollow and numb. *Broland never got the chance to see or touch snow. Now...it's too late.* The thought of what might have been rekindled her sorrow and sent fresh tears down her cheeks. Using the corner of her cloak, she wiped them dry and noticed someone standing beside the stables.

It took Cassie but a moment to realize it was Rena, wearing a gray cloak that matched her own. White flakes dotted the girl's auburn hair, and concern filled her green eyes. As Cassie drew near, Rena called out.

"I was hoping you would return sooner. It's cold out here."

"Didn't you grow up in Cinti Mor?" Cassie asked.

"Yes. But we knew better than to linger in winter weather for no reason."

"I have my reasons…" Cassie left the rest unsaid. Rena knew why.

"How are you today?" Rena asked. "You had already left the room when I woke."

"I…couldn't sleep." *Not that I tried.*

"You attempted to reach your mother again last night?"

"Yes." There was no reason to hide it. "I am able to enter the dream world with ease, and I can sense which dream is yours. My mother, however… There are so many dream bubbles. I don't know how to locate hers among the thousands of others."

Rena turned. "Come on. Let's go inside."

Cassie followed, stepping in Rena's tracks. The snow was already halfway up her boots and it left Cassie wondering how much would accumulate by the time the storm finally passed through the valley.

Rena opened the door and Cassie hurried inside, stamping her feet and littering the rug with clumps of snow. She lowered her hood and fluffed her cloak to add more snow to the entryway, leaving the floor damp and glistening.

"It sounds as if your attempts would be more productive if fewer people were sleeping." Rena said as she dusted herself off.

Cassie gasped. "Of course. Why didn't I think of that?"

Rena's eyes narrowed. "Are you messing with me?"

"No. I'm serious. I was thinking that dream walking needed to take place at night. Since my mother remains unconscious, she is sleeping during the day when there are far fewer dreams occurring."

"So, you are saying…"

"I'm saying that I should try it now."

"It's almost time for lunch."

"Exactly."

Rena stared into Cassie's eyes. "If you wish to try now, I will come watch over you."

"I would...appreciate that, so long as you don't interrupt me."

Without waiting for a response, Cassie dashed up the stairs with Rena following. As she walked to her room, Cassie sought her source of Order. Within the blue, calm presence, she settled into a walking meditation. Rena unlocked the door and Cassie shuffled inside, shedding her damp cloak before heading to her bedroom. She sat on the bed while Rena closed the curtain. By the time she was lying on her back, Cassie's eyes were closed, and she was in full meditation.

She extended herself into the blue presence of Order and pushed through into the other place, beyond.

The void was quiet and far less populated than in the past. A smattering of bubbles remained close to Cassie, but the one she needed was in Kantar. Thinking of her home, she willed herself there, and her surroundings shifted, a new group of bubbles appearing. *Am I really in Kantar...or the dream version of it?* she wondered. *If so, how do I know which dream is hers?*

She extended toward a bubble, touched it, and poked her head inside. She sensed a man's presence, his dream coalescing to a bedroom with a massive bed covered in red blankets. What Cassie saw next made her gasp and recoil in embarrassment. When she withdrew, the bubble sealed behind her with a soft pop.

Oh, my, she thought. *I must remember that these bubbles are filled with private thoughts. Sometimes,* very *private thoughts.* Rather than continuing to try every random bubble, Cassie chose a new tactic.

Thinking of her mother, Cassie tried to focus on her mother's spirit, her honest nature, her compassion. She visualized her mother in her mind and again willed herself to *shift*.

Three bubbles floated near her, one of them somehow drawing her attention. Cassie responded and carefully slid her hand through the bubble's wall. Within, she sensed something familiar.

Eager to see her mother, Cassie pushed herself into the bubble. What she found was unexpected.

She and Ashland were in a closet. The door was closed, a slice of daylight coming from the crack beneath it. An oppressive sense of hopelessness hung in the air. Shadows and cobwebs and worse waited in the dark corners.

Cassie's eyes adjusted, and her gaze fell upon her mother. Ashland was just a girl, no more than eleven or twelve years old. Her face was bruised, her eye swollen shut, her arm held close to her chest while blood dripped from her elbow. Concern for this poor girl welled up inside Cassie. She knelt and put her hand on the girl's head.

"You are injured. I can heal you."

Ashland blinked. "I've been waiting for the Master Herrin to heal me, but Tyrin will not allow them near me. He says I will learn nothing if I am not allowed to feel pain."

"Tyrin?"

"My uncle." The word was bereft of affection. "He's training me so I can one day attend the Academy in Fallbrandt."

Cassie had never heard her mother mention an uncle. "Did he do this to you?"

Ashland gave a weak nod and turned away in shame. "I...must learn respect."

Cassie made a decision, touching the girl on the arm while seeking her source of Order. Ashland gasped and chill wracked her body. The girl morphed, her appearance aging.

"What did you do to me?" Ashland's voice sounded older.

"I healed you."

Silence for two beats.

"Cassie?"

Hope welled up inside Cassie, her eyes blurring from tears. "Yes, Mother. I'm here to help you."

"Where are we?"

Cassie wiped her eyes. "This is a dream. I need you to wake."

"A dream?"

Ashland stood and tried the door, but it did not open. "It's locked. I...I don't know how to get out."

"Use your magic, Mother."

Ashland blinked "My...magic?"

Cassie set her jaw, drew the knife at her hip, and began carving a symbol into the door. She then reached out for Chaos, and took it in. Raw energy flared inside her until she poured the energy into the rune. It, too, flared to life, illuminating the closet with crimson light until the symbol pulsed and faded. Spinning, Cassie kicked the door with her heel and it shattered, splinters swirling in the air and dissipating in a wisp of smoke.

Beyond the door, was a pale, shapeless space lit by white light.

Ashland stared at it. "I…am afraid."

Cassie took her arm. "Don't fear, mother. I'm with you. You can do this. You must wake."

Ashland stared into Cassie's eyes and nodded. "Yes. I must wake. Brock needs me. My people need me."

Tears of loss blurred Cassie's vision as she turned away. *I cannot tell her about Broland and father. Not yet. Not now.*

"Let's go," Ashland said as she headed toward the door.

Cassie moved with her mother, through the doorway, and into the light.

The bubble popped and the void returned. Cassie ignored the other bubbles and willed herself toward her own distant source of Order. Relief stoked dormant happiness inside her. She had done it. Her mother was awake, but new fears had surfaced, and there was little time to act.

Cassie opened her eyes and sat upright. Rena jumped and put her hand to her chest.

"You startled me," Rena's breathed heavily. "Is everything all right?"

"I found my mother." Cassie flung her legs off the bed and stood. "She is awake, but she's in danger."

Cassie waited in the quiet corridor, leaning against the wall. The briefing room door opened and she strode forward, ready.

"Cassie?" Master Hedgewick arched his brow while looking up and down the corridor. "Were you waiting this entire time?"

Cassie nodded firmly. "Yes. It is imperative I speak with you and the other leaders."

Hedgewick moved aside and waved Cassie into the briefing room.

Delvin leaned forward in his chair, appearing alarmed – an unusual display of emotion from him. "Is this about your brother? Are Quinn and Brandt in trouble?"

"No." Cassie shook her head as she approached the table. "He hasn't contacted me today."

"What's this about, Cassilyn?" Firellus said.

Her gaze swept the faces of the three men as she considered where to begin.

"My mother is awake."

Hedgewick leaned forward, his brow furrowed. "Ashland? How do you know this?"

"I…" She could not think of a response that wouldn't also reveal her secret. *Oh, well. They would find out eventually.* "I contacted her in a dream."

Delvin chuckled. "I contact many women in my dreams. Some are queens, some…not so much."

Cassie scowled at him. "I'm serious. I have been able to…visit other people's dreams. I entered Rena's dream a few days ago and have since been trying to do the same to contact my mother. Earlier today, I was able to do so. I found her, helped her, and she woke."

"That is…incredible." The awe was apparent in Hedgewick's voice. "How does it work?"

With a huff, Cassie rolled her eyes. "That's not important. She's *awake.*" The men stared at her. "Don't you see? Once word gets out that she survived, she becomes the target of another attack. My mother, the queen of Kantaria, is in danger. We have to help her."

Delvin's eyes narrowed, and he turned toward Firellus. "She has a point, Elias."

"True," Master Firellus leaned back, his finger tapping the table as he considered the situation. "But, who can we assign? We just agreed that we must send a squad out to deal with the latest disaster in Vallerton. If we have a rogue arcanist, as we suspect, it will only grow worse if we ignore it. With Bilchard, Rena, Kirk, and Nalah set to depart with Kwai-Lan, that leaves only Cassilyn, Curan, and ourselves."

Cassie's brow furrowed. *Rena is leaving? On a mission? I wonder if she knows, yet.*

A grimace crossed Delvin's face. "You're right. We dare not send Cassie because she is too valuable…especially now that she can communicate in dreams. I suspect we can utilize this new skill in a number of interesting ways." The man grinned at the thought before shaking his head, as if to clear it. "The only option is Curan, whose fighting skill and natural abilities make him a solid fit, but he's only been here for a few weeks. Sending him out on a mission this early would go against protocol."

The room fell silent. Cassie's gaze moved from one man to another. All remained silent.

"So, that's it?" Cassie blurted, her voice rising in pitch. "You say you want to help my mother, but you won't do it?"

Firellus sighed. "Cassie..."

"No!" She slapped the table so hard it stung her hand, but she didn't care. "I'll not listen to your excuses. If you won't find a way to help my mother, I will."

Cassie turned, ripped the door open, and slammed it behind her. Her stomping footsteps echoed down the hall as she headed toward the stairwell. The door behind her opened and Delvin's voice called out from behind her.

"Don't even consider leaving the Ward, Cassie. If you try it, we'll hunt you down and lock you up. If you were captured by the enemy, it would create an even greater danger, not just to Kantaria, but to the whole of Issalia."

She darted up the stairwell, his words ringing in her head with the sound of truth – a truth she would rather deny. Still, she would not sit idle and lose her mother. She had already lost too much.

Delvin had a point. There was only one solution. Her mind was set, and she was determined to be more convincing during her next conversation.

I'll make him listen, and I'll send him off tonight, when everyone is asleep.

8

AWAKENINGS

Ashland opened her eyes, only to close them again. It was bright. Too bright. Her head hurt and her throat was dry from thirst. She heard a voice nearby...Wharton's voice, too muffled for her to make out the words. With effort, she was able to turn her head toward the sound and away from the light.

Through blurry eyes, she saw Wharton talking to Master Beldon, the citadel temple minister. The short, pudgy man appeared small beside the captain of the guard. Wharton had his back facing her, his arms motioning as he spoke with the minister. Beldon shook his head and glanced toward Ashland, his eyes widening and his mouth gaping open.

"She's awake!" the minister exclaimed as he pushed past Wharton and rushed toward Ashland. When Beldon reached the room, he fumbled for a pitcher on the nightstand and filled a small cup with a spout. He knelt beside her bed and held the spout to her lips.

"Drink, my Queen."

Ashland opened her mouth, and glorious water filled it. She swallowed and coughed when some slid down the wrong pipe. Even the cough required effort. When it receded, she opened her mouth, and he gave her another drink. She swallowed and saw Wharton standing in the doorway, staring at her with a look she could not ignore.

"What happened?" she croaked. "Where am I?"

Beldon's gaze shifted to Wharton. The captain of the guard appeared fierce as usual, with wavy dark hair that grazed the shoulders of his leather uniform – black and trimmed with gold and red. The sight of Wharton's weathered face – framed by a dark goatee – usually brought Ashland comfort and a sense of safety. Instead, something about his expression gave her pause. With a grim nod, Wharton indicated that Beldon should continue. Ashland's unease grew worse.

When the master minister turned toward her, his eyes refused to meet hers. Beldon ran his free hand over his balding head, smoothing the wisps of gray hair he had combed across it.

"There was an incident, Your Highness. An explosion. The injury to your head was severe, and you came very close to death. I was able to heal you, but it left your life force badly weakened."

An explosion, Ashland repeated in her head. She vaguely recalled Broland's friend in the royal apartment before he fled over the railing. What happened next, she was unsure. A sense of panic lingered in the memory.

She blinked and cleared her throat. "How long have I been asleep?"

The minister brought a wet cloth to her face and wiped her brow. "Ten days."

Ten days. So long. Without food. "I need to eat…and more water." She tried to sit up, but her muscles failed and her head hardly came off the pillow. "Can you help me sit?"

"There is more," Beldon's apologetic tone stirred fear inside her. He held the cloth in both hands, his fingers working it as he bit his lip. His mouth opened but no sound came out. He turned away and tried again, this time successful.

"The King – your husband – did not survive. Nor did the Prince."

A gasp caught in Ashland's throat, her heart skipping a beat as she drew a ragged breath. She shook her head, the effort requiring far more energy than the result might convey.

"No. No. It cannot be true," Ashland's plea was barely audible, even to herself.

Brock and Broland, both gone? Shock. Pain. Sorrow. Her world was crashing down, the fortifications on which she had built her life, now crumbling. A lonely tear tracked down her cheek – all that her parched body could muster.

Wharton leaned forward and put his hand on Beldon's shoulder. "She requested food, Beldon. Your focus must remain on her health" Although Wharton's tone was subdued, it still carried the weight of a command. "Go find something suitable while I console our Queen."

Beldon nodded and climbed to his feet with a groan. When the minister's purple cloak faded from view, Wharton closed the door and turned toward Ashland.

"I am sorry you had to experience that, Your Highness." Wharton knelt beside the bed, his voice dropping to whisper. "I must share a secret and spare you further pain. Your husband forbade me from telling anyone but you." He leaned even closer, his whisper filled with excitement. "King Brock lives, as does Prince Broland."

Ashland blinked in confusion and stared into Wharton's eyes, searching for the truth. "I don't understand."

Wharton glanced back at the closed door before responding. "There was an assassination attempt. It was Kony..." He grimaced. "If that is even his real name. A search was conducted after the explosion, but to no avail. We found the rope he used to climb the western wall and escape the citadel, but we were unable to track him down.

"Brock feared another attempt would follow if our enemies knew of his survival. While under a disguise, he and Broland departed the city the day after the attack."

Lingering effects of her extended sleep still clouded Ashland's mind. Through the murk, she sorted through Wharton's words and the conflicting emotions inside her.

She stared into his eyes, searching for answers. "It's true?" *Please, let it be true.* "They are truly alive?"

"Yes." Wharton gripped her hand. "I swear it, my Queen."

The pain in her heart eased, and another tear tracked down her face. She closed her eyes and breathed in a deep sigh of relief. The pit of sorrow that had briefly formed now filled with joy. When she opened them, she saw Wharton staring at her in concern. *Be strong, Ashland. You are still queen of Kantaria.*

"How were you able to convince Beldon and the others that...?" she couldn't say it aloud.

"That Brock and Broland were dead?" When Ashland gave the slightest nod, his eyes lowered. "Others did die during the attack: General Budakis, Burke, and Lorna."

"Gunther?" With their friendship lasting more than two decades, Ashland had always been fond of the general. His loss left a hollowness in the joy of her husband's and son's survival.

Wharton paused and turned away to collect himself. Ashland knew how much Wharton had respected Budakis. He took a deep breath and continued.

"Their bodies were badly burned, which made them difficult to recognize. We dressed up the two guards to appear as the king and prince before we set them ablaze in a public funeral, along with General Budakis. We were sure to spread the word that the king and prince were dead and you were deathly ill from your injuries. That bought us time without fear of another attack. Now that you have awakened, you must get well soon. Once word is out that you live, your life is in jeopardy."

Ashland considered his words and knew them as fact. With the crown came responsibility. In that responsibility, she sought resolve. She would eat, drink, and gather her strength. A quick recovery was required, for Kantaria needed her.

"There is one last thing you should know before Beldon returns." Wharton's face darkened. "With you in a coma, the king and prince both thought dead, and Cassie and Brandt out of the country, someone had to take control and manage the kingdom."

"Yes. Of course."

"The person who assumed the role did so based on his own court ruling. As we speak, Magistrate Filbert sits on the throne. I don't have to tell you that the situation is bound to be…complicated."

Hearing a knock, Wharton stood, turned toward the door, and opened it to reveal Master Beldon and his apprentice, Terissa.

"We have porridge, dried beef, and fruit for you, my Queen." Beldon rushed in with a thick pillow under one arm, a bed tray under the other. "While it's not a lavish meal, it will give you strength." Beldon looked across the bed, toward Wharton. "Captain, will you please help her sit, so I can slide this pillow behind her?"

Wharton did as requested, scooping his hand beneath Ashland's pillow and lifting so Beldon could prop her up with the second pillow. Once the bed table was placed across Ashland's lap, Terissa scurried in to place a steaming bowl of porridge, a bowl of chopped fruit, and two strips of dried beef on it. Beldon appeared with a glass of water.

"Will you need anything else, Your Highness?" The minister kneaded his hands nervously.

"No. Thank you, Master Beldon."

"Very well," Beldon shuffled to the door. "Ring the bell on your nightstand when you need me."

When the minister and his assistant departed, Wharton turned toward her. "I need to check on a few things. I'll be back later this afternoon to see how you fare."

"Thank you, Wharton."

With a salute, Wharton turned and marched out the door. The room fell silent.

Ashland stared down at the food and found herself reaching for her resolve just to eat. While she wasn't fond of porridge, she knew that regaining her health was more important than taste. Her thoughts shifted to her husband, and she reached out to him…fearful that he might not respond.

Brock. Silence. *Please answer. I cannot bear losing you.*

After a beat, she received his response.

Ashland? Is it really you?

A fresh wave of relief washed over her, creating tears of joy joined by soft laughter. *Yes, my heart. I'm awake and well, and I miss you dearly.*

Thank Issal. I had begun to dread attempting to contact you. With each day that passed without you responding, my fears grew stronger. Ashland sensed his pain through their bond. *Leaving you behind was the hardest decision I have ever made. You are my light, and my world is darkness without you.*

As is mine without you. Please tell me that you and Broland are safe.

Broland is with me…for now. We are both safe and are in Nor Torin.

Ashland held tight to her joy until Brock interrupted.

You must take over and rule Kantaria as if I am gone. I intend to keep my survival a secret until I am in position to respond to the Empire. It will take a few weeks, maybe longer, before I am ready.

What do you intend to do, Brock?

I am aware of the ideals The Hand intends to spread. I know Varius and Kardan and how they think. Archon Varius believes she had to kill me because she sees me as a threat to her, to the Empire, and to the beliefs The Hand would have others follow. Although I have done nothing to provoke an attack, she sent an assassin to kill me and the people I love. Since she believes I am too dangerous to live, Ashland sensed the heat of Brock's anger through their bond, *I intend to prove her correct.*

9

RANGERS

A rumble shook beneath Chuli's feet. The weapons hanging on the wall shook, threatening to fall to the floor. Squeaks coming from above forced her to look up in concern. Shadows of crossbeams stretched across the slanted logs that formed the ceiling – shadows cast by the lone glowlamp in the room.

"Why did they build this place out of wood?" Chuli muttered.

"They likely believed that the garrison was temporary," Jonah guessed. "Wood makes for easy construction. It takes many hours and a lot of sweat to cut bricks, haul them, stack them, and mortar them together."

"It still seems…unnatural."

Jonah snorted. "This is coming from someone who grew up in a city carved from stone – a city hidden in a secret cave above a box canyon, nonetheless."

Chuli glared at him. "Hush. We do not speak of Mondomi where Outlanders might hear us." Still glaring, she leaned closer. "Don't make me have to kill you, Jonah Selbin."

With alarm in his eyes, Jonah turned to Thiron, who shrugged. Torney chuckled.

Jonah blinked and turned toward Chuli. "You do know we're the only people in here, right?"

"Others may be listening." Her eyes shifted from side to side as she leaned close and whispered. "We have spies. The Empire might as well."

"She does have a point, Jonah." Thiron said in his deep voice.

The door opened and Captain Marcella entered, wearing an even heavier scowl than normal. Her scribe, Samantha, followed Marcella in and closed the door.

"What's wrong, Captain?" Jonah asked. "Did something go wrong with the tunnel?"

While Marcella had red hair and green eyes like Jonah, the similarities between the two ended there. Tall for a woman, Marcella appeared forever stern, as if the weight of the world rested on her shoulders. Perhaps a small portion of it did.

"Another week has passed without the garrison receiving reinforcements."

Thiron sat back with his hands behind his head. "How many soldiers do you have now? Five hundred?"

"Five hundred and twenty."

"You were expecting more?"

"Chadwick was to secretly drain his city of the nine hundred soldiers stationed in Wayport. They were to arrive here in small groups, leaving Wayport with eighty guards to hold it should an attack come from the sea."

"How many has he sent?"

"None."

"The others were all sent by King Brock?"

"Yes. I first arrived twelve weeks ago, accompanied by two hundred soldiers, a dozen miners, and a handful of carpenters. We spent the next eight weeks rebuilding the compound, including three new bunkhouses. Brock then began sending additional troops, twenty soldiers at a time to make it difficult for the Empire to keep track. Chadwick was to do the same."

Thiron's brow furrowed. "You haven't been notified of any trouble in Wayport?"

"No" Marcella grimaced at Samantha, the young scribe writing at a fierce pace. "Do you have to record *everything*?"

The timid blond, just a few years older than Chuli, shrunk from the captain while hugging her journal. "But, these are the details that define history."

Marcella rolled her eyes. "You and your history."

Samantha straightened her back, seemingly recovering her pride as she said, "Remember, he who does not learn from mistakes of the past…"

"Is doomed to repeat them." Marcella glowered at the girl, who, again, wilted under the stern woman's gaze. "You've said it often enough that *I* have it memorized."

A knock drew everyone's attention.

"Come in," Marcella bellowed.

A man stepped inside and thumped his fist against his chest plate. "I have news from the miners, Captain. The tunnel is complete. They are cleaning away the debris now."

"Thank you, Sergeant. Gather a few soldiers, and help get it cleared so we can get these people out tonight."

The soldier nodded and stepped outside.

Marcella turned toward Thiron. "You heard the man. The tunnel is ready, so you two can be on your way. I hope you slept well last night because tonight might be a long one."

Chuli's gaze flicked toward Thiron before addressing Marcella. "You are positive we cannot take the road, even at night?"

"It won't work. The Empire barricaded the road ten miles southeast of here. They post scouts to watch us. We captured a few and killed a few others. Since then, they have been more careful, but I am sure they exist. Our position is critical to anything they might try, and they won't be caught unaware, even if the troops arrive in small groups in the middle of the night." Marcella shook her head. "I am sure of it. Through the tunnel is the only way."

Thiron's bird-like gaze shifted to Chuli, and she nodded, indicating she was ready. After three weeks in the garrison, her real mission would finally begin.

The pale blue glow from the stone in Thiron's hand was Chuli's guide in the darkness. Just wide enough for two men to walk astride and with a ceiling that sometimes required Chuli to crouch, the tunnel was unlike those she grew up roaming in Mondomi. Her childhood home was all rock – hard, often smooth, and rarely dirty. Here, rocks occupied sections while other tunnel sections were nothing but clay. The less stable areas were reinforced with wooden frames, like doorways without a door. The floor was all dirt and debris, interrupted by the occasional boulder that was easier to tunnel around than through.

Ahead, the light shone upon swirls of dust lingering in the air. Thiron stopped and pulled out the swatch of cloth Sergeant Rios had given him, and Chuli did the same. The miners had said that dust stirred from tonight's blast might take hours to settle. Until then, the dry particles would fill the back half of the tunnel. With the cloth covering their nose and mouth, they again advanced. Chuli tried to imagine where they were in relation to the surface above them.

The garrison had been built against a steep canyon wall, too steep to scale. It provided a natural defense from the north, while forcing any approaching army to funnel between the garrison and the cliff that dropped to the sea at the south. That narrow strip of land created the perfect location for a military outpost. Chuli was bewildered as to why a more formidable structure had not replaced it many years ago.

Logically, Chuli and Thiron were somewhere beneath the plateau that formed the canyon wall. After five minutes of navigating the tunnel, she began to wonder how far it went before it returned to the surface.

It was gradual at first, but the tunnel began sloping upward, the dust in the air thickening. After a dozen more strides, the incline steepened until Thiron and Chuli climbed from the tunnel. After removing the cloth from their faces, they surveyed their surroundings.

They had emerged in a box canyon with steep walls a quarter mile apart, both sides rising hundreds of feet up. The visible starlit sky above was a narrow strip that ran east and west, the stars providing enough light for her to see the scrub and rocks surrounding them.

"We will head east until we find a way out of the canyon," Thiron said softly. "We may need to wait for daylight to scale a wall if there is no opening at the end."

Holding the glowing rock held before him, Thiron began weaving his way through the brush with Chuli a step behind.

The going was slow...methodical. More than once, they were forced to backtrack when they came to a dead end of rock, cacti, or shrubbery. Loose gravel crunched beneath their feet with each step, becoming louder in the low areas that acted as a wash. The wash made Chuli think of rain. Having grown up with box canyons, she knew how dangerous they could become during heavy rainfall. The water had to go somewhere and it often did so at a swift pace.

Numerous times, Thiron stopped and held his hand up, listening. Hearing movement, Chuli would stare into the darkness with one hand on her bow, the other holding the fletching of an arrow in her quiver. The second of such an instance was made more intense by the reflection of eyes shining in the brush, green and unblinking. Suddenly, the animal bolted, scurried across the canyon floor, and disappeared into a thicket.

"Coyote," Thiron said as he resumed his trek eastward.

After what seemed like many hours, the canyon narrowed until the walls stood no more than fifty feet apart. Towering, dark, and imposing, the canyon walls seemed as if they sought to consume Chuli and Thiron. In that narrow gap, they came upon a pile of massive boulders that ran uphill.

Thiron said his second word of the past three hours, "Landslide," and began to climb the rocks.

Moving with even more care, their pace slowed further. Halfway up, Chuli stepped on an unstable rock, caught her balance, and pulled back as it broke loose and began a long, noisy tumble down the pile. Thiron glared at her with the glowing stone held between them, and Chuli winced at the commotion. Minutes seemed to pass before the rock came to a stop, the noise stopping with it.

"Sorry," she whispered.

With a grunt in response, Thiron turned and resumed his ascent.

Concentrating on each step while following her mentor and his glowing stone, Chuli didn't notice the sky above growing lighter until the surrounding rocks had grown noticeably more visible. She paused and noticed the top of the surrounding ridges standing just two stories above her. Hurrying, she caught up to Thiron, scrambled up the embankment, and climbed atop a narrow plateau.

The sky to the east glowed with the pale blue of impending dawn.

Twilight covered the plateau in purple light, mixing with the shadows that left Chuli imagining the night resisting the coming day, reluctant to release its grip on the land.

Thiron led her across the ridge and slowed when he reached the downslope on the other side. The man stopped and Chuli stopped beside him, both staring at the scene below as the sun edged over the horizon.

An expansive, flat basin stretched before them, covered in trees that stretched for miles. To the south, Chuli could just make out the strip of roadway that ran along the cliffs overlooking the Sea of Fates. Directly south of their position, in a narrow choke point between the ridge and the sea, a wooden structure blocked the road. It was miles away and the light still pale, yet Chuli could see soldiers moving about the area. *That must be the blockade Marcella described – the border of Empire lands.*

Turning north, she found mountains and plateaus similar to the one where they currently stood. The sun further eased its way into the sky and forced Chuli to squint at the glare. She held her hand over her eyes and peered to the southeast. From deep in the forest, thin trails of smoke rose toward the sky.

"The enemy camp," Thiron said. "It must be ten miles away."

Chuli eased forward and peeked over the edge. The drop was likely a thousand feet – the cliff wall too steep to navigate.

"How do we get down?"

"Come," Thiron turned and walked along the cliff edge, heading north. "We will find a way, and then, we will rest until it grows dark."

A nightrill call echoed from a tree somewhere above. Another bird repeated the call, somewhere to the west. Although the forest was dark, it lacked the overwhelming presence of the Red Towers, north of Vallerton. The thought stirred memories – images of a giant badger flashing in Chuli's head. The monster's attack had wounded Wyck and nearly killed Thiron. Chuli's arrows had done nothing to stop the beast nor had they reduced the terror that had gripped her. If not for Jonah's healing abilities and the augmentation he had applied to Wyck, they all would have died. A chill ran down Chuli's spine. She hoped never to face anything like that monster again.

The meager remaining leaves in the surrounding trees allowed starlight to filter through and extended her field of view. Ahead of her, Thiron gripped the small glowstone in his fist, covering much of it while a narrow slice of pale light shone upon the ground before him. Rather than moving with speed, they focused on stealth.

Placing each footstep softly while avoiding fallen twigs or wilted leaves required concentration and patience – an effort that wore on Chuli. The short naps she had been able to capture during the day didn't help the situation, leaving her unrested. She and Thiron had spent the daylight hours in a cave-like recess atop the plateau. Once the sun had finally neared the western horizon, Thiron led Chuli down a series of ledges and slopes toward the bottom of the cliff. By the time they had reached the bottom, dusk was upon them. Chuli recalled looking up at the dark wall of rock they had descended and thinking that only a goat might decide to climb it.

Thiron stopped and gestured for her to stop as well. Chuli listened and heard...laughter? The sound was distant and from somewhere east of their position. Adjusting his course, Thiron angled to the left, toward the sound.

Thiron pocketed the glowstone and the darkness grew more bold, the shadows deeper. Moving with care and only starlight to guide them, they circled around a thicket and ducked beneath low branches before stopping. Orange flickering light appeared in the distance and then faded, only to reappear again.

"Quiet, now," Thiron whispered.

Chuli frowned at him. As if that needed saying. *You may as well remind me to breathe.*

The man gestured to the north, indicating for Chuli to head in that direction. Crouching, Thiron snuck off to the east, circled around a tree, and slid beneath the bough of a lonely pine.

Pausing to collect herself, Chuli took a calming breath and crept northward. Laughter came from ahead, along with the hum of people talking. She caught a glimpse of flickering firelight and the peaked silhouettes of tents nearby.

Using the light as a beacon, she eased toward the edge of the wood, got down on her hands and knees, and crawled through some long grass growing between two thick shrubs. Careful not to shake the branches, she continued forward until the camp came into view.

Dozens of men sat around the fire while others milled about, some slipping into tents for the night. Within the camp, she counted five tents, each spacious enough to sleep six or eight men. Beyond, she spotted other camps, with the flickering orange of fires extending as far as she could see.

Two men stood from beside the fire and said goodnight to their fellow soldiers. Turning, they headed toward the gap between tents and straight for Chuli's position. She remained still, scarcely breathing as the men approached.

"How long do we wait here?"

"Capt'n says not long, now. More soldiers comin' from the north. They get here, an' we march."

Both men stopped before the shrubs to Chuli's left and right and then began to relieve themselves. The way her heart pounded from anxiety, Chuli feared that the men might hear it above the sound of their streams.

"I'll be happy to go. I've been itching to try those muskets against something other than a practice target."

The other man snorted. "Those little pea shooters ain't gonna make no difference."

The acrid scent of urine began to waft up Chuli's nose. She held her breath and prayed to the Spirit of Nature that the men leave.

"I'll take those against a sword any day. Before anyone can get close enough to poke you, bang, they're dead."

"I'll put my money on the flash bombs." The men turned and began walking toward the tents. "Launch a few o' those, and there won't be nobody left t' fight."

Their voices faded to murmurs as the distance increased, leaving Chuli alone with the thump of her pulse.

Chuli backed away on her elbows and knees, rose to a crouch, and tried to catch her breath. Movement in the periphery made her jump with start. Her hand went to her chest when she realized it was Thiron, passing just a few strides away. He waved for her to follow as he headed north.

—+ ϕ +—

Chuli squatted beside the brook, the air bubbling from her water skin as she filled it. Tilting the water skin to her mouth, the cool water soothed her throat as it slid down. After dunking it back in the water and filling it again, she capped it and climbed back up the rise. She ducked beneath the pines that lined the water and crouched while she approached Thiron's position.

The light of the setting sun painted the basin with an amber hue and made Chuli think of looking at the world through a brown-tinted bottle. The forest stretched out below for a good half mile before it opened to the clearing where the army was camped. Thiron was not looking in that direction.

Turning toward the east, Chuli spotted another force approaching. The reflection of the sun off metal drew her eyes farther south.

"Those steam carriages look big beside the men on horseback," she said.

"They are big. And they are pulling something as well."

Chuli counted four machines, each generating a combination of black smoke and white steam. Watching in silence, she tried to identify what each carriage was towing.

"This is not good," Chuli said when she recognized the machines rolling behind each carriage. "Those catapults are big."

Thiron backed away from the edge, and Chuli mirrored his action, with neither standing upright until they were beyond the trees.

"We have seen enough," Thiron said. "We must return as quickly as possible. The garrison must be warned. They cannot stand up to what they are about to face."

"It will be a difficult climb up the cliffside if you plan to return through the canyon."

Thiron stared into the distance, his eyes narrowed in thought. "Speed is more important than stealth. Night is coming soon. We will loop around the western perimeter of the forest and will follow the road back to Hipoint."

Chuli turned in that direction, frowning. "What about the barricade? There are guards. How do we get past it?"

With a grim look from Thiron, Chuli knew the answer.

—+ φ +—

Clouds rolled in from the sea after nightfall, blotting out the stars and leaving the night as black as ink. The blue glow of lamps provided light for the guards on the eastern side of the wall – light that was to their backs as they stared west.

Built in haste to barricade the hundred-foot gap between the steep cliffside to the north and the precipitous drop to the sea on the south, the wooden wall stood fourteen feet tall. The gate at the center remained closed and barred. A ten-foot-high scaffold ran across the interior to each side of the gate. Four bowmen stood upon the scaffold, staring over the wall, ready to attack anyone approaching from Hipoint. They apparently had not considered a threat approaching from behind them.

Crouched in shadows so thick that she could not see the bow she held before her, Chuli waited while Thiron crept around the backside of the barracks. She stared hard into the blackness and tried to determine his position. A shadow shifted along the barracks wall, barely visible from the indirect light of the glowlamp around the corner. Thiron eased along the wall with his back to it and neared the corner. Moving quickly, Thiron snuck a peek and pulled back. A moment later, he slipped around the corner. That was her signal.

Remaining in a crouch, Chuli climbed down from the rock pile and crept toward the wall, careful to remain in the shadow cast by the barracks. Timing her strides with the crashing waves below the cliffs, Chuli hoped the sound was enough to mask the crunch of gravel beneath each step she took. The entire time, she watched the men atop the wall, ready to loose an arrow if one turned around.

When she neared the barracks, Thiron reappeared with a rope trailing behind him. He wrapped it about a log sticking from the wall and tied it off. He turned toward her, slid his bow off his shoulder, and gave a nod.

Chuli ran to the road, drew, and took aim. Her target – the furthest guard upon the wall – stood fifty paces away. She held the bowstring back, steady, and her target seemed to grow as she focused upon him. Adjusting for the breeze coming from the sea, she shifted her aim and released. Before the arrow even struck, her hand was at her quiver, her fingers gripping the fletching of another arrow. The first arrow struck her target between the shoulder blades. He stumbled to his knees while she nocked her bow. Chuli drew back as the guard nearest turned toward his companion. The first guard fell backward off the scaffold as she released the second arrow, it striking the other guard in the ribs. The guard twisted about and saw her. She instantly nocked another arrow and shot, but not before the guard could call out.

"Attack!"

Her second arrow took the guard in the throat. He collapsed on the scaffold. The other two bowmen were already dead, both victims of Thiron's arrows. Thiron ran toward the gate with Chuli a few strides behind him. He tried to lift the bar, but it barely moved. It was a long, heavy slab of wood treated to resist flames.

A commotion from the barracks caused Chuli to turn toward it. The door opened, but only a few inches. Soldiers inside bellowed and struggled to pull it free, but the rope Thiron had tied to the handle held firm.

"Help me with this." Thiron said.

Chuli shouldered her bow and got beneath the bar. Using her legs, she pushed upward with all her might while Thiron did the same. The bar lifted, cleared the supports, and they both leaped backward as it fell to the road. Thiron then pulled on the gate, opening it enough for Chuli to slide through. Hearing a cry of pain, Chuli turned to find Thiron spun around, leaning against the inside of the gate. Grabbing his wrist, Chuli pulled him through the opening, and then she saw the arrow sticking from the back of his shoulder.

"You're hit," she said.

"I'll be fine. Just break it off. Someone will heal it when we reach the garrison."

With one hand, she gripped the arrow tightly at the base where it met his skin. Using the other, she broke the shaft and he gasped in pain, stumbling forward. Chuli dropped the broken arrow and found her hand covered in his blood.

"Don't just stand there," Thiron said as he waved her forward. "Run."

Chuli followed him past the glowlamps posted beside the road. The man was wounded – the back of his jerkin damp with blood. It was easily ten miles to Hipoint, assuming he made it that far. As the lights faded behind them, the darkness thickened. An image formed in her mind, one of her and Thiron stumbling blindly over the cliff's edge. Running in the dark, she heard only rasping breaths, footsteps on the gravel, and the surf far below.

10

ALL FOR A MAP

The wait staff poured through the kitchen doors and into the corridor. Among them, Brandt Talenz carried a carafe of wine in one hand and a tray of goblets in the other, careful to ensure that the swinging door did not strike the tray. He had made that mistake once the previous week. The result was a disaster that had nearly seen him fired. Memories of Master Sheen's screaming resurfaced. At the time, Brandt thought the veins in the man's temples might burst. Once Sheen had said his piece, and the broken glass had been cleaned up, Brandt resumed his duty as a steward. Not one word of the incident had been spoken since.

Up the stairs, the wait staff climbed with Sheen in the lead. Jurgan and Poul, the other two stewards, bracketed Brandt while the food servers followed. An official walked past, paying them no heed. Brandt thought back to his life in Kantar, all the times he had duly ignored servants, never giving them a second thought – never considering that they were the same as anyone else. He now knew better. *They all have families, hopes, and dreams of a better life. I wonder how many honestly love what they do and how many see such service as a yoke about their neck.* The observation made him wonder how he had not realized it earlier.

Reaching the door to the dining room, Sheen stopped, and the others stopped behind him. Sheen stepped inside and announced that drinks had arrived. On that signal, Brandt and the other stewards entered the room.

Tonight's dinner was an important one with all eight Council members, Archon Varius, General Kardan, and Captain Sculdin in attendance. Brandt had heard talk of another captain named Rorrick, but had not seen the man since his arrival in Sol Polis, two weeks past. Standing at the far end of the room was the girl who drew his attention.

Quinn was leaning against the wall in a casual manner, arms crossed beneath her breasts while her steely blue eyes surveyed her surroundings. Those eyes met Brandt's and her expression altered slightly. She ran one hand through her blond hair and tugged at the tail hanging over her shoulder. Two tugs meant to meet her two hours after nightfall.

Brandt nodded and began filling goblets with wine, working his way along one side of the table. Once finished, he stood to the side of the room and waited for the other wine steward and the one who served water. With drinks served, Brandt poured the remainder of his carafe into Poul's, who was to remain and refill goblets as needed. Jurgan and Brandt departed together, clearing the way for the food servers who entered and began performing their assigned tasks.

As Brandt ran down the stairs, he found himself grinning. It had been three days since he had been alone with Quinn. His wait would end tonight.

Brandt crept up the stairs, listening for movement from the floor above. Behind him, the servants' quarters were quiet, as usual at this late hour. He frowned at the thought of waking early after a short night of sleep. *I should have given sleep more appreciation when I still lived in Kantar.* At the time, he thought his life was busy. The volume of pranks he had concocted over the years was a telling sign that he had had too much time on his hands back then.

He turned the corner at the landing and eased up the stairs. A female guard walked past, twenty feet away. Brandt crouched low with his hands on the steps, hoping the guard had not spotted him.

The soft tap of her footsteps faded as she crossed the main hall, oblivious.

Moving to the top of the stairs, Brandt snuck a glance around the corner and found the guard moving away, the woman now halfway to the council chamber doors at the rear of the building. He slipped around the corner, padded along the wall, and carefully opened the side door. It let out the smallest of squeaks and Brandt winced. A sidelong glance revealed the guard approaching the far end of the hall. He slithered through the narrow opening and closed the door behind him. When it clicked shut, the pale blue light from inside fell away and darkness enveloped him.

As his eyes adjusted to the dim starlight, the garden before him began to coalesce. He crept away from the building and headed toward the shadowy silhouette of trees ahead. A cool breeze blew from the east, and the shrubs beside him whispered softly, the flowers near his knees rustling in response. A nightrill call echoed from above. Brandt peered up into the tree, but saw only shadows, and beyond those, only stars.

"Psst."

The sound came from his left. He adjusted his path, twisted to squeeze between a pair of tall shrubs, and found Quinn waiting in a small clearing.

"Why must you always be late?"

He shrugged in the darkness. "Old habits die hard."

"See what happens when you grow up as a spoiled brat?"

"Ouch," Brandt stopped before Quinn and touched her face. "I wish I could see your eyes. Meeting in the darkness like this…it deprives me of their beauty."

She snorted. "Does that line work with the daughters of other royals?"

He chuckled. "Not the smart ones."

"Good. I'd hate to think they lacked the capacity for reason."

"Well, I never said that." He shifted closer until he stood with his cheek beside hers, his voice dropping even lower. "Besides, they lack your fire, your strength."

He felt the warmth of her breath on his neck, the heat of her palm on his upper arm. His hand cupped her chin and guided her lips to his.

A rush of warmth ran through him, leaving his pulse racing and head dizzy by the time the kiss ended.

"How are you?" he asked.

"I'm fine...surviving." He sensed resignation in her voice. "It helps that you're here, even if we can rarely be together."

"By your side is where I wish to be, Quinn." He grinned. "That's where all the excitement happens."

"You're incorrigible."

"I've been called worse."

A moment passed with both of them quiet. Finally, Brandt decided it best not to avoid reality.

"While I am more than happy to spend time alone with you, I assume there was another reason you wished to meet me."

Quinn sighed. "Yes. A man arrived two days ago and gave a report to Varius and Kardan while I was in the room. He brought an army of hired soldiers, mercenaries gathered across Torinland and Hurnsdom. Somehow, he had gathered thousands."

Brandt frowned. "That doesn't sound good."

"They are to meet Mollis at a rendezvous point somewhere to the north. We need to figure out where they are heading."

"I agree, but what can I do? Other than serving them wine, I'm never close to those people."

"Kardan has maps in his office. He uses them for planning, and they are marked with Imperial troop locations." Quinn sighed. "I haven't figured out how to get close enough to read the maps. Both Varius and Kardan are in the room whenever I'm there. Kardan keeps long hours, often sleeping in his office rather than in his room on the floor below. Worse, whenever they are both away, I'm stuck following them around like a nursemaid."

"That does make it difficult," Brandt agreed. "Too bad there aren't copies elsewhere."

Quinn gasped, her eyes widening. "That's it!"

His brow furrowed. "What's *it*?"

"I saw similar maps on Sculdin's desk a few weeks ago."

"Captain Sculdin?" Brandt found himself nodding. "That makes sense. He is likely supporting Kardan and might be sent into the field himself."

"Why do you say that?"

"Did you forget? My father is the king of Kantaria. Between him and General Budakis, I've had my fill of military strategy discussions." Brandt thought about the maps and decided it was likely for Sculdin to become highly involved. "Kardan must trust Sculdin to give him copies. A general cannot function alone. I suspect Sculdin is his second in command. If so, he will take the field at some point."

"Well, we need to get into Sculdin's office and have a look at those maps." Quinn turned away. "Follow me."

"Now?" He asked but received no response as Quinn disappeared past the shrubs. "Something tells me I'm going to be tired come morning," he muttered.

Hurrying to catch up, Brandt slipped between the shrubs and spotted Quinn scurrying toward the rear of the castle. With light but hurried footsteps, he caught up to her as she put her back to the wall and peered around the corner. A moment later, she resumed her journey with him in tow.

As they approached the rear wing, Brandt realized where they were headed. Reaching out, he grabbed her shoulder, and she spun around to face him.

"Are you crazy?" he asked in a harsh whisper.

"Hush. You don't want to wake the guards."

"Exactly! This is where they sleep."

"It's also where Sculdin's office is located."

She turned and continued forward, toward the door leading to the guard barracks.

Stifling a groan, Brandt again hurried along. He caught up to Quinn as she slowed before the door. She pressed her ear against it, listened, and then tested the handle. Turning it, she eased the door open, and pale blue light leaked out. They both peered inside and saw nothing but an empty corridor. From somewhere inside, they heard the soft rumble of a snore.

Quinn opened the door further and slipped inside with Brandt a pace behind. Stepping softly on the balls of their feet, they crept down the hallway toward a single glowlamp sconce mounted beside an open door. When she reached the open doorway, Quinn peeked in and pulled back. She glanced at Brandt and tilted her head to the side, indicating that they continue. After she slithered beyond the doorway, he scurried past, glancing in to see rows of bunks along the walls, most occupied by sleeping guards. There were easily two dozen bunks, perhaps more.

When they reached the end of the corridor, Quinn opened the door and he followed her through.

They stepped down to a dirt surface, fifty paces long and half the width. An arched ceiling stood three stories above them, and the pale blue glow of a dormant glowlamp came from the loft overlooking the room. Quinn pointed toward the loft.

"Sculdin's office is up there." She eyed Brandt. "Can you...you know...use your magic to make yourself light and just jump up there?"

"Actually, I'd rather not."

"Why not?"

"Once Chaos is used, it takes a long time to recover. What if we are discovered, and I need to use it to escape or to save you? I'll be help-less and all...floaty."

"Really?" Her eyes narrowed at him. "What do you propose, then?"

"Well, I can boost you up, and you can climb to the loft. I've seen your climbing skills on the Jungle. This should be easy."

"Why me? You can climb just as well."

"True, but I'm stronger than you and you're lighter, so you're easier to lift."

She snorted. "Well, we agree on the last statement."

Quinn walked toward the wall, looking up as she decided on her best route.

"Lift me here." She pointed up. "I'll grab the ledge, shimmy over, and climb the railing."

Brandt stood with his back to the wall, clasped his hands together, and squatted. Quinn put her boot into his hands and he stood, grunting as he lifted. With her other foot, she pushed off his shoulders and climbed up.

He turned to watch as she gripped the first ledge, climbed to the next ledge above, shimmied to the side, gripped a balcony baluster, and began to climb up it hand-over-hand. Seconds later, she disappeared over the railing. The room fell quiet save for the sound of shuffling papers above. Nervous, Brandt stared at the door to the barracks, fearing it would open at any moment. If caught while Quinn was in Sculdin's office, they'd be doomed.

Hearing a noise above, he saw Quinn climbing over the rail. She lowered herself until she dangled from two balusters and let go, bending her knees with the landing. Still, the thud of her boots striking the dirt sent alarms off in Brandt's head, spinning like the puff of dust she created.

"I have it. Let's go." Quinn turned about.

"Wait." Brandt caught her shoulder and spun her back toward him. "What do you mean, you have it?"

"The map I need." She patted her torso. "I rolled it up and stuffed it in my jerkin."

"You stole it?" Brandt struggled to keep his voice down. "I thought you were going to look at it, memorize it. If you steal it, they'll know it is missing."

"Too late for that." She turned and ran toward the door.

"Chuli was right," Brandt mumbled to himself. "Quinn is even worse than I am."

Releasing a sigh, he again hurried to follow. Hurrying along, he wondered what crazy plan she would come up with next.

11

RECLAMATION

Ashland waved Wharton aside and leaned into the cane as she stood. Using the cane reminded her of Budakis, who had used one for his last six years. Those final years were difficult on him, yet he rarely showed it. She missed his strength and wished he could be at her side now. *Farewell, Gunther. I pray that Issal rewards you for the goodness you brought to the world.*

The captain of the guard turned toward the door, gripped the handle and glanced back at her.

Ashland gave Wharton a nod. "I'm ready."

The man opened the door and held it for her. She grunted at the effort of each step, her muscles still weak, her body stiff from lying in bed for two weeks.

Two guards waited outside the temple apartments. Nels, she recognized. The young woman to the other side was unfamiliar. With Wharton in the lead, and both guards following behind, Ashland descended the stairs and entered the courtyard that led to the main keep.

Gray skies greeted her, along with a cool winter breeze. Ashland held her royal robes together with her free hand and frowned at the lack of color in the courtyard. While Kantar rarely experienced rain outside of winter, the season had just begun and the gardens thirsted mightily. The shrubs appeared dry and dormant from months of dry weather, the flowers wilted and forlorn.

Her gaze was drawn toward the top floor where she saw remnants of the wreckage. An attack on her family, her home, had rendered damage that might take years to repair. Yet, they had survived. The image left her longing to reach out to Brock. *Restrain yourself, Ashland,* she told herself. *Remember, you are the queen. You can do this.*

Wharton approached the side door, and the guard stationed there gave him a brief nod. The captain of the guard held the door while Ashland entered. He then reclaimed the lead while she limped down the corridor toward the main hall.

It was busy, as usual. The doors to all four courtrooms and the royal throne room were closed. Without pause, she followed Wharton toward the wide-eyed guards who stood beside the closed throne room doors.

"The Queen would have an audience with Magistrate Filbert," Wharton announced.

One guard, a young man with dark eyes, black hair, and a deep tan, turned toward his companion. Clearly the senior of the two, the other man was tall and lean with a hatchet face and beady brown eyes.

"The Magistrate said he was to be left alone. He's meetin' with his clerk, fixin' laws and such."

Wharton shifted closer to the guard. "You appear old enough to possess a bit of wisdom. Tell me, is there any kingdom where a magistrate outranks a queen?"

The guard's thick brow furrowed and his eyes shifted back and forth. "Um...no. I don't think so."

"Exactly." Wharton pushed past the man and into the room. "The Queen is going in."

Ashland followed him inside, trailed by her two guards.

Although it was mid-day, the cloud-covered sky did a poor job of lighting the throne room and made the murals on the domed ceiling all but imperceptible. Likewise, the distant corners were dark beyond the rows of benches along the center aisle.

The room stood empty save for two people upon the dais. The

magistrate lounged upon the king's throne, dictating to a skinny young man with curly brown hair. Ashland's throne, which normally stood beside Brock's, was notably absent.

Filbert stopped in mid-sentence, his eyes going wide as he sat forward. "You…Your Highness," the old man stammered. "What are you doing out of bed?"

Ashland continued forward, leaning on her cane with each step, wishing she had the strength to discard it.

"While my body still recovers, I assure you that my mind is sharp, and my will is strong."

The man opened his mouth, but Ashland continued before he could reply.

"I hear talk of you drafting a law to repurpose the city temples toward worship every day of the week rather than using them to educate the city's youth, save for Seventh Day, as they do now." She stopped before the throne and allowed anger to seep into her voice. "The education system King Brock established was among my husband's most revered accomplishments. You cannot discard it on a whim."

"I assure you, it is no whim, my Queen." Filbert's voice was firm, demanding. "Rescinding that enactment would both increase the public's connection with Issal and would save the kingdom's coffers a fair sum."

"At what cost? Would you not invest in our future? Knowledge is power, and sharing knowledge with our youth ensures a better tomorrow for our people."

"Bah!" The magistrate decried. "It's a waste! If we revert to teaching skilled youth trades, then we will ensure our future with better blacksmiths, more skilled bakers, trained hunters, and more."

"We can have those things, and those people will also know how to read, write, and do basic math, making our society that much stronger."

Filbert stood. "You'll not…"

The ring of a sword withdrawing from a scabbard echoed throughout the courtroom. The magistrate's eyes grew wide and his mouth dropped open as Wharton leveled his sword at his chest, the point mere inches away.

Filbert's wrinkled face had grown pasty white. "I am a magistrate of the law. You wouldn't…"

"Don't attempt to tell me what I will and will not do, old man," Wharton growled. "I report to Queen Ashland and nobody else. As long as she lives, she holds the power in Kantaria."

Wharton flicked his sword to the left, and Filbert shuffled in that direction, circling around the guards.

I must regain control of the conversation. "Thank you for stepping in while I was recovering, *Magistrate*," Ashland said. "You may return to your courtroom and resume your normal duties."

Filbert's expression darkened to a scowl. He turned, rushed past the armed guards, and fled from the room with his black and purple cloaking billowing behind him. With a gulp, the scrawny clerk scurried after the old man.

"Follow him," Wharton said to the guards. "Be sure he doesn't cause a stir. I'm sure he'll be fine once his anger has simmered."

The two guards nodded and headed out the door.

When she heard Wharton's blade returning to his scabbard, Ashland turned toward him.

"Thank you, Wharton. If the confrontation had escalated much further, I would have been forced to issue punishment. I am already at a disadvantage, and I don't need the other magistrates backing him based on what they might perceive as abuse of my station."

"You are their Queen, and it's best they remember that fact." With his jaw set, Wharton glared toward the door where Filbert had exited. "You should know that we lost a few guards in the explosion, and a few more quit afterward. I'm still filling positions, but I find it difficult to determine which ones I can trust. I thought it prudent to warn you."

Ashland nodded. "Trust given is a delicate thing, easily damaged and extremely difficult to repair. We trusted Kony…and look at what happened."

Wharton's brow furrowed and his eyes found the floor. "I apologize, Your Highness. My job is to protect you and your family. With young Kony, I…failed you."

Extending her free hand, Ashland gripped his. "Nonsense. You couldn't have known. He fooled everyone. Most of all, my son." A tear slid down her cheek. "Broland thought he had found a friend. He gave much of himself to Kony and their relationship. Spurred by that friendship, I saw Broland growing into the person I had always hoped he might become. To have been betrayed like that..." Another tear emerged.

"That is what I mean." Wharton mumbled. "I failed him most of all."

"Stop!" Ashland said with more force than intended. "Dwelling on the past and assigning blame will do neither of us good. We must focus on the future and find our way beyond the troubles affecting Kantaria, both inside and outside her borders."

Ashland realized her hand was clenched in a fist, the statement eliciting more passion than she had expected.

Wharton's stoic expression softened to a wry smile. "Well said, my Queen."

She gaped at him. "You did that on purpose."

He shrugged. "I do not know what you mean, Your Highness."

Ashland laughed in return, shifting to take a seat on the throne. She leaned the cane against it and took a deep, contemplative breath. "What must I do first, Wharton? Where do I begin?"

The man reached into his coat and withdrew a folded sheet of paper.

"As I was saying, I am concerned about the elite guard. I am trying to fill positions, yet more than ever, I find myself doubting new recruits." He extended the paper toward her. "A new potential guard arrived today with this letter. He claims that you will know him and can trust him."

She accepted the note, still sealed with a drop of red wax. "What is his name?"

"Randall or something. He wouldn't tell me his last name."

"Randall? I don't know anyone with that name." Her brow furrowed. "Not revealing his last name hardly sounds trustworthy."

"I told him as much. Regardless, he requested that you read the missive and decide for yourself."

Curious, Ashland opened the letter and immediately recognized the handwriting inside. A smile crossed her face, and tears filled her eyes as she read it to herself. When finished, she wiped her eyes clear and held the note to her chest.

"Are you all right, my Queen?" Wharton asked.

She laughed, happier than she had been in days. "Yes. I'm fine. Please bring this young man in. I would very much like to meet him."

12

TENSION

Jonah Selbin maintained his connection with his own source of Order, simultaneously coaxing the latent Order surrounding him into the breastplate, trapping the Chaos bound within it. The process was tedious and exhausting. Worse, successfully completing an Infusion lacked the sense of accomplishment one might feel from actually crafting something.

With a groan, he opened his eyes and frowned at the armor.

"Who would have thought that enchanting would end up being so boring?"

Torney set his own breastplate aside with a sigh. "I know. After three weeks of this, I never want to see another sword or a piece of armor as long as I live."

"I agree. I almost wish the Empire would attack just to end the monotony."

Torney grunted in response.

Jonah turned toward the cluster of soldiers who sat around the dormant fire, three of them running their blades across whetstones while the others told stories. During their stay at the garrison, Jonah had discovered that soldiers enjoyed telling raunchy stories, each with an obvious effort to outdo the others. He had also learned that the women were the worst of the lot. His ears still turned red when he recalled the things he had heard.

"Olusk!" Jonah shouted. The squat, muscular man turned toward him. "Your armor is ready."

The soldier set his whetstone aside, sheathed his blade, and strolled over. Olusk's brow furrowed beneath an expansive forehead that met his shorn hair. He wore a grimace as he stared at the breastplate. Gripping it, Olusk picked it up and grunted.

"Feels odd, like it's hollow or something."

"That's the idea," Jonah replied. "I made it lighter. It won't wear you down while you're fighting."

"Will it break?"

Jonah struck it with the side of his fist. Rather than a clang, the sound was a deep thump with a hint of a metallic ring at the end.

"It's just as strong as before, but I added an Elastic augmentation. Most weapons will bounce right off it. It would take a massive blow to cut through it. Even with blunt weapons, you should feel a fraction of the impact."

The soldier stared at Jonah for a long moment before a grin spread across his face. With his deep-set, dark eyes and facial scar, the expression was more creepy than friendly. Olusk thumped Jonah on the back, the blow forcing him to cough.

"You're not half bad, Ginger," Olusk said as he spun away.

Jonah frowned at the name but chose not to poke the bear while he was happy. "Thanks."

Olusk walked over to the other soldiers and struck one on the head with the armor. It bounced off, undamaged, although the man brought a hand to his head and glared at Olusk.

"What's that for?" the soldier grumbled.

"Just testin' it is all," Olusk said before reclaiming his seat.

"Someone's approaching from the east!" a female guard cried from the scaffold along the wall. "They appear injured!"

Jonah glanced toward Torney, who appeared deep in meditation as he worked on another enchantment. Deciding that someone might be in need of healing, and thinking that any diversion from enchanting sounded good, Jonah jogged toward the gate.

A group of guards had gathered there, listening to Sergeant Rios. He issued a series of orders and called for the gate to open. The eight soldiers shuffled out while the archers manning the wall nocked their bows. Jonah slid in behind the soldiers who were stepping outside.

A half-mile down the road, Jonah saw two people – one of whom leaned heavily on the other. With the morning sun still low in the sky behind them, the people were shadowy silhouettes and difficult to see properly. Yet, in two breaths, Jonah realized who it was.

He burst past the soldiers and ran down the road.

"Get back here!" Rios ordered.

Jonah didn't listen. Instead, he ran faster. When he reached the barricade of stakes, secured in the ground and pointing east, he slipped through and resumed his run. As he drew closer, he was able to see more clearly.

Chuli's arm was covered in blood, her face dirty and streaked from sweat. Worse, Thiron's normally dark skin had paled, his eyes at half-mast. An arrow stuck out from his abdomen and blood covered his thigh. Thiron stumbled and fell to his knees, twisting as Chuli clung to him. Then, Jonah saw a second arrow protruding from his shoulder.

Jonah rushed forward and knelt beside Thiron.

"What happened?"

"He took an arrow in the back when we passed through the Empire barricade." Chuli gasped for air. "I thought we would make it, but we ran into an ambush a mile back. Two bowmen. They're dead, but… they got him in the process."

Jonah nodded toward Chuli's bloody arm. "What about you?"

She shook her head. "It's just a graze, from a bowshot that likely would have killed me. I stumbled over a rock when the ambush struck, and the arrow sliced my arm instead."

Turning back to Thiron, Jonah considered the two arrows and decided on a course of action.

"Sorry, Thiron. This is going to hurt, but we don't have time to waste. We are going to pull the arrow from your shoulder and then lay you down to pull the one from your stomach. I can heal you once they are both removed."

The man grunted. "Do…it."

Jonah drew his knife – the only weapon he carried – and sliced through Thiron's bowstring.

"What are you doing?" Chuli asked, clearly appalled.

"Saving his life."

Jonah slid his blade beneath the strap of Thiron's pack and water skin, cutting both free. Last was the quiver, which required more effort before the knife cut through the leather strap.

"Hold him tightly, Chuli."

Circling behind Thiron, Jonah wrapped his fingers around the broken shaft, twisted it, and yanked it free. A cry of pain came from the wounded man, joined by groans and ragged breathing through clenched teeth. Jonah cringed at the broken arrow in his hand, flesh still clinging to the arrowhead. Disgusted, he tossed the arrow aside.

"Lay him down," he said. "We have little time."

Jonah and Chuli helped Thiron to a sitting position before laying him down. The man's eyes were pinned shut, his face contorted in pain.

The guards arrived, surrounding the trio while Jonah put one hand on the arrow sticking from Thiron's abdomen, his other hand on the man's bare arm.

"Hold him down, Chuli." Jonah winced when he looked down at the arrow, the front of Thiron's jerkin soaked in blood. "Sorry, Thiron, but it's the only way."

Giving it a quick jerk, the arrow moved, but didn't come free. Thiron cried out, his back arching as he gasped a ragged breath. His eyes rolled back in his head and he fell limp.

"He fainted," Chuli said.

Jonah clenched his teeth, twisted the arrow, and pulled as hard as he could.

The arrow came free in a trail of blood. Tossing it aside, Jonah pushed the heel of his hand against the oozing wound and closed his eyes. In moments, he settled into a meditative state and found his center. Through the hand resting on Thiron's arm, Jonah extended his awareness into the injured man and sought Thiron's source of Order.

It was weak, far dimmer than it should be. In contrast, Thiron's wounds raged with a bright red glow. Stoking the man's source of Order the best he could, Jonah first attacked the abdomen wound, smothering the Chaos lurking there while mending his arrow-mangled innards. The complexity of the injury, combined with the weak condition of Thiron's life force, made the process a long and tortuous one.

Only when the area was free of Chaos did Jonah turn his attention to the wound in the man's back. While not as grievous as the stomach wound, Thiron's life force was even weaker than before. Jonah slowed the process, working cautiously, gently, to reduce the Chaos in the area without completely draining Thiron of his life force. With the injury only half healed, Jonah released the connection and opened his eyes.

Chuli's pleaded. "Were you able to heal him? Will he live?"

"I did the best I could, Chuli. He is weak. I fear if I push any further, he won't survive it."

Jonah studied the guards standing around him. Their faces were somber...even Sergeant Rios. Rising to his feet, Jonah found his hands stained with blood. His stomach lurched with a threat to revolt.

"His stomach wound is healed. The arrow hole in his back is not. We must move him to a bed and bandage him up."

"You heard him," Rios said, pointing toward the soldiers. "Four of you, pick the man up and carry him to the infirmary."

Soldiers shifted about as Chuli and Jonah backed away to give them room. Gripping Thiron's arms and legs, they lifted him and headed back toward the garrison.

Rios patted Jonah on the shoulder. "You did what you could, son. It's now down to the man's will and Issal's blessing."

The sergeant and his soldiers marched toward the garrison with Jonah watching in silence. A soft touch on his arm drew his attention. He turned toward Chuli, meeting her dark eyes.

"Thank you, Jonah." Her tone was earnest, emotional. "You saved his life...again."

An internal struggle waged inside Jonah. He considered hugging her and fought the urge to cry. As usual, he turned it around and made a wry face, burying such emotions.

"It almost makes my complaining worth it, huh?"

She chuckled, and his weariness lifted like a sunrise.

"Almost."

Jonah sat at the table in Captain Marcella's office, watching Chuli clean dried blood from her arm with a damp rag. With the gash in her arm healed, cleaning it erased any evidence of its existence. Jonah realized how dangerous Chuli's mission had been and how lucky she was to have returned safely.

In the chair beside Jonah, Torney fidgeted nervously. He ran his hand through his wavy red hair, his eyes continuously surveying the room.

Rios stood in the corner with his arms crossed over his barrel chest. The sergeant's glare and frown might have made Jonah fidget as well if he weren't so exhausted. Enchanting and healing both required more energy than one might guess. It was not quite time for lunch, and Jonah was already looking forward to sleep.

The door opened and Marcella stepped into the room.

"How is he?" Chuli asked.

"The medicus is...uncertain. His wound appears minor at this point, but he has lost a lot of blood." Marcella gripped Jonah's shoulder. "He most assuredly would have died without the healing, but the cost was high."

Jonah nodded in silence. He knew he had pressed Thiron's life force close to the edge. The gap between overtaxing Thiron's resources and sufficiently healing the man's wounds was narrow at best...a hairline crack, impossible to navigate, at worst.

Marcella strode across the room and pulled out a chair, sitting and waving for Rios to join them.

"We must set our worries about Thiron aside." Marcella stared at Chuli. "What have you discovered?"

Chuli's eyes narrowed as she stared into space. "Their force is more significant than we thought. Thiron and I estimate more than three thousand soldiers gathered in the woods north of Yarth."

Marcella glanced toward Rios. "Even if the squads Chadwick was to supply had arrived, we wouldn't have enough soldiers to hold off a force that size, not without a proper keep and far superior battlements."

Rios shook his head. "No. Not a chance."

"There is more," Chuli said. "We suspected they had access to explosives, but what we face now appears worse than what we feared. The Empire has found new ways to use this...flash powder. In addition, they have steam carriages towing catapults. I overheard a man talking about using them to launch flash bombs – something that could blow up a building."

Marcella stared at Chuli in silence, a long, uncomfortable silence. "You make it sound as if we are trapped here, waiting to die."

"Honestly, I believe that is what will happen if we remain. Thiron thought so as well. When we decided to head back, it was to warn you…to let you know that you had no hope of defeating what you faced."

Marcella pounded a fist on the table as she rose to her feet. "My duty is to prevent the Empire from advancing into Kantaria."

"What if that outcome is impossible?" Jonah asked. "Is it your duty to throw away soldiers' lives without hope or anything to gain?"

Backing away from the table, Marcella began pacing with her hands clasped behind her back. "If we fight, perhaps we can wound them, reduce their numbers. What would you have me do? Abandon the garrison and let the Empire army just march on past without us striking a blow?"

Jonah knew that their situation was dire, like a rat caught in a trap with no way to escape. *A trap*, he repeated in his mind as an idea began to form. His worried face turned to a grin. "Abandoning the garrison is exactly what we must do."

The captain stopped pacing to scowl at Jonah. "There was a reason King Brock entrusted me with this post. He knew I would not bend to our enemy's will."

Jonah shook his head. "You don't understand." He stood, facing the group. "My parents own a farm outside of Nor Torin. About eight years back, we had problems with a particularly smart coyote who would raid us of our livestock. Despite locking the barn up at night, we would come out in the morning to find a calf missing or a pig dead. My father finally had enough and moved the remaining livestock out before climbing into the barn loft and waiting with a crossbow. Sure enough, the coyote appeared, wiggling through a gap below a wall, a narrow tunnel hidden by a pile of hay. While the animal sniffed around, my father shot it and ended the coyote's reign of terror."

Jonah grinned as he waited for the story to sink in. Confused expressions were all he received until Rios threw his arms in the air.

"What the blazes are you talking about?" Rios was incredulous.

"We are discussing war, and you tell stories about coyotes and livestock?"

Jonah waved his hands in an attempt to calm the sergeant. "Hold on. Hear me out." He turned toward Marcella. "As you told us earlier, the Empire is watching us. The ambush on Chuli and Thiron, just a mile away, proves it. They know we're here and likely know how many soldiers we have gathered."

"Yes. And…"

"And they will believe we are still here even if we evacuate." Jonah pointed toward the north. "They don't know about the tunnel. We can send soldiers through, one squad at a time, until all are out except a core group who will be used as bait."

Jonah turned toward Chuli. "How long before the Empire army arrives?"

Chuli's brow furrowed. "They likely need a day to break camp. A force that size won't move very fast, and they have twenty miles to cover. The soonest they'll arrive is mid-day, tomorrow. More likely, tomorrow evening."

Jonah turned toward Marcella. "That doesn't leave us much time, but I have some ideas. If we start now, we can turn this place into a deathtrap before they arrive."

Seconds passed before Marcella's grimace softened and morphed into a smirk. "Rios, get me an inventory list that covers weapons, food, armor, supplies…everything. We have plans to make and little time to execute them."

13

DIRE STRAITS

Everson took a deep breath and knocked. Shuffling sounds came from inside, followed by approaching footsteps. The door opened to reveal a middle-aged man, clean shaven and wearing rectangular spectacles. Smoothing his thick, dark hair with one hand, the man gave Everson an affable grin.

"Everson. What can I do for you?"

"I'm sorry to bother you, Master Hedgewick." Everson kneaded his hands and glanced down the corridor. It remained empty but for him. "I'm seeking specific information, and I believe you are the best source."

Hedgewick's grin widened. "I do strive to be a source of information." He moved aside, holding the door open. "Come in and have a seat. By the way, you can call me Benny."

Walking past the engineering master, Everson said, "Thank you, sir. Er...Benny."

Benny closed the door and walked to his sitting area. Morning light from the Atrium streamed through the open curtains and provided ample light. His Ratio Bellicus table was covered with books, the game pieces pushed aside. The man sat in a cushioned chair and gestured for Everson to sit on the sofa. Everson's mechanical legs whirred, air hissing from them as he bent his knees to sit.

Benny shook his head. "I don't think my amazement at your augmented legs will ever cease. Discovering how to harness Chaos as a power source was a stroke of genius. I'm envious that I didn't figure it out myself."

"Thank you."

Everson's heart hummed with pride. Benny Hedgewick was a man he admired, a man respected by many. Recent information regarding Benny's role in the Battle at the Brink only served to increase Hedgewick's legendary status in Everson's mind. That lingering sense of awe also made speaking to the man much more difficult.

Benny leaned back, striking a relaxed pose as he crossed his legs. A smirk remained on his lips as he eyed Everson.

"You came here seeking information. Usually, that means you have questions requiring answers." Benny gestured toward Everson. "Let's hear it."

Everson took a deep breath and considered where to begin. "It appears that we will be unable to avoid a war with the Empire. If we can't prevent it, I would like to help our side win."

The man's eyes narrowed. "While I find that commendable, it's hardly news. In fact, it's among the reasons we recruited you."

"Yeah. I guess." Everson shrugged. "But having never seen a battle, I don't know much about what transpires – what elements matter most and what actions might sway victory for one side or the other. Accordingly, I sought more information."

"Did you go to the academy library?" Benny's grin reappeared. "You do know that they named it after my ancestor, not after me, right?"

Everson shook his head. "No. Research would take more time than I wanted to commit. For quicker answers, I went to Master Alridge."

"Yes. Salina was there." Benny nodded. "She knows a thing or two about what really happened."

"Exactly. The recorded information surrounding the Battle at the Brink is vague at best."

"The lack of details is intentional. There is knowledge about what transpired that can be used against us if it were to fall into the wrong hands."

"Yet, that's what happened, didn't it? Some of the knowledge is being used against us."

The man's face darkened at Everson's statement. Benny turned and stared toward the Atrium with his lips pressed together. A long, uncomfortable moment of silence passed before he spoke.

"Karl Jarlish and I were rivals while I was at the academy. His father was famous for inventing the steam engine, so when Karl arrived, he was already well known. Of course, I was young. Jealousy is particularly common before wisdom makes one aware of how ugly it actually is.

"In hindsight, I believe that my envy of the attention Karl received worked in my favor. It fueled my ambition. If I wanted to become the greatest inventor of my time, then my creations needed to surpass anything Karl attempted. There is a chance that the Hedgewick Flyer might have never existed if not for my rivalry with Karl."

A wistful expression remained on Benny's face as he stared into space. He then shook his head as if to clear away cobwebs of stray thoughts and resumed his tale.

"Certain events led to my leaving the school during my second year. That journey was filled with adventure and discovery, marred by the death of a friend. Yet, events of the wider world changed my perspective as a new enemy arose. With my mind focused on saving mankind from annihilation, I returned to the Academy.

"At the time, The Horde was tearing the east coast to shreds and would soon turn west. I witnessed the aftermath of what they had done to Sol Polis. Even now, approaching twenty years later, those horrific images remain fixed in my memory and often resurface in nightmares. A small group of us, led by King Brock, scrambled to gather the best force we could manage to stop this horde of monsters. Our army was drastically outnumbered, and we couldn't even comprehend what we were to face. Perhaps that was for the best. If we had known, we may have abandoned the plan."

Hedgewick ran his hand through his hair, as if he were weary.

"When I came back to the school, I sought to turn my discovery of flash powder into a weapon. Karl and I set our rivalry aside, and he became my partner. Together, we crafted the very first flash bombs – small glass canisters with a brass cap. On impact, the cap would compress and cause the trigger to strike a flint, which created a spark and ignited the powder in the jar. The result was quite impressive. Without a doubt, the flash bombs helped us win the battle. Mankind survived, but, sometimes, mankind is its own worst enemy."

Benny's focus shifted back to Everson, their eyes meeting. "Afterward, Karl and I drifted apart. My inventions spurred my career, while his languished. Within a few years, he moved from Fallbrandt, and I never heard from him again. That is, until his name resurfaced in Quinn's report."

Everson nodded. "He's the inventor who now works for the Empire."

"It appears so." Benny leaned forward. "You should know that he has access to more flash powder than we had back then, more than anyone in recorded history."

"How do you know this?"

"About six years ago, there was a prison break. Many people escaped. This was not a typical prison. It also happened to be the richest gold mine in all of Issalia."

Everson's face pinched. "Gold? It's too soft. What can you make from gold other than jewelry?"

Benny shook his head. "You misunderstand. It's not what you can make from gold, but what you can buy with it. People. Loyalty. Land. Power.

"In addition, the very same mine was our primary source for flash powder."

Everson leaned forward. "Wait. Are you saying that the same people who currently lead the Empire were prisoners?"

"Yes."

"And when they escaped, they acquired the gold and flash powder stored at these mines?"

"Yes."

"How much?"

"Gold?" Benny shrugged. "I don't know. Enough to make a difference, I assure you."

"What about the flash powder?"

"Records from the mine state that numerous barrels of flash powder had been stocked there. Twenty-four barrels to be exact."

Everson's eyes grew wide. "They took all of it?"

"I'm afraid so."

Everson sat back and considered the revelation. His mind spun it about and examined it from numerous angles. "You mentioned the mine as a source for flash powder. Can we get more there?"

Benny shook his head. "It appears that all flashstone veins have been mined from that location, but it doesn't leave us without hope. I happen to know of an old, forgotten quarry near Selbin with a vein or two. Anticipating the need, I sent a team there last week to gather what they could. When they return, we shall see what they found."

Something in the back of Everson's mind stirred, a question itching for an answer. "I suspect that most prison escapees would rather do their best to blend in with society, happy to be free while doing what they could to avoid a return to such dire straits. Yet, not only did these people not blend in, they overthrew Vinacci, Kalimar, and half of Hurnsdom. Those kingdoms now form an Empire that can challenge the rest of Issalia."

"Who are these people? How are they so resourceful? Despite the advantages of gold and flash powder, it takes far more than money and weapons to achieve such power. It requires experienced leaders."

Benny's eyes shifted to stare at the Ratio Bellicus table. "Yes. There is more to the tale than prison escapees and flash bombs."

His head tilted up to lock eyes with Everson. Inside them was a seriousness that seemed rare from this light-hearted, kind man. In Benny's gaze, Everson saw a dread that made him shiver.

"You see, the leaders of this new Empire were once masters at the Fallbrandt Academy of Magic and Science. Even back then, they served another purpose – one with a hidden agenda. Under that old regime, before the kingdoms of Issalia were reformed, these men and women were the leaders of a secret organization within the Ministry, a group known as The Hand. They are extremists whose ideals guide them without pause. As proven by their actions, they will go to extreme measures to ensure a solitary outcome: the end of Chaos.

"Driven by this objective, I fear for what the future holds should they prove victorious."

14

SPURETTI

A cool ocean breeze balanced the afternoon heat, the cliff edge looming above Chuli partially blocking the sun. She longed for the shadows to shift toward her and provide relief. Even sitting among a pile of boulders, she felt exposed by the sunlight.

A snore arose from Gillup, the soldier still asleep. Chuli envied the man's ability to sleep sitting upright...in direct sunlight, nonetheless. Her attempt at sleeping the night prior had produced little success and a grogginess lingered. A sigh slipped out as she rose to her feet and peered down the road.

Of course, the road remained empty. From her position, she had a clear eastern view for a half mile before the road rounded a bend. The steep hillside of a tall plateau created a boundary to the north side of the road while a cliff edge ran along the south side with a frightening drop to the sea. This road was the only path to Hipoint, so the Imperial was forced to take this route. Chuli's gaze shifted nearer and settled on a track that crossed the gravel road.

When she and Gillup had first arrived at the post, they found two Imperial soldiers, both dead and oblivious to the coyotes nosing around them. Apparently, nobody had come to relieve the men after Chuli and Thiron had foiled their ambush – a confrontation that ended the two men's lives. It immediately became obvious that the bodies, and the smell, had to be addressed before anything else. They had chased the coyotes off before discussing their options. Holding their breath from the stench, Chuli and Gillup had then performed the unpleasant task of dragging the corpses across the road and dumping them over the cliff edge.

A pair of seabirds circled overhead, their lonely calls joining the distant sound of surf until their flight path took them beyond the line of Chuli's view. She cast another glance down the road and paused. Something glinted in the distance, metal reflecting sunlight. The relection moved, rounding the bend as a machine appeared.

Chuli turned and tapped Gillup on the shoulder. The man blinked awake, rubbed his eyes, and then ran his fingers down his face and through his thick, brown beard.

"What is it?"

"Look." She pointed to the east.

The man groaned as he leaned forward, got his feet beneath him, and rose to a crouch beside Chuli. Gillup grunted as a second steam carriage came into view. "Finally."

While Chuli didn't relish what was to come, a part of her agreed with him. Two days of lying in wait was long enough.

"See the catapults they are towing?"

He nodded. "They are moving at a slow pace. I bet soldiers come around the corner next."

Sure enough, the Imperial infantry unit appeared, trailing the two steam carriages.

"We had better go," Chuli said.

The man nodded, shouldered his bow, quiver, and pack, and began the short descent to the road. Chuli followed with one hand gripping her pack, the other her bowstring. They broke into a jog, heading west while keeping the rocks between them and the approaching army. As they ran, Chuli found herself wondering if Thiron remained unconscious. She had grown used to her mentor's presence, and it seemed odd not to have him around. She had come to rely on his wisdom.

As they rounded a long, gradual bend, the garrison came into view. A quarter mile from the garrison, she glanced up at the rock wall to the north and saw a rune marking it. At Jonah's direction, one of the miners had climbed the cliff wall and drawn the symbol with a chunk

of coal. Turning to look forward, she found herself approaching a catapult positioned in the middle of the road – the only siege engine
stationed at the garrison.

Chuli and Gillup slowed to a walk as they passed the catapult. Just
behind the siege engine was a barrier of sharpened stakes, sticking up
from the ground at an angle. After a backward glance, Gillup slid
between a gap in the stakes with Chuli a step behind. Gillup held his
hands to his mouth as he marched toward the garrison.

"Enemy approaching!" he shouted. "They are minutes away."

The man stopped and turned toward Chuli, both breathing heavily
from their run. Chuli looked backward, toward the road that led to the
approaching army. It remained empty, nothing in sight save for the
lonely catapult, loaded and waiting for use.

The gate opened and Marcella strode out, joined by Rios, Samantha, Jonah, and Torney.

"Report, Gillup," Marcella said.

"The enemy approaches at a marching pace. They are about a mile
away, led by two steam carriages, each towing a catapult. Infantry
follow, likely leading the cavalry and the other steam carriages that
were reported earlier."

Marcella turned toward Jonah. "At that pace, they'll be visible in
ten minutes…fifteen at most."

Jonah nodded. "I'm ready. Be sure to have the catapult manned
when I return."

Without another word, Jonah broke into a run, skirting the catapult
as he headed east, away from the garrison.

Marcella turned to Rios. "Send Spuretti out and get the soldiers into
position. We have to make a good show of it, or they may not take
the bait."

Rios nodded, turned, and disappeared back into the garrison.

The captain then put her hand on Samantha's shoulder, the scribe
jerking with a start as if she were stabbed. "You are to take my message
to King Brock. The ship is yours, and the captain is waiting for you.
You may linger and watch the events as they unfold, but do not risk
capture nor an attack. If you don't make it to Kantar, Brock will not be
aware of what transpired here."

Samantha nodded firmly, but Chuli noted the nervousness in the young woman's eyes. "Yes, Captain. I will not let you down." She began her walk toward the city, stopped, and looked back. "May Issal be with you." She then scurried off, toward the steps that led down to the docks. There, a single ship waited since the rest had departed during the evacuation.

"While that girl drives me crazy with her endless writing, I'll miss her. Maybe she will make me famous someday." Marcella's voice carried a wistful tone that seemed much out of character. She then turned toward Chuli. "Your friend remains unconscious. We have him strapped to your horse, as we agreed. I have assigned three others to take your mounts, including the medicus. They were instructed to leave when the enemy was sighted."

Chuli nodded. "Thank you, Captain."

Marcella stared down the road with her eyes narrowed. "I hope your friend knows what he's doing. If this doesn't work, we won't have time to evacuate."

Turning, Chuli followed Marcella's gaze and spotted Jonah eight hundred feet beyond the catapult. The rune scrawled on the cliffside flared red, pulsed and faded. Jonah spun about and began jogging back.

The garrison gates opened wider and soldiers began marching out with Rios in the lead. He spun about and walked backward while shouting orders to the trailing troops.

"Align in ranks twenty across!" He stopped and held his arms out. "Soldiers in front, stop here. We don't want to get too close to the barrier. Our siege engine will inevitably become a target when they are in range."

Minutes passed as five hundred soldiers poured from the garrison, shuffled about, and lined up in twenty separate columns. The clopping of hooves arose as horses rode from the garrison. Hurrying, Chuli jogged between the rows of Kantarian soldiers to meet the riders coming through the gate.

Two soldiers, a man named Meeks and a woman named Jilli, led the group. Thiron followed, strapped to Rhychue, with Medicus Tilbrick bringing up the rear. The horses in the lead stopped while Marcella said some quiet words to the two soldiers. Chuli approached Rhychue and caressed the horse's neck.

"Take care of him, girl."

Chuli found herself concerned as she examined the man who had trained her. His eyes remained closed, his face still pale as he slept. The medicus had strapped Thiron to the saddle such that his upper body rested on pillows stuffed between him and the horse's back.

"If anything bad should happen, return to Mondomi," she said to her horse.

"Don't worry," Tilbrick said. "We will take care of him and meet you tonight at camp."

"I plan to be there...should the fates allow it." Chuli could not keep the worry from affecting her words.

Marcella finished her conversation with Meeks and Jilli. Meeks waved his arm forward and kicked his horse into an easy walk. The other three trailed behind, the horses circling the garrison wall before heading west. Chuli found herself wondering if she would ever see them again.

"Here they come!" someone shouted.

When Chuli turned around, she saw distant movement and the gleam of metal at the far end of the road. Her stomach twisted, and her heart fluttered as the reality of what was to come became tangible. She looped around the ranks of soldiers and approached Marcella as Jonah arrived from the other direction.

"It's done," Jonah said as he came to a stop.

A short, older soldier named Nick Spuretti stood beside Marcella. With one arm that ended at his elbow and four angry scars that ran down his neck, Spuretti had clearly seen the worst of a battlefield. In contrast to the anxiety Chuli was experiencing, Spuretti appeared calm, focused, despite his task. Captain Marcella put her hand on the man's shoulder.

"It is time, Nick," Marcella said, her tone somber. "The catapult is loaded and in position. You simply need to pull the trigger, but you must wait until my command."

Spuretti turned toward the catapult and nodded. "I understand, Captain. I survived a war against an army of banshees. If Issal wills it, I'll survive this as well."

Without another word, he broke into a run. Chuli watched him cross the open ground, wiggle between the spiked barricade, and approach the armed catapult.

At the end of the road, the second steam carriage had come into view, both moving closer at a methodical pace, trailed by two columns of smoke and a mass of marching soldiers. Around the bend, the enemy army continued to advance, a force of thousands coming to face a garrison manned by hundreds. Regardless, Chuli did not fear the army itself. She feared the weapons they possessed.

"Oh, no," Jonah said, pointing to the east. "They've stopped."

Chuli grimaced while staring at the steam carriages, stopped more than a quarter mile down the road. Her focus shifted to the location with the rune on the cliff wall. Although it was difficult to notice in the shadows cast by the evening sun, she could tell that the enemy had not yet advanced far enough.

Jonah shook his head. "If they stop for more than an hour, this won't work."

"Come on," Marcella muttered. "Keep moving, you toad lickers."

The machines at the front remained in place while the trailing column of Imperial soldiers gathered. In the distance, behind the army, Chuli observed rising smoke trails from the other steam carriages. Everyone waited in quiet, the only sounds coming from the rush of surf below and the whistle of the wind slipping through the tiny gaps in the garrison palisade.

Nobody moved, not among the kingdom troops nor among the distant Imperial army. A tension filled the air as the two forces faced one another from a distance. Then, smoke began to billow from the steam carriages at the fore, and the machines resumed their advance.

Recalling the catapults towed behind the machines, Chuli wondered how far they could launch their projectiles. Her attention shifted from the approaching machines to the rune on the cliff as she attempted to gauge the distance. As if the enemy had read her mind, her question was answered.

A small object flew up from the first catapult, the metal on it glinting in the sun as it spun and hurtled toward them.

"Launch!" Marcella shouted. "Now, Spuretti! Launch and run!"

With a thump, Spuretti's catapult arm flung forward, sending the boulder in the launch basket sailing through the air. Rather than heading toward the advancing enemy, the rock angled toward the cliff face.

The object fired by the Imperial catapult fell from the sky, the bronze glinting in the sun as it spun about. Too late, Spuretti turned to run. An explosion blasted the catapult apart, sent a massive spray of earth into the air, and caused the remains to erupt in a tower of green flame. Debris rained upon the kingdom army and forced Chuli to cover her head for protection. When she lowered her arms, she found the catapult destroyed, burning components littering the road, and a crater where the bomb had struck. Similarly, Spuretti was dead, his mangled corpse on fire.

The rock Spuretti had launched struck the cliff face with a loud crack. A massive rumble came from the cliff as it shattered and collapsed in a landslide. Millions of tons of rock tumbled down and rolled toward the sea – a wall of earth that plowed through both Imperial steam carriages and the war machines behind them. Flash bombs on board the machines ignited, resulting in distant booming explosions and eruptions of green flame. Seconds passed and the landslide continued, filling the air with a cloud of dust that mixed with the black smoke rising from the burning carriages. The tide of rock swept one of the carriages over the cliff edge, and it disappeared while the other was buried. A mixture of dust and smoke churned amidst the landslide and made it impossible to see anything of the army beyond it.

As the dust settled, the reality of what had happened set in. The destruction was massive, leaving a wall of rock and earth across the entire road, obscuring the enemy army from view. During the entire scene, the people surrounding Chuli had remained silent. That is, until Jonah's voice broke the spell.

"That worked even better than I had hoped." Jonah sounded impressed with himself.

Someone among the soldiers behind them cheered. Another cheer joined the first, calling out Marcella's name. Others joined in with cheers of their own, the soldiers breaking ranks as their fists pumped toward the sky. It was a small victory, but a victory regardless.

The first part of their plan had worked. Jonah's idea to use the Brittle rune on the cliff face had created a new obstacle between the approaching army and the garrison while also depleting the enemy of two catapults and a portion of their flash bombs. Yet, Chuli's gaze fell on the still-burning fire as it feasted on the remains of their only catapult.

Among the flames, she saw the outline of Spuretti's burning body, charred beyond recognition. *How many others will die before the day is through?*

15

DEATHTRAP

J onah stood atop the scaffold inside the garrison walls, his hands gripping two of the wooden posts that formed the wall. Touching the wood left his hands oily – a side effect of whatever was used to make the wood fire retardant. After seeing how quickly a flash bomb had destroyed the catapult, he doubted that anything could prevent flash powder from burning the wooden palisades. Jonah hoped the use of magic might delay the inevitable. That task was up to him and Torney. *Where is Torney? He should be back by now*, Jonah thought.

Archers lined the scaffold to both sides of him, a dozen to his left, more to his right. All the other soldiers had already vacated through the tunnel. He glanced at Chuli, who stood beside him, and found her staring toward the Imperial Army...out there...somewhere.

Ten glowstones lined each side of the road before them, lighting the area between the garrison wall and the barrier of stakes that stood hundreds of feet away. Beyond the barrier was darkness.

Another flash of green lit up the night. A beat later, the thump of an explosion shook the ground. It was the eighth such explosion in the past hour.

"How many of those flash bombs do they have?" Jonah muttered.

"I do not know, Jonah Selbin," Chuli said, her tone contemplative. "Perhaps we should sneak out and get a count of them."

He gave Chuli a sidelong glance and found her faintly lit by the pale blue light from the road. "You're messing with me again, aren't you?"

"Perhaps." The hint of a smile turned the corners of her lips.

Jonah smiled in return but it quickly slid away as he stared out upon the night, wondering what the enemy might be planning. "I wish we could see past the barrier. I feel like the entire army is standing just beyond the light and those bombs are just some sort of distraction."

Chuli glared out into the night and then nodded. "That is likely what they are doing."

"Why waste the bombs, then?"

"It's doubtful they sent the steam carriages and catapults without the intent to use them." Chuli's tone was, again, thoughtful. "Men on foot, and even those on horseback, can scale the landslide without serious difficulty, but there is no way for the machines to pass the landslide. If they must remove it, bombs seem like a good way to do so."

Jonah appraised Chuli for a long moment before nodding. "You're smarter than I thought. Perhaps it's because you are so quiet."

Torney appeared from behind Chuli, walking toward her and Jonah. "Have you two been up here yapping this entire time?"

"It took you long enough," Jonah chided. "Did you lose your way to the jakes, or did you take a nap while you were away?"

Torney snorted. "I wish. A nap sounds wonderful." He fell quiet for a moment as he stared down the road. "I miss Rena. This whole thing...I have a bad feeling about it. It makes me wish I had never agreed to join this mission...that I was instead back at the Ward with her beside me."

Chuli put her hand on his shoulder. "It is well that you care so much about her. You might find solace in knowing what we do here is important. Her life might be among those we save tonight."

He nodded. "Thanks, Chuli. That gives me a good reason to fight... and to survive. I can't wait to see her again."

"Good. Now be quiet." Chuli hushed him. "They're out there, and they might attack at any moment."

With a glance toward the road, Torney grimaced. "It's odd, but I find the waiting worse than the idea of the Imperial troops attacking. I swear my anxiety doubles every five minutes and doubles again each time I hear an explosion." He frowned at Chuli. "You're sure we are out of bowshot?"

Chuli nodded. "Those stakes are over six hundred feet away, and the wind is blowing at our backs. Even using longbows, they would need to be well inside the stakes for an arrow to clear the wall."

Torney's eyes grew wide. "What's that?"

Jonah turned to find a something moving in the shadows beyond the barrier. Dim light reflected off surfaces as he tried to make out what it was.

"Those are raised shields," Chuli said. "It looks like three or more soldiers in a cluster."

A twang sounded from their right as an archer loosed an arrow. Moments later, the distant clang of an arrow striking metal rang in the night. The soldiers behind the shield cluster did not slow until they reached the barricade of stakes. A hand emerged and set something on the ground while the cluster of shields began moving along the row of stakes.

"It's flash powder!" Jonah exclaimed. "They're pouring it at the base of the stakes. They intend to burn the barricade."

Chuli looked at Jonah with alarm in her eyes and then looked down at the bucket of grease-soaked rags beside her.

"Do one of you have a flint? I have an idea." She drew an arrow, grabbed a strip cloth, and wrapped it about the arrowhead. "They are going to burn it, anyway. Why not do it on our terms?"

By then, Torney had his flint and striker out. Turning toward him, Chuli held the arrow out and he began to strike it, creating sparks. At the third strike, the rag caught fire.

Chuli turned toward the road with her bow nocked, the flaming arrow flickering in the breeze. She held steady and loosed. A streak of orange sailed into the sky and landed near one of the stakes. The fire momentarily snuffed out, but then came back to life, licking the neighboring stake as the flame climbed the arrow shaft.

"Huh." Chuli said. "I expected more..."

A flare of green burst from the area and streaked across the road, toward the men behind the cluster of shields. The barricade of stakes caught on fire while yelps of surprise arose. The men, four in all, scattered. The man with the bucket of flash powder realized that the flame was burning toward him, following the trail of powder. He dropped the bucket just before the flame reached it. A towering flash of green flame shot up, turning orange as it receded. Three of the men were on fire. One fell to the ground and began to roll about. The other two flailed mindlessly, one stumbling to the ground and the other launching himself over the cliff edge.

In the light of the fire, Jonah saw the mass of enemy soldiers beyond it, waiting for the fire to die down. He suspected the enemy would wait for the fire to burn out and then attack.

He was wrong.

Small green blasts appeared in the distance, joined by a staccato of *bangs*. Something thudded against the wall right in front of Jonah, other thuds coming from his left and right. A man cried out and stumbled, holding his shoulder. Another soldier's head jerked backward, the man's eye socket oozing blood as he staggered and fell from the scaffold.

"Get down!" Marcella screamed from below. "Everyone get down!"

Squatting with his back to the wall, Jonah found Chuli and Torney doing the same.

"So much for being beyond the range of their bows," Jonah said.

"What are those things?" Torney asked, flinching when the thud from a shot struck the log behind him.

"I don't know. Judging by the green blasts, whatever they are, they use flash powder."

The bangs of the odd enemy weapons fell quiet, replaced by the rumble of approaching footsteps on the wooden scaffolding. Marcella emerged from the darkness in a crouch, keeping her head below the top of the wall. The woman slowed as she reached them, her face a thundercloud as she growled at Chuli.

"Who told you to loose your arrow?"

Chuli blinked. "Nobody, Captain. I had an idea..."

"Our barricade is now on fire and there will be nothing between us and the enemy but dirt and a few glowstones!"

Jonah interjected. "They were going to burn the barricade, anyway. Chuli merely beat them to it, and she took out a few of the enemy in the process." Marcella glared at Jonah and he hastily added, "They were spreading flash powder, using a cluster of shields to protect them while they did it."

The fire in the captain's eyes simmered "Well, next time, be sure to communicate with me. I command this post, and the lives of everyone here are my responsibility."

"You are correct, Captain" Chuli nodded, her eyes flicking toward Marcella and away in shame. "I apologize."

Jonah turned and peeked over the wall. The fires had died down, and the enemy had advanced, the front line waiting just beyond the remnants of the barricade.

"If it's all the same with you, Captain, I think it's time to initiate the next part of the plan."

Marcella cupped her hands to her mouth and shouted. "Archers, ready yourselves. When they advance, fire at will." She then put one hand on Jonah's shoulder, the other on Torney's. "You two be ready. And, for Issal's sake, don't die. If we lose you, we'll never hold them long enough to evacuate."

The captain turned and scurried down the scaffold, crouching down while offering words of encouragement to the soldiers as they waited for the attack. They didn't have to wait long.

With a roar, the enemy army charged. Archers inside the garrison raised their bows and began loosing arrows that arced through the air to rain death down upon the enemy. Dozens of Imperial soldiers fell, but others replaced them. In mere moments, a smattering of them slowed at around three hundred feet. They lifted oddly shaped metal tubes, aimed, and a flash of green blasted from them. A female archer to Jonah's left staggered backward. Jonah's eyes widened as blood oozed from a hole in the woman's forehead. She fell backward, off the scaffold, to the ground below.

He turned and saw other soldiers with the same weapons. A small flash of green flame lit the night and a soldier beyond Torney screamed when struck.

Jonah ducked behind the wall as terror raced through his veins. People were dying and he could be next. He needed to act.

"Now, Torney!" Jonah roared. "Do it now!"

Jonah closed his eyes and latched on to his fear. Chaos surrounded him – raw, angry energy he absorbed until he thought he might burst. He opened his eyes, stood, and stared down at the rune he had carefully traced at the side of the road. Releasing the energy into the rune, it began to glow. A wave of exhaustion struck and caused his knees to buckle. He gripped two of the sharpened log ends for support and glanced to his left.

Torney charged his own symbol, fifty feet inland from Jonah's rune. Jonah watched his own rune pulse and fade, curious as to the effect that would occur. This particular rune remained among the few augmentations he had yet to see attempted.

The ground before the rune suddenly burst upward in a shockwave, expanding as it rolled toward the attackers. Enemy soldiers cried out and tried to scramble away, but the wave of earth moved too quickly. It blasted through, over and beyond the men, tossing them as if they were leaves before a stiff autumn breeze. Torney's shockwave followed, rolling eastward toward the attacking army in an ever-widening path until it eclipsed the torn earth from Jonah's shockwave. In moments, nothing remained standing within the six-hundred-foot battleground that had briefly existed.

Another shockwave blasted out from Jonah's rune, pulverizing the earth as it headed east, trailed by Torney's shockwave.

"How long will this continue?" Chuli asked.

Jonah shrugged. "I guess the same as any other rune. They will begin to weaken in about an hour and will die off shortly after that."

Torney wiped his brow and ran his hand down his face, appearing exhausted. "Well, now we know why Alridge refused to let us test this one near the Ward."

"Yes we do." Jonah agreed as cries of pain and calls for help came from nearby. "We had better go see if we can heal any of the wounded."

Torney grunted. "Now? I'm exhausted, and I could really use some rest."

Jonah turned away, speaking back at Torney over his shoulder. "As King Cassius used to say to me, *you can rest when you're dead*."

The three Wardens moved down the scaffold, toward a woman who held her hand to her chest, her back against the wall. Squatting beside her, Jonah put his hand on her hand, which covered her wound.

Chuli moved past Jonah and knelt to the other side of the injured woman. Her face was pale, her forehead covered in sweat, her breathing ragged. He closed his eyes, sank into meditation, and found his source of Order.

The woman's life force was dim, weak. Inside her, he found a storm of Chaos surrounding an object that appeared black in his mind's eye – an object Order could not heal.

Jonah opened his eyes. "There's something in your shoulder. We need to cut it out so I can heal you."

The wounded woman nodded weakly. Chuli gripped her hand and moved it from the wound. Dark blood oozed from it and Jonah steeled himself for what he must do. He drew his knife and found himself wishing that the medicus had not left with Thiron.

A blast of heat and flash of green light erupted behind Jonah. The explosion was deafening. Torney fell over Jonah, struck the scaffold, and rolled off. He hit the ground below, hard, and fell still. Debris rained down upon the garrison interior, joined by shouts and screams.

Jonah turned and found a portion of the wall missing, the sections standing beside it ablaze. A man beyond the breach was on fire, screaming as he flailed and fell from the scaffold. With his knife still in hand, Jonah turned back toward his patient. Her eyes were open but vacant, her breathing stilled. Too late. He put the knife away as another explosion struck, this one just short of the garrison walls.

"She's dead." He pointed past Chuli. "We need to go!"

Chuli nodded, turned, and scrambled after the other archers as they headed toward the ladder. Jonah stood and peeked over the wall, pausing when he saw a hole in the ground, surrounded by flames that licked the bottom of the garrison wall directly below where he stood. His Shockwave rune was gone, the shockwaves taken with it. Turning, he found Torney's rune also destroyed. Without the Shockwaves to hold them back, the enemy army would be upon them in minutes.

Jonah ran down the scaffold, which was now empty save for himself. Reaching the end, he sped down the ladder and almost knocked Chuli off.

"Ouch!" Chuli yelled. "Wait until I'm down!"

Jonah shouted, "We have to hurry! The Shockwave runes are gone. The army will be here any minute!"

Chuli reached the ground and ran toward Torney. "We can't leave him!"

Dropping to his feet, Jonah released a sigh and ran to follow her.

"You heard him," Marcella shouted, waving to the remaining soldiers. "Evacuate now! To the tunnel!"

Another explosion struck, beyond the original breach, chased by a flash of green flames. Parts of the wall sprayed into the air. A thin section between the two breaches remained for a moment before tipping inward, spilling hot, orange flames into the compound. The remaining soldiers circled around the backside of a bunkhouse and disappeared while Jonah and Chuli knelt beside their friend.

Torney lay with his face down. In the flickering light of the fire, Jonah saw a wound on the back of Torney's head, his hair matted with blood. Jonah put his hand on his friend's head and dove straight into healing, only to find a foreign object lodged in Torney's skull, obstructing the healing process.

Jonah opened his eyes and shook his head. "I can't heal him without a little surgery. We don't have time and will have to carry him."

Chuli grimaced and scooped her hand beneath Torney's shoulder. Jonah did the same, with each of them looping one of Torney's arms around their necks before dragging him around the barracks.

"Why couldn't it have been you who got injured?" Chuli said with a grunt.

"Why would you say that?" Jonah gasped, his breathing labored at Torney's dead weight. "You do know I have feelings, right?"

"Sorry. Nothing personal," she grunted as they turned the corner. "I'd just rather carry you instead of him. You are a fair bit lighter than Torney, you know."

Jonah grunted "Yes. *That*, I can understand."

The cave came into view as another explosion erupted behind them. Jonah found himself thankful for it. "At least we know they aren't rushing the compound yet. I doubt they would try to blow up their own soldiers."

"True," Chuli said.

As they drew closer to the cave, Jonah peered at the device hanging above the entrance. The reflection of the fires behind them flickered off the brass housing, the shape of the thing reminding Jonah of a large turtle shell. Secured to a rope, the Chaos trap dangled from a hastily built, twelve-foot-tall frame. Jonah's gaze followed the rope from the frame to the tunnel entrance. When they reached the tunnel, he slowed.

"We need to stop." Jonah gasped for air. "I have to draw the rune."

Chuli nodded, panting as she leaned against the rock wall.

Jonah ducked from beneath Torney's arm, and Chuli grunted at the added weight. Torney's head flopped to the side, and he slid to the ground.

"Sorry," Chuli wiped her brow, still panting. "He's too heavy to carry by myself."

Rather than reply, Jonah set himself to drawing a symbol beneath the Chaos trap. Once finished, the Cold rune was six feet in diameter. Jonah stared at it to ensure he had drawn it correctly. The fog bank would engulf the garrison, mask the cave entrance, and provide a clean escape. If he had drawn it incorrectly, bad things could happen.

Bad things could happen.

"Wait," Jonah said aloud. "Bad things happen if an incomplete rune is used!"

"What are you talking about?"

He spoke while erasing part of one line. "Remember our Chaos lessons? What did Alridge say about a misdrawn rune?" Without waiting for her response, he scrambled beside Torney. "Let's pick him up and get out of here."

They both bent, grunting as they lifted Torney as they had done before.

"Does he feel heavier now, or is it just me?" Jonah said between clenched teeth.

Chuli groaned. "Perhaps he stuffed rocks in his pockets when we weren't looking."

They entered the black maw of the tunnel, following the rope that held the Chaos trap in place. Twenty paces ahead, a glowstone offered light to help guide the way. The going was slow, the tunnel too narrow for three people to walk astride. They passed the first glowstone and the blue light of another came into view. When they reached it, they leaned Torney against the cave wall and paused to catch their breath.

"You know," Jonah panted, "I haven't heard an explosion for a while."

Shouts arose from the garrison behind them. Among the shouting, Jonah heard the word *tunnel*. Alarmed, he scrambled for his dagger, drew it, and frantically began sawing at the rope.

"They escaped through here!" A man shouted from the tunnel mouth.

Jonah cut faster, but the rope was thick. It began to fray as other voices joined the first. All of a sudden, the rope snapped, the tail end flying toward the tunnel entrance as a man appeared near the first glowstone.

A thunderous boom came from the direction of the garrison. Red crackling energy engulfed the enemy soldier in the tunnel, his hair and eyes and clothing bursting into flames as he collapsed to the ground, shaking in convulsions. A tremor ran through the tunnel, sending rocks and dirt raining down upon Jonah, Chuli, and Torney. The three Wardens fell to the ground with Torney on top. They covered their heads as debris hit them and left Jonah praying to Issal that they would not be buried alive.

The rocks stopped falling, leaving stirred dust in the air. Jonah freed his arm from the dirt that had gathered and pushed Torney off him. Chuli coughed and wiped dirt from her eyes before helping to push Torney aside. The tunnel behind them had collapsed completely, blocking a retreat. Jonah turned to look in the other direction, and found the tunnel intact. He released a sigh of relief and began working his legs free. With his feet beneath him, he rose to a crouch and pulled Torney off of Chuli. She sat up and checked herself for wounds, appearing dirty but whole.

While he waited for her to clean herself off so they could resume the trek up the tunnel, Jonah put his hand on Torney and closed his eyes to check for any new injuries. He found his own center in seconds and extended his awareness toward Torney, but found nothing. Panicking, he tried again, but Torney's body was a hollow chamber, devoid of life.

Jonah opened his eyes and gazed upon his friend – dirty, bloody, and lifeless. He opened his mouth, and words came out but they sounded as if someone else, someone distant, said them.

"He's dead."

Like a damn breaking, sadness burst through and filled him until it flowed from his eyes. Tears ran down his face, and he rubbed them away with a dirt-covered sleeve. Chuli's arm wrapped around his back and her chest pressed up against his side. He turned toward her, resting his head on her shoulder while he sobbed.

Losing a fellow warden had always been a possibility. He'd known that. The reality had never truly struck him until now.

My friend is dead.

Acknowledging the fact was painful. Jonah was saddened by the hole Torney's death would leave in his life. And then, he arrived at a realization – one even worse.

Oh, Issal, what will I tell Rena?

16

GHOST TOWN

Rena Dimas opened and clenched her mitted hand. Her fingers were stiff, numb from the cold. Every few minutes, she would switch which hand held the reins while attempting to warm the other. The rabbit-fur lining of the mitts helped, but after a full day of riding in freezing temperatures, the cold had found a way beyond her defenses. Even the fur stole wrapped about her neck could not completely keep the cold at bay nor could the wool-hooded cloak that covered her head and shoulders. Rena found herself thankful that the surrounding forest blocked the wind.

Kwai-Lan raised his hand, stopping his horse beneath the falling flakes. Kirk, Nalah, and Bilchard also paused their steeds. Rena gripped the reins, although she couldn't actually feel them, and pulled. The mare beneath her whinnied, shook her head, and came to a stop. With the horses stilled, silence filled the air – the heavy stillness that often accompanied falling snow.

The Red Towers loomed over the small party, the forest's presence thick and foreboding, unable to be ignored. While a narrow strip of gray sky was visible above the road, shadowy gloom ruled the forest. Rena found it difficult to see beyond fifty feet, despite the blanket of white that covered the forest floor. A quarter mile ahead of them, light waited, an opening that beckoned. She wondered why they had stopped so near the forest's edge.

Kwai-Lan frowned, his thin mustache bending with his lips. "It is quiet."

Kirk snorted. "What a brilliant observation."

The combat instructor gave Kirk a flat look. "Perhaps you should use your wits toward something constructive. What have we seen since we entered the wood? What have we heard?"

Kirk pulled his hood back, revealing dark, shoulder-length hair. In silence, his narrowed eyes surveyed his surroundings. The man's face was unshaven, his complexion swarthy. Rena knew little of the espion other than he was among the eldest wardens.

"I see nothing and hear even less."

"Precisely."

Kirk huffed a sigh, his breath swirling in the air. "Enough of the cryptic talk, Kwai-Lan. What's your point?"

"My point," Kwai-Lan's tone was serious, his glare heavy. "Is that we have seen nothing. No animals. No tracks in the snow. Nothing since we entered the Red Towers." He held his hand out, pointing south. "The edge of the wood is just ahead. Doesn't it seem odd to you that we have seen zero signs of life all day?"

The man's comment stirred memories of the farm they had passed before entering the forest. All that remained were broken fences, a destroyed barn, dilapidated outbuildings, and the shell of a farmhouse that had burned to the ground. By then, the weather had already cast a melancholy shadow over the party. An abandoned farm and a foreboding forest had further darkened Rena's thoughts and left her longing to return to the safety of the Ward. *Why did you leave me, Torney?*

"Even though we are leaving the forest, I suggest everyone remain alert." Kwai-Lan said, his expression grim as he paused to look each companion in the eye. "Something is wrong here. I can feel it."

He kicked his horse into a trot and the others followed. The light ahead called to Rena and urged her toward it. When the tall trees fell away and more typical-sized trees replaced them, Rena felt a sense of relief. A breeze hit her and found its way into her cloak. The return of the wind gave Rena the impression that even *it* avoided venturing through the ominous forest.

A rise appeared and the horses climbed it, reaching the top a half hour later. They crested the hill and a town came into view. A cluster of a few dozen snow-covered buildings waited in the valley below. Vallerton.

The idea of a warm fire and a soft bed stirred a whisper of hope inside Rena, the emotion fleeting, losing out to melancholy. *If only Torney were waiting there for me.* The thought left her with a hollowness that screamed to be filled. *I need someone to trust.* She thought about her companions. *I hardly know these people. I don't even know their last names.*

Kwai-Lan led them toward the quiet town, the tracks left by his horse disturbing the virgin snow. It was growing late, the gray sky darkening. Without tracks to guide them, not even ruts from a wagon, it had already been difficult to follow the road. In the dark, it would be near impossible.

Rena surveyed the houses as they drew nearer. The first was a farm beside the road, strangely deserted. The fence was broken, the barn door missing. The house stood whole, but it was boarded up and lacked signs of life. No tracks ran to the door, no smoke came from the chimney. The idea of smoke caused Rena to turn toward the approaching village and the chimneys among it. Nothing. A chill ran down her spine – a chill unrelated to the cold weather.

"Why are there no fires burning?" she said aloud.

Bilchard's brow furrowed. "You're right. I knew something was missing. Every one of these homes should have a fire going in this weather."

The group fell silent again as they reached the edge of the city.

Continuing what the group had repeatedly observed throughout the day, all was quiet, not a single person or animal in sight. They passed a bake shop, the front door and window smashed in. The butcher shop across the street was even worse, the building damaged to the point that the roof had collapsed and snow filled the interior. The party then came across the town's inn. A sign marked *Wishing Well Inn* clung precariously by one nail as it hung upside down at an odd angle. The front door had been smashed in, the windows shattered. A breeze whistled through the building, a howl that added to the eeriness of the place.

Kwai-Lan swung his leg over and dismounted. "Bilchard, Nalah, you're with me. Kirk, you stay here and make sure nothing happens to Rena. She's our only healer."

As commanded, Bilchard and Nalah both climbed down, Bilchard drawing his sword, and Nalah ready with her short bow. Kwai-Lan produced a glass stick filled with glowing powder. A quick shake and the stick flared to life, the powder inside shining with a blue light.

Stepping over the smashed door, the trio entered and faded from view. Rena stared at the doorway for a moment and then turned to study her surroundings.

The streets were quiet but for the wind. She watched Kirk for a moment, fearing the moment alone with him. The man's horse shuffled beside hers. Upon it, he remained alert, his eyes flicking this way and that, but never at Rena. With an effort, she looked away, and her gaze settled on a building made of stone at the south end of town. Unlike the other buildings, it appeared intact. There was no smoke rising from it, but perhaps it was occupied.

Moments later, Kwai-Lan emerged with Bilchard and Nalah trailing him. The combat master's face was fixed in a grim expression. Bilchard's eyes appeared a bit wild. Nalah appeared shaken. She scurried toward a snow bank, leaned forward with her hands on her knees, and began to retch.

"What did you find?" Kirk asked. "Is anyone here?"

Kwai-Lan climbed on his horse. "No. At least, not anybody who's alive."

"Someone...or something killed some people in there," Bilchard said, sheathing his sword. "Worse, what's left...something has been chewing on them...eating them. The smell..."

The imagery caused Rena to clench her eyes closed and think of something...anything else. She recalled the stone structure, opened her eyes, and addressed Kwai-Lan.

"There's a brick building at the other end of town," Rena pointed toward it. "That must be the town keep we read about in Thiron's report."

Without a word, Kwai-Lan urged his horse forward and rode

toward the keep. Rena and the others followed, each of them warily watching the buildings they rode past. Houses lay vacant, some partially destroyed. A smithy stood to one side of the road, or what remained of it. Only the forge was intact, but it was blackened by soot. The building that had surrounded it was gone, and nothing but dormant black coals remained.

The keep itself was a modest, square, two-story building. A wooden palisade had once surrounded it, but most of the logs had fallen, some outward, some inward. Snow-covered shards of what remained of the gate lay between the broken palisade and the keep itself. Similar to the rest of the city, no tracks had disturbed the area until Kwai-Lan dismounted and walked to the door.

Kwai-Lan's heavy knock echoed inside the building. Seconds trickled by, and he knocked again. Minutes passed. No response.

"Locked and no answer." Kwai-Lan turned toward Kirk. "Can you get us in?"

A smirk appeared on Kirk's face, the first smile Rena had seen since they left Selbin. He slid off his horse and drew a set of needles from a sheath on his hip. Kirk knelt before the door and began picking the lock.

Rena and the others climbed off their horses, each following Kwai-Lan's lead as he tied his mount to an intact section of the palisade wall. Removing her mitts, Rena flexed her fingers and looped the rope around a post before securing it. She then blew warm air into her hands and rubbed them together. Kirk stood, stepped aside, and turned the knob. The door swung open with a deep creak.

The interior was dark, quiet.

Kwai-Lan drew one of his strange star-shaped knives from the sash that hung over his shoulder. Holding the knife ready, he crossed through the open doorway.

Without looking back, Kwai-Lan called out instructions. "Nalah, you follow me. Rena, you're in the middle. Kirk and Bilchard can take the rear. Remain quiet and ready."

Everyone except Rena held a weapon, Nalah with her short bow, Kirk with his knives, Bilchard with his longsword in one hand, shield strapped to the other. Kwai-Lan produced his glowstick and entered the building while the rest trailed him.

They passed closed doors with Kwai-Lan stopping to open them. The first was a sleeping quarters with six beds, stacked in pairs. The room was cold and appeared unused. Across the hall was what appeared to be an armory, severely lacking anything that resembled a weapon.

They continued down the hall, which opened to a common room dimly lit by small, snow-covered windows. A kitchen stood to one side, the cupboards bare of food. Broken plates and dirty dishes lay stacked on the counter and table. The sitting area beside the kitchen appeared very disturbed, as if a fight had occurred. Broken chairs and a torn, blood-stained sofa occupied the space before a dormant fireplace. Across from the common area was a stairwell leading up, and another leading down. Another hallway, darker than the first, waited ahead of them.

Kwai-Lan gazed upon their surroundings with narrowed eyes. After a moment, he pointed toward the stairs.

"Bilchard and Kirk, you go up and see what you can find. Try not to kill anyone who doesn't need killing. Nalah and I will go downstairs." The man addressed Rena, "Stay put. If anything happens, we are but a shout away."

Rena nodded, and he turned toward the dark stairwell. With his glowstick held before him, Kwai-Lan led a very nervous Nalah in a careful descent.

"What are you waiting for, big guy?" Kirk said, giving Bilchard a nudge as he passed him. "Let's go see if anyone is home."

The duo crept up the stairs and faded around the corner, leaving Rena alone.

She noticed that the front door remained open. It was growing dark outside. The wind howled, the sound the only thing she heard beyond her own, rasping breath.

Like a corpse clawing its way out of a grave, thoughts of her father arose. His dark specter hovered over her, encouraging her to cower.

To fear Issal is to love him, her father had often said. *Fear is the only way he knows we are genuinely repentant.*

Accordingly, fear is how Rena's father controlled her.

Rena recalled the time her father had nailed her in a crate and had left her outside overnight. Although it was autumn at the time, autumn evenings in Cinti Mor could grow quite cold. After her screaming had stopped, after her voice was shredded and the tears would no longer fall, she feared she might die in that dark, cold, lonely crate. The secrets Rena and her father shared, his secrets, had driven him to it. Even though she had sworn to never tell, he insisted that fear was the best way, the only way to be certain. When he had opened the crate the next morning, her father lifted her out, held her, and expressed his love. *Our relationship is special, Rena. It must remain a secret. Others wouldn't understand.*

The thick scent of an unwashed body arose, stirring the pit of fear in Rena's stomach. Arms suddenly appeared from behind and wrapped about her, squeezing. She screamed in horror, the image of her father locked in her mind. She heard his angry snarls in her ear, felt the heat of his breath on her neck. *He has returned. He knows about Torney. He know about Cassie…about my dream. He has discovered that they know what he did to me.*

The rush of hurried steps came from above, rapidly descending the stairwell. The man holding her dragged her backward as she sobbed and shrieked. Bilchard burst from the stairwell, big and bulky in his winter gear, his longsword held before him, his face in a scowl of fury – a scowl like her father's.

Something snapped inside Rena. All her strength left her in one ragged gasp. She stumbled, collapsed, and slipped from the man's grip. The side of her head struck something. All fell dark as her father reached for her.

17

MADNESS

Darkness. It surrounded Rena. Within the gloom, her father's face appeared, his hands reaching for her, shaking her.

"Rena!" he shouted. "Rena! Wake up!"

Her eyes opened with a start. She gasped, blinking in confusion. Kwai-Lan was looking down at her with a furrowed brow.

"You hit your head when you fell," Kwai-Lan said.

Rena sat up. Her head hurt. When she lifted her hand to it, she felt a lump.

"Are you all right?" Nalah asked.

"Yes. I'll be fine. It's just a headache."

Kwai-Lan held his hand out and helped Rena to her feet. "It does not bode well to see our only healer as the first person injured."

Rena found Bilchard standing with his sword drawn, the weapon pointed at a tall, thin man with a scraggly beard. The man's eyes were wild and constantly shifting.

"Who's that?" Rena asked.

"Good question." Kwai-Lan turned toward the man. "What is your name?"

The man ran a hand through his untamed brown hair. "Name?"

Kwai-Lan moved closer to the man. Despite his short stature, the menacing weight to his glare was impressive.

"Are you Constable Hardy?"

The man nodded with obvious trepidation.

"What happened here? Where are the town folk?"

Hardy's eyes shifted toward the open door at the end of the hallway. "Madness. It's madness out there. Please close the door."

Kwai-Lan nodded toward Kirk. "Do it.

Rolling his eyes, Kirk turned and walked down the corridor. With the front door closed, he returned and Kwai-Lan addressed the constable.

"You speak of madness. What happened, man?"

Hardy's gaze remained on the closed door, but Rena had the feeling he was looking past it, recalling something.

"Vallerton...is cursed."

Kirk guffawed. "Cursed! You *are* mad."

The constable's focus shifted toward Kirk. "You would be, too, if you had seen it."

"Seen what, Hardy?" Kwai-Lan demanded.

"It began a few weeks back. Just as before, the first incident was at Vernon's farm, but it wasn't just a few cows and a broken fence this time." Hardy's gaze fell toward the floor. He shook his head. "Vernon and Ingrid, both dead. Their bodies were mangled, parts eaten. Their child, Olive. We never did find her."

Hardy fell silent again.

"Listen, Hardy." The hardness was gone from Kwai-Lan's voice, his tone shifting toward compassion. "We are here to help. Do you recall the hunters who came to Vallerton this past summer? The ones who killed the monstrous badger?"

The constable nodded.

"We are part of the same group." Kwai-Lan gestured toward his fellow wardens. "We are here to help you, but we must know what it is we face."

"You wouldn't believe me if I told you. It sounds...ridiculous."

Kirk crossed his arms and leaned against the wall. "More ridiculous than a ten-foot-tall badger?"

"Honestly...yes."

Rena couldn't stop thinking about the farmer and his family. The description matched what they had found at the abandoned inn. "What about the rest of the people? Are they all...dead?"

Hardy's haunted eyes met hers, and she saw madness inside them. "I honestly don't know if any survived." He stared down the hallway, toward the front door. "The men came here and took the weapons. They wanted me to come with them, but I refused. This keep is too small to house everyone, so they planned to hole up in the one place that can." Hardy's bulging eyes stared at Kwai-Lan. "Dead or alive, you should find them in the mines."

Kwai-Lan frowned. "The mines." He took a deep breath and exhaled. "We had best go there now. It's getting dark."

Hardy began shaking his head from side to side while kneading his thin hands. "No, no, no, no. Don't go out there. Not now. Not if it's growing dark."

A chill ran down Rena's spine. "Why not?" She found herself fearing his response.

He leaned toward her with wild eyes and whispered, "They come at night."

Kirk stalked toward the constable. "Enough of your cryptic tales. Who comes at night? What is it we face here?"

Hardy broke and began blabbering gibberish. Spittle sprayed from his mouth, and his head twitched with each unintelligible syllable. The look in his eyes had grown even worse, and Rena found herself backing from him despite Bilchard's sword still held ready.

Kwai-Lan watched Hardy for a moment and then spun on his heel. "Everyone outside. Let's see what we find at the mine."

The group left the mad constable behind, emerging outside to falling snow, heavy enough that it had already partially buried their tracks.

Bilchard came out last, closing the door behind him. "What happened to that man?"

Kwai-Lan shook his head as he untied his horse. "Something has broken his mind. Based on what Nalah and I saw in the basement, the constable has been living in a cell down there for some time now. Whatever it is, he's scared enough to lock himself up in the basement every night rather than sleeping in a bed upstairs." Kwai-Lan climbed into his saddle. "Perhaps we will learn more if we can find the missing people."

When the others were mounted and ready, Kwai-Lan led them back down the street, through the ghost of a town, and turned at the first fork in the road. Thiron's report said that the mine itself was only a mile outside of town. Rena found herself searching the shadowy woods beside the road, fearing what hid in the darkness. *Torney. I need you. Why couldn't you be here with me?*

They crested a rise and found open pits surrounded by ten-foot piles of earth, now covered in snow. At the bottom of one pit was a well. A trough of snow-covered tracks ran from the well, toward a cliff face at the far end of the pit.

"There's a mining tunnel. Those tracks run from the tunnel to the well, so someone has been coming out to fetch drinking water."

Following a man-made ramp that circled half of the pit, Kwai-Lan led the other mounted riders down. Upon reaching the well, they all dismounted and tied their horses to it. Rena's stomach rumbled in hunger. The trail rations she had eaten offered little sustenance. She then considered the horses and wondered where they would get food. Finding Vallerton abandoned had not crossed their minds when they set out on this journey.

With Kwai-Lan in the lead, Rena in the middle, and Bilchard bringing up the rear, they tromped through the snow toward the dark tunnel. Kwai-Lan and Kirk entered but Rena stopped outside the tunnel. From the depths of her consciousness, terror clawed up, constricting her throat and causing her breathing to become rapid, shallow gasps.

A hand gripped her shoulder and she jumped. She turned and saw Bilchard looking down with concern in his eyes.

"It's all right, Rena." He lifted his sword. "We'll protect you."

She nodded and forced herself forward, into the gloom.

The light from Kwai-Lan's glowstick shined ahead, creating silhouettes of both him and Kirk. Rena hurried forward and found the tunnel larger than she had first imagined. The roof was eight feet tall, the tunnel wide enough for the entire party to walk astride one another. They rounded a bend and came to a recently built block wall. Within the wall, was a door, thick and sturdy.

Kwai-Lan paused briefly before raising his fist to the door. The knock echoed off the rock walls of the tunnel. Moments passed. He raised his fist to knock again, and a sound arose from inside. The door opened.

Two men stood inside, one holding the door, the other aiming a crossbow at Kwai-Lan. The man holding the door had hair the color of straw. His blue eyes were free of wrinkles, his skin smooth, but tanned. In contrast, the other man was balding and what remained on his hair had gone gray. His face was weathered, his shoulders broad. Thick, calloused fingers gripped the crossbow and held it up with ease. The older man leaned forward, craning his neck to see down the tunnel. Lowering the crossbow, he exhaled in relief.

"Thank, Issal. Please tell me that you've come to save us," the man said in a deep voice.

Kwai-Lan nodded. "Yes. My name is Kwai-Lan Chen. We have journeyed here from Fallbrandt, sent here to help the town of Vallerton. I assume you live there?"

Nodding, he replied, "Yes. I'm Grady...Grady Unger. I'm the town blacksmith. Or, I was before..." his voice trailed off.

"May we come in?" Kwai-Lan asked. "I assure you, we mean no harm."

"Of course." Grady turned to his tall companion. "Tindle, be sure to close and bar the door behind us."

The blond man nodded while stepping aside to hold the door open. Grady led them down a tunnel that gradually curved to the left. At the first opening, he turned down another tunnel that opened to a natural cavern lit by lanterns, glowing with a pale blue light.

Pallets with bedding ran along two walls. A fire burned at the far end, the smoke rising up what appeared to be a natural chimney. A half-dozen wooden tables sat in the center, encircled by a mish-mash of chairs and benches, all occupied.

Men, women, and children, perhaps fifty in all, turned toward them. Their faces were dirty, but they appeared in good health... certainly in better shape than the constable.

"We have visitors," Grady announced in a booming voice. "I suggest that the men join me while we meet with them."

The sixteen men seated at the tables stood and crossed the room. Grady grabbed the nearest lantern and turned toward Kwai-Lan.

"Let's meet in another chamber. I'd rather not discuss this around the children."

Grady led them further down the tunnel and came to another cavern, this one half the size of the previous gallery. A table waited in the center, beside a shallow pool of water with stalactites hanging high above it. Nine chairs surrounded the table. Grady took one and gestured for Kwai-Lan to join him. As Rena sat beside Kwai-Lan, a drop of water fell into the pool, disturbing the tranquil surface and sending a ring of ripples toward the water's edge. Rena's companions each took a seat, along with Grady, Tindle, and two others. The remaining men stood behind Grady, their faces unshaven, bags beneath their eyes from lack of sleep.

"We call this the planning chamber," Grady said, his voice echoing off the uneven cave roof. "This is where we meet and make the difficult decisions – the ones we would rather avoid but must face, regardless." His gaze settled on Kwai-Lan. "How did you find us?"

"When we found the town abandoned, we went to the keep. Constable Hardy is there, but…he is not well. He seems to be maddened by what happened."

"Maddened?" Tindle asked.

"His mind appears…broken."

"What we have seen and endured…" Grady shook his head. "It might be enough to break a man, and Hardy has been involved from the onset. Honestly, I think he was still spooked from the badger this past summer. Then, when this all began…"

Kirk rolled his eyes. "Oh, for the love of Issal. You're as bad as Hardy." He slapped his palm on the table. "Just tell us what we face."

Grady scowled so hard at Kirk, Rena thought he might reach across the table and attack him. After a glance toward his companions, his expression softened, and he began his tale.

"It began a few weeks back, the night before our first snowfall. I was out working in the smithy, cleaning up before dinner. As usual, it was hot inside the workshop, so I had the doors open. When I thought I heard a scream, I hurried out and listened. Again, screams arose from the north end of town, distant but sure.

"I ran to the keep and alerted Hardy. I armed myself with an axe. He grabbed a crossbow and sword. The keep stable had two horses, used for emergencies. I took one, he took the other, and off we went. After racing across town, we slowed and listened. Another scream and cries for help came from the direction of Vernon's farm. When we got there, we saw a sight we weren't prepared to see.

"The fence was broken, the front door missing, windows shattered. Dead cows littered the area, some partially eaten. We dismounted and entered the house, wary of an attack. None came. Vernon lay face-first on the floor, a bloody scythe lying beside him. Using my boot, I rolled him over and found his face missing, bitten right off. We searched the house and found his wife dead, mutilated, but his young child was nowhere to be seen. It was a long, horrible night. One I will never forget."

He gazed down at his hands as if blood covered them. "At first, I could only wonder at what might cause such horror. I now wish I didn't know." He looked up, his eyes meeting Kwai-Lan's. "It's odd how the unknown is often more frightening than the truth. In this case, the truth was much worse.

"Five nights later – nights where everyone in town had been on high alert – they returned. We were ready, or we thought we were. If there had been only one or two, we would have been fine. However, we had no idea of what we faced, particularly in the dark of night. These monsters move fast, in rapid bursts. Yet, they are deathly quiet. You would never know one was coming if not for their eyes.

"When they attacked, they smashed through doors and windows with ease, ransacking buildings and killing the people who were in them. I fought hard, killing one in my own workshop, but these beasts are mindless in their violence. Another one burst in and smashed into a beam that supported the smithy roof. The beam broke. With the weight of snow atop it, the roof caved in, crushing the monster and pinning me to the ground. With the forge still hot, it only took moments for the fallen wood to catch fire. I was able to work myself free and crawl out as the blaze took hold. In the light of the fire, I saw them."

"What was it?" Kirk insisted. "What did you see?"

Grady frowned. "This is far worse than it sounds."

"Just say it, Grady." Kwai'Lan urged the man.

"Rabbits."

"What?" Rena asked. "Bunnies?"

Grady shook his head. "Not bunnies. Monsters." He held his arm out, his hand five feet off the ground. "About this tall. Black as night. Eyes that glow red with the evil that drives them. They are fast and ferocious."

"Rabbits?" Kwai'Lan's brow furrowed. "They don't eat meat. Rabbits are plant eaters. Animals prey on them, not the other way around."

"These are different. If you stopped by the inn, you would have seen what they do."

"So, what happened after the smithy caught fire?"

"The blaze was big and bright as you can imagine. The light of the fire also seemed to frighten them away. It was a long night, even worse than the night when Vernon and Ingrid died. When day broke, we went to the keep and demanded that Hardy do something. He gave us access to the weapons, but he would not leave the building. In fact, he vowed to *never* leave the keep again. I tried to appeal to the man, but… something had changed inside him. I later discovered that he had witnessed the monsters dragging away children as he tried to save their mother.

"We told Hardy we were sending a man to Nor Torin and planned to hole up in the mines until help arrived. The remaining towns folk gathered their belongings, as much food as we had stored, and made this place our home. It will remain as such until this scourge is gone."

Rena listened to the stories, the images playing out in her head until something occurred to her.

"Oh, no," she uttered.

Everyone turned toward her.

"What is it?" Kwai-Lan asked.

"Rabbits are meant to be prey. They breed fast – perhaps faster than any other animal. If they are that massive and have become the hunters instead of the hunted, what's to stop them from multiplying? A handful of these monsters could produce a swarm within weeks."

Oh, Torney. Where are you?

18

THE RETURN

As the pale walls of Sol Polis drew closer, anxiety twisted Iko's innards. *Now I know how it feels to be seasick.* Having sailed many times without experiencing the illness, he was guessing because the source of his malady had nothing to do with the sea.

Motion to his left drew his attention to Percy, who was climbing up the stairs from the cabin they shared. Percy approached and handed Iko his pack, which he accepted with a nod. Once again, Iko found himself longing for a sword at his hip, something he had grown used to during his stay in Kantar. Having nothing but the dagger strapped to his belt made him uncomfortable, like a part of him was missing.

In his deep voice, Captain Sterling shouted orders that set the crew scurrying to their posts – some climbed masts, some held the lines, others waited beside the rail. When the sails were furled, the ship slowed and drifted toward the pier. The sailors at the rail made ready, the one closer to Iko tossing a loop over the thick post sticking up from the pier as they drifted past. When the rope drew taught, the ship stopped, pulling against it for a moment before settling beside the pier.

Iko turned to Percy. "Why don't you go pay Sterling? I'll meet you on the docks."

With a nod, Percy turned and headed toward the quarterdeck.

Sailors shuffled past Iko as they slid the boarding plank through an opening in the rail and let it drop to the dock. Moments later, Iko descended the plank and stepped onto solid footing for the first time since leaving Wayport.

He looked toward Sol Polis, his gaze settling on the citadel that overlooked the city. The shorter, scorched and broken tower seemed an oddity standing beside the two that remained intact – their alabaster walls appearing like bright white teeth in the afternoon sun. Iko's mother waited somewhere inside the citadel. Although he wished otherwise, his duty was to report to her immediately – a conversation he dreaded.

Percy climbed off the boarding plank and clapped Iko on the shoulder. "We made it. Let's get this over with, and then we can relax for a bit."

Iko gave his friend a sidelong glance. Percy stood a few inches shorter than Iko, with a head of brown hair that seemed to curl more with the humidity. His smile was affable, as always, his manner at ease.

Iko raised a brow in response. "Haven't we just spent the better part of two weeks relaxing on a ship?"

"Yes. But I didn't have an ale in my hand, so it doesn't count." Percy flashed a broad smile.

Finding his friend's grin infectious, Iko smiled in return. "Good point." He waved Percy forward. "Let's complete our duty, and then we'll have a few mugs."

"Only a few?" Percy shook his head as he began walking. "I'm thinking double digits are more appropriate after this mission."

Iko's smile faded as memories of the past month resurfaced.

When he first left for Kantar, his mission had been clear and the objective made sense. Unexpectedly, Iko had found a kindred spirit in Broland. He had anticipated a spoiled, pretentious prince whose attention was focused on balls, dinners, and fashion. Instead, Iko had discovered Broland to be honest, friendly, and compassionate. As he spent time with the prince, the walls around the feigned friendship began to crack and fall away. What remained was a friend, the only friend Iko had outside of Percy. Killing Broland had taken every bit of Iko's will. The wound it had rendered was still fresh, raw, and refused to heal. *Forgive me, my friend.* The words sounded hollow in his head.

A cloud of melancholy hovered over Iko as they passed through Downside, crossed beneath the outer wall, and entered Sol Polis proper. The foot traffic thickened, parted, and faded. Carts and carriages rolled by, the rumble of their wheels swallowed by the hum of the city. Beggars at the corner, shops lining the street, and guards on patrol were lost in the haze of Iko's thoughts until the citadel suddenly loomed before them, as if it had appeared from nowhere.

Built upon a hilltop and surrounded by a tall wall, the complex of alabaster buildings and towers stood over the city like a guardian – a guardian that had failed more than once. Two decades prior, The Horde had crushed the city, destroying it and everyone within. More recently – less than a year past – Sol Polis had been assaulted, captured, and taken from King Dalwin, the man Iko's mother had replaced. That day marked the rebirth of the Empire.

Percy moved ahead of Iko and began scaling the stairs to the western gate. Following, Iko shook his head in an attempt to clear it. *Focus, Iko.*

They reached the top, and one of the guards on duty held his hand up.

"Hold. State your name and your reason for visiting the citadel."

"It's me, Tarshal. Ikonis Eldarro."

The guard lowered his hand, stared at Iko for a moment, and then nodded. "Sorry, Iko. I didn't recognize you with the facial hair." He studied Iko from head to toe. "You've grown into a man. Although, you appear a bit tired."

"Tired, I am. We just arrived and are travel weary."

"I assume you are here to see your mother."

I'd rather be elsewhere. Perhaps a tavern, behind a bar lined with mugs of ale. "Yes."

"She's in a meeting with the Council today. Kardan is with them. Things are…brewing."

Iko nodded. "I should have guessed as much." *Feared as much.*

"Go on in and report to Sculdin in the barracks. He'll walk you to your mother's chambers."

Scully. Him, I do wish to see. "Thanks, Tarshal."

They passed through the gate and headed north, following a brick path through the western garden. Long shadows covered the path, casting the area in a gloom that matched Iko's mood. Unlike his last visit, the garden lacked color, the flowers now dormant until spring. Winter in Sol Polis simply meant rain and reasonable temperatures, nothing like a winter in Fallbrandt. The thought stirred memories of a pleasant carriage ride across the snow-covered valley. He found himself missing Quinn, the sentiment eliciting a sigh. *Another betrayal I must live with. Another friend lost because of my actions. Another sacrifice made for our cause.*

Emerging from the garden, they turned the corner and crossed an open courtyard where an empty carriage waited, the harnesses empty with the horses likely off in the stable. Percy opened the door to the barracks and led Iko down the corridor inside. They passed an open door. Inside, Iko spotted three males and a female playing dice at a table, the walls surrounding them lined with empty bunks. The guards glanced in his direction, and then resumed their game. A cheer arose at the throw, countered by one of the guards cursing his bad luck. Reaching the door at the end, Percy opened it to a shout.

Two guards were sparring, one with a lean frame and standing over six feet tall, the other sporting a squat, thick build. Wooden swords clashed, the clacking of wood on wood filling the air. The tall guard swung his shield about and blocked a massive blow from his opponent before attempting a counterstrike that missed. The two men circled, the tall man swinging a chest-high strike. The squat guard lifted his shield, redirecting the strike while executing a thrust toward his opponent's abdomen. With an *oof*, the tall man bent and collapsed. As a healer ran in from the side of the room, Iko glanced up and found Sculdin leaning over the rail of his lofted office.

"Is that young Ikonis?" Sculdin shouted. "And Percilus as well?"

"Yo, Sculdin." Percy waved.

"We came to see you, Scully," Iko said.

"Come on up. The stairs are at the far end of the practice yard."

Stepping down on the dirt floor, Iko crossed the yard, nodding toward the two guards as he walked past. Iko recognized the shorter guard and nodded toward him when their eyes met. *Tarvick. The man might be a member of the elite guard, but I could defeat him in a duel. Despite his strength, his motion is slow, his moves predictable.*

Percy opened the door and led Iko up the stairs to Sculdin's office.

They entered the loft to find Sculdin waiting. Sculdin gripped Percy's forearm and clapped his back before doing the same to Iko.

"It's good to see you have returned safely," Sculdin said. "Your mother didn't tell me where you were, only that you were on a dangerous and important mission."

Iko nodded. "Thank you, Scully. Percy and I just arrived via ship. We'll need a place to sleep, but first, I must speak with my mother."

"Your mother has been in the Council chambers all day, but I can escort you to her chambers if you wish to wait there." Sculdin turned toward Percy. "Come along. I'll have Sheen find you two a room."

Sculdin led them out the door, up the stairs to the top floor, and down another long corridor. Another guard Iko knew, a woman named Ydith, was patrolling the hallway. Ydith nodded to Sculdin and eyed Iko as he passed by – her narrowed eyes following him the entire time. Sculdin opened the second to last door and stepped aside.

"Wait in here. Dinner time approaches, and I expect your mother will be along shortly."

Sculdin pulled the door closed, leaving Iko alone in the room.

Iko turned to find a desk and chairs before him. To his left, a sitting area, a tub and vanity, and a four-poster bed occupied the length of the room. Beams of light from the setting sun streamed through the open curtains, tinting everything with an amber hue. Drawn toward the light, Iko crossed the room, toward the open window. The tap of each step echoed off the polished marble floor, the sound ominous in the quiet room.

Looking outside, he found the sun nearing the horizon, casting a long reflection across the sea. The silhouette of a ship split the bright reflection, its sails raised as it drifted into port. Closer in, the streets teemed with life, the activity sure to fade as darkness settled over the city. The taverns would fill at that time, and Iko hoped to find himself in one of them. Drinking himself to a stupor had never held much appeal…until now.

With a sigh, Iko turned from the window and strolled toward the desk, his thoughts drifting to his mother's role as Archon. While she had spent three years leading the Council while they ruled Vinacci, he still had not grown used to her position as Archon of the Empire. With Kalimar and the entire east coast under her rule, she was likely the most powerful person in all of Issalia. Even then, it seemed as if her ambition, and that of the Council, would not be sated until they ruled the entire continent.

He stopped at the desk, and his gaze landed on a pile of papers. Curious, he spun the top sheet around and found it to be a letter to Karl Jarlish. Iko began reading the letter when he heard the door open. Realizing that his mother wouldn't approve of his snooping, he spun around and blinked in surprise.

He couldn't have been more shocked if Issal himself had appeared and offered him salvation.

"Quinn?"

19

CONFRONTATION

Quinn crossed her arms and leaned against the wall, resisting a sigh. Her strong distaste for boredom had taken hold and left her impatient to do something. Anything.

The two guards beside the Council Chamber door eyed her with expressions that left words unnecessary. *No sympathy there*, Quinn thought. *I'm sure they prefer boredom to the alternative. Guards and soldiers tend to die when things aren't boring.* Deciding to occupy her mind with something pleasant, she recalled her rendezvous with Brandt from the previous evening.

They had met in the abandoned tower, three hours after sunset. After Brandt produced a glowstone, Quinn rolled out the map she had stolen the night before. Using Brandt's telepathic connection with his sister, they had relayed the latest events to their leaders at the Ward.

"They want to know what we see on the map," Brandt had said.

Quinn had then leaned over it while holding the glowstone close. "I see a big black X marked in a forest just north of Yarth. Black arrows point from Vinacci to the X, while a red arrow points from the X to Hipoint."

Brandt had closed his eyes and Quinn waited while he communicated with his sister. After a moment, he said, "The Empire attempting an advance past Hipoint is expected. Kantarian soldiers now occupy the garrison at Hipoint, and wardens are stationed at the garrison for support. What else do you see on the map?"

"There's a star beside Yarth, along with notes about wagons, supplies, and more arrows that come from various cities."

Moments later, Brandt said, "They are guessing that the star is a collection point for supplies and possibly for their army as well."

While he relayed the response, Quinn moved the glowstone and shifted her focus with it, locating a name she didn't recognize. "There's also a circle that might mean something. What is..." she squinted to read the scribbled text, "Castile Corvichi?"

With his eyes still closed, Brandt said, "Before they respond, they wish to know where it's located."

"It appears to be located in the mountains east of Vinata, beside a river."

Brandt's eyes had remained closed as he relayed the message. "Master Firellus remembers a famous Vinacci merchant name Corvichi who built a castle far from the city. There, he sought to secure his wealth in a protective location. However, Corvichi died only a few years after the castle was completed, and he had no heirs. Firellus believes that the castle was then abandoned." Brandt opened his eyes and frowned. "That can't be right."

"What can't be right?"

"This Corvichi lived over four hundred years ago."

"What does that have to do with anything?"

He shrugged. "I have no idea."

Quinn frowned in frustration. She had hoped the map would provide them an advantage. Instead, stealing it now seemed like a pointless risk she could not undo. That feeling clung to her as the memory faded and her focus shifted back to the present, to her location in the citadel main hall.

She began to pace before the doors, knowing it annoyed the guards. *Good. I hope they're annoyed. They annoy me with their attitude.*

The doors suddenly opened as the eight Council members exited the chambers. With grim expressions and mouths bent into frowns, they crossed the hall to the stairwell, their blue-trimmed white cloaks swaying with each step. Kardan and Varius then appeared, both wearing a scowl. *I wonder what has left everyone so upset.*

With a glance and the flick of her wrist, Varius indicated that Quinn should take the lead. Presuming that the Archon was heading back to her chambers, Quinn crossed the hall with Varius and Kardan in tow. They climbed the stairs to the top floor, where Varius tapped Quinn on the shoulder.

"Glynnis, you go on and meet me in my room." Varius turned toward Kardan. "I need a moment alone with Leo."

The Archon turn toward her general, and Quinn's curiosity screamed to remain and listen, but the Archon's orders were clear. She spun about, approached the door, and noticed Ydith down the corridor, leaning against the wall with her arms crossed. A knowing smirk was painted across the woman's face, causing Quinn to frown in return. *What is it with that hateful woman?* She continued to glare at Ydith as she opened the door and stepped inside.

When Quinn turned forward, she saw someone in the room. His back faced her, his fingers touching the papers on the Archon's desk. Alarmed, Quinn prepared to defend herself as the man turned around. However, nothing could have prepared her for that moment.

"Quinn?" Iko said aloud.

Quinn gritted her teeth and lunged with a jab to his throat, striking him hard. Iko staggered back a step, but Quinn rushed forward, using her momentum to thrust a knee into his groin. Choking with one hand around his throat, he doubled-over, his eyes bulging. A backward thrust of her arm drove an elbow into his temple and Iko spun about, falling to one knee. Quinn drew the knife from his belt, wrapped her arm about his head, and held the blade to his neck, allowing the tip to pierce his skin.

"Glynnis!" Varius shouted from the open doorway. "What are you doing to my son?"

Still panting with adrenaline, Quinn blinked at Varius, whose expression teetered between alarm and outrage. The Archon's words replayed in Quinn's head. *Her son?*

"Release him!" Varius commanded as she strode into the room.

Responding to the order, Quinn pulled the knife away and stepped back, numbly confused. Iko leaned forward with one hand on the floor, the other to his throat as he coughed. A drip of blood tracked down his neck, onto his fingers. Varius put her hand on his head and closed her eyes. He then shuddered – a telling sign of the healing that had taken place. His choking shifted to gasps for air as he stood and looked at his hand, still streaked with blood.

"You'll have to excuse Glynnis, Ikonis. Her concern for my well-being leaves her somewhat over-protective, but I can think of worse traits for a bodyguard."

Iko blinked and turned toward Quinn. "Bodyguard?"

Quinn glared at him, not daring to respond. She had shared a piece of herself with Iko, and he had betrayed her. Half a year later, he now stood five feet away. Her fist clenched, wishing she could strike him again.

The shock of him reappearing began to wear off, replaced by anxiety as she realized the gravity of her situation. Again, he would betray her – this time to his mother. The truth would paint an ugly picture, and Varius would see Quinn imprisoned or worse. She was doomed.

Varius didn't notice the exchange, instead, she circled her desk. "Things have transpired since you left, son." She sat in her desk chair. "There was an assassination attempt, one that Glynnis foiled. It appears that the kingdoms would see me dead. I prefer otherwise. Glynnis now remains by my side to prevent such an outcome."

Iko looked at Varius and then back at Quinn, his eyes narrowing, but he said nothing.

"Glynnis," Varius said. "Go find Jeshica and have her arrange dinner for two in my chamber. You are then free for the remainder of the evening." Varius leaned back with an easy smile. "Don't worry about me. I assure you, I am safe in the presence of my son."

Gathering herself, Quinn nodded. "Very well. If you need me, I'll be in my room after I eat."

Quinn walked out the door, which had remained open during the exchange. She pulled it closed and faced Ydith, who now stood directly across the hall, leaning against the corridor wall with that smirk still on her face.

"You knew he was in there," Quinn said in a challenge.

"I wouldn't be doing my job if I didn't know," Ydith retorted.

"Yet, you did nothing to warn me."

Ydith moved closer, her face twisted in a sneer. The woman stood a few inches taller than Quinn, allowing her to look down her nose as she spoke. "Since when do you need our help? I thought you were special." Her voice took on a nasal quality. "The great Glynnis can do everything on her own...including taking credit for murder."

"I didn't murder Warrick." Quinn had to restrain herself from shouting. "In fact, I did everything I could to *not* kill the man. Regardless, he wasn't going to stop until the Archon was dead."

"You'd have others believe you're some grand hero." Ydith poked Quinn in the chest with her finger, putting weight behind it to force Quinn backward. "I think you're a fake and a liar. If you care to meet me in the practice yards, I'd be happy to show you how I deal with liars."

Rather than respond, Quinn snatched Ydith's finger from her chest and gave it a brutal wrench, dislocating it.

"Argh!" Ydith cried and stumbled against the wall with her hand cradled to herself. "You wench!"

Quinn turned and walked away, her thoughts shifting to Iko. He was sure to tell Varius the truth. She needed to prepare for that outcome.

20

INTERNAL CONFLICT

The door closed and Iko stared at it in shock, his mind racing with questions clouded by confusion. *Why is Quinn here? Did my mother call her Glynnis?*

"Take a seat, Ikonis."

Iko turned to find his mother staring at him from behind her desk. He numbly moved toward the empty chair across from her, sitting as instructed.

"I pray you have good news to report," she said, prompting him.

Thoughts of Quinn washed away, replaced by the painful memories of what he had done. He had known this moment was coming for weeks, yet he had to steel himself to speak. Burying his internal conflict, he forced his emotions aside and responded.

"Yes, Mother." *You can do this.* "As we planned, I was able to befriend Prince Broland. Soon after my arrival, we began spending many hours together, day and at night. As a sparring partner and a drinking companion, he and I grew close."

He rubbed his eyes clear of the tears that had begun to form. *Stop it.*

"Sorry. My eyes are dry from lack of sleep and the wind on the ship." *Keep it together, Iko.* "Although I found myself in a position of confidence, I discovered little that we do not already know. King Brock had reinstated the garrison at Hipoint and had been sending soldiers there to secure it. How many, I was never able to determine until the end.

"When Percy arrived and delivered the flash bomb, I..." Iko took a calming breath, "I initiated the assassination. I began by killing General Budakis but was forced to kill a guard in the process. I stole the general's plans to defend Kantaria, which included details regarding the garrison and more. I then snuck to the top floor, killed the guard on duty, and entered the king's chamber. While I was preparing my escape, Prince Broland appeared with a sword and interrupted me. I..." *Oh, Issal. Why?* "I was able to arm the flash bomb and escape over the balcony rail before it ignited. The prince, the king, and the queen were in the room at the time."

Iko's heartache threatened to overwhelm him, so he pressed on, ignoring it as he finished the story. However, he could not look his mother in the eye for fear that she recognize his inner turmoil.

"Percy and I remained in Kantar for a few days while the search for the assassin lost momentum." *A torturous six days. Six days of loneliness, despite Percy's presence.* "Before we left, I was able to confirm that both King Brock and Prince Broland were killed in the blast. Queen Ashland remained alive but unconscious."

He fell silent, but refused to look into his mother's eyes, instead focusing on the marble tiled floor.

"This is wonderful news, Ikonis." She stood and circled the desk to stand before him. Her hand cupped his chin and lifted it until he faced her. "You make me proud. With Budakis, Brock, and Broland dead, Kantaria is a ship without a rudder, lost to the whims of the wind. We will blow through the kingdom and make it ours."

He swallowed hard and nodded. "There is more I must tell you."

She turned toward the window, staring out with her hands clasped behind her back, the setting sun painting her face orange. "Go on."

"When we left Kantar, Percy and I sailed to Wayport. While there, I chose to seek an audience with Chadwick and Illiri. I wished to ensure their loyalty by informing them of King Brock and Prince Broland's fate, anticipating that they might fear a similar fate should they cross the Empire. When I arrived, Captain Sharene informed me of another guest who was meeting with the Duke and Duchess." Iko paused, knowing his mother would be angry. "It was Pretencia."

Iko's mother spun about with a fire in her eyes. "Dalwin was there?"

"Yes, along with Admiral Thanes and Parker Thanes. Hearing this unexpected turn of events, I requested that Sharene gather a squad of guards to accompany me into the courtroom. Given the news from Kantar and the ultimatum that he commit, Chadwick told the guards to arrest Pretencia." Again, he paused, knowing her anger. "Unfortunately, Tenzi escaped through a broken window and jumped into the river. Sharene promised that her soldiers would search for the woman, but I doubt they will find her. Regardless, Pretencia and Parker Thanes are both now locked in cells while Chadwick awaits orders from you."

With eyes narrowed and lips pressed together, Iko's mother stared at him as she considered the news. Finally, her stern gaze relaxed and she reclaimed her seat behind the desk.

"I will draft a missive for Chadwick, giving him instructions to execute Pretencia and Thanes. There was a time where I thought keeping Dalwin around might prove useful, but I cannot abide the man escaping again. The risk is too high."

Iko found himself, again, staring at the floor, unable to meet his mother's gaze. He knew she considered King Brock's assassination a practical necessity, but the act had stained his soul and discussing it left his stomach sour. *What has happened to me? How have I become so weak?* He closed his eyes for a beat and then spoke again.

"I completed the task you requested of me, Mother." Iko swallowed hard and forced himself to ask the question. "What would you have of me now?"

Before she could respond, a bellowing voice carried from the adjacent room. His mother's brow furrowed as she stood and strode toward the door to Kardan's office. Curious, Iko found himself compelled to follow. She opened it to reveal Kardan's face, red with anger. A messenger stood before the general with shoulders hunched, his hands kneading one another.

"What's this about?" Varius asked.

Kardan turned toward her and waved a fist wrapped about a crumpled message.

"This is about that imbecile, Mollis."

Varius frowned. "Didn't you task Mollis with leading the mercenary army in the capture of Hipoint?"

"Don't remind me."

The paper crumpled further in Kardan's shaking fist, his veins bulging in his temple before he turned, stomped to his desk, and scribbled something on a sheet of paper. Once finished, he stabbed the pen point into the desk, breaking it.

Kardan spun and handed the paper to the messenger. "Get yourself some food and supplies for the road. You are to give this note to Sergeant Mollis as soon as possible. Tell Mollis to remain in Hipoint. While it's of little use, we can't allow the kingdoms to reclaim it. He is to hold the city, and the garrison, until reinforcements arrive."

With a nod, the messenger turned toward the door.

"One more thing," Kardan added, stopping the messenger in mid stride. "Go down one floor and knock on the third door on the right. If a young man answers, send him up here to speak with me. He will be joining you on your journey."

The messenger, again, nodded before leaving.

When the door closed, Varius spoke. "What is this about, Leo?"

The general glared at her for a moment, shifted to his desk chair, and collapsed in it with a sigh. "Despite four siege engines, a full complement of flash bombs, and three thousand soldiers, Mollis was barely able to defeat a wooden-walled garrison occupied by a few hundred of the enemy."

Iko's brow furrowed. "But, he was successful?"

"Yes, but at what cost?" The general ran his hand through his thinning hair. "In the process, the enemy killed over half our soldiers. When they finally took the garrison, only a few enemy bodies were found. The bulk of Kantarian soldiers stationed there apparently escaped through a tunnel that later collapsed. Worse, our remaining mercenaries abandoned Mollis and fled north after the battle. All that remains are Mollis and sixty Imperial soldiers, who now hold Hipoint."

Varius gave Kardan a stern look. "We paid with gold and promised them more. Why would the soldiers abandon us after one battle?"

Kardan rubbed his eyes and ran a hand down his face. "Mollis claims to have faced dozens of arcanists, wielding deadly magic. His report mentions landslides, shockwaves, and powerful explosions, all caused by Chaos magic. Apparently, such a display of mystical power put fear into the hearts of the mercenaries. They chose survival over the chance to earn more gold." Kardan's brow furrowed. "It's all very strange. We've been monitoring the comings and goings from Fallbrandt. The only group we saw leave the valley, and later appear in Hipoint, consisted of four people. A squad so small couldn't have done this much damage, yet I don't see how they could have equipped the garrison with so many arcanists without our knowledge."

"At least the garrison no longer stands in our way," Varius said. "What of Rhone?"

"While the rest of Hipoint had been evacuated, Rhone opted to remain at his manor with the hope of our forces winning the day. He has since sent word for the citizens to return. The city is ours to use as we see fit."

"You don't intend for Mollis to remain in charge, do you?"

Kardan shook his head. "No. He is detailed and can follow orders but lacks the creativity to lead when facing the unknown."

"You could send Sculdin," Iko suggested.

His mother looked at him with an arched brow before nodding. "True. Sculdin is suitable for such a task."

Kardan stared at her for a moment before responding. "While I value Sculdin's input and his strategic mind, I will certainly need to put him in the field...but I would rather wait until it is time to advance beyond Hipoint."

A thudding knock came from the door.

"Come in," Kardan bellowed.

The door opened and Percy strode in. "You wished to see me?"

Kardan crossed the room and put his hand on Percy's shoulder. "Yes. I have a task that requires special skills. Mollis is holding Hipoint with a small force. I need you to meet him there and then track down the Kantarian army that escaped." His serious gaze held Percy captive. "Scout out their position well. Count their numbers. Assess their weakness. When we move against them, I intend to be well prepared."

Percy nodded. "You can count on me, Kardan."

"Good." The general nodded and removed his hand from Percy's shoulder. "Gather your things and visit Hundley in the stables. Tell him I gave you leave to take a horse. You are to travel with the messenger who visited your room. Don't dally, because you leave inside the hour."

"You can count on me, Kardan." Percy noted turned toward Iko, clasping his forearm. "I'll see you soon."

Iko nodded. "Farewell, Percy."

Percy slipped out the door, closing it behind himself. Kardan stared at the door for a long moment that was interrupted when Iko's mother cleared her throat.

"Although things did not go as you had wished, our plans remain intact, Leo."

"We lost one quarter of our army, Meryl." Kardan grimaced. "Worse, we have gained almost nothing in the process."

"That may be true, but we have gained in other areas." Her mouth turned up in a smile. "Ikonis was successful in cutting the head off the snake. Kantar is leaderless, and Chadwick has committed in full. Wayport is ours as are the eight hundred soldiers Brock had stationed there." She strolled to Kardan's desk and placed her hands on it, leaning close. "We now hold all the lands along the Sea of Fates and the east coast, from Wayport to the northern tip of Hurnsdom. With nothing at our backs, we can advance without fear."

"Yes." Kardan dipped his head in a nod, his expression determined. "Some planning is yet required, but we can do as you say, placing us in position as we wait for spring. When the weather turns, and the snows melt, we will attack."

"Precisely," Varius said. "We will soon see the end of Chaos."

21

IMPERIAL GAMBIT

Q uinn slipped the cord over her head, her keys dangling from it before she found the one that unlocked her door. Light from the setting sun lit the interior, warming the room. She closed the door and noticed a sheet of paper on her nightstand. The handwriting was recognizable, the message simple and direct: *We must talk. Now.*

Varius, Quinn thought. *Why does she wish to see me? What did Iko tell her?* Images of prison cells and executioners appeared in her head. *This could be bad.*

Discarding the note, she opened the drawer, scooped up her remaining Chaos trap and a chunk of coal, and traced a rune on her palm. Staring at it, she thought *I hope I don't have to use it.* She then gripped the false makeup case in the same hand and approached the door connecting her room to the Archon's chamber. Her knock was answered with a muffled response.

"Come in."

Quinn opened the door to find Varius far across the room, staring out the window. The Archon's face was lit orange, her shadow cast across the floor and up the far wall to create a tall, ominous silhouette of the real thing. Quinn's stomach fluttered as she crossed the room, toward the waiting Archon.

"You wished to see me," Quinn said.

Varius remained quiet for a number of breaths, her hands clasped at her waist.

"There are very few who genuinely understand my motives," the Archon began. "Others often mistake my ambition as a lust for power. Those people are wrong. I am simply doing my best to shape the world into a place of peace, and hope, and prosperity. And, yet, the position of Archon, as leader of the Empire, has become a constant struggle.

"There are times where I feel as if I am playing a massive game of Ratio Bellicus, moving my units against an unknown, invisible enemy. Worse, my opponent's moves remain hidden until it is too late, similar to a gambit maneuver in the game itself. I find my ranks thinning, my perceived advantage waning with each mysterious shift of the game board."

Quinn's brow furrowed in confusion. "What do you wish of me, Meryl?"

The Archon turned from the window, moved to her desk, and opened the bottom drawer. From the drawer, she removed two leather-bound scabbards. She gripped one of the hilts and pulled the sword free. Sunlight reflected off the blade as Varius twisted it in examination. The short sword was a work of art, beautiful and deadly.

Varius shifted her focus from the sword to Quinn. "We have spies among us…right here in the citadel."

Swallowing hard, Quinn forced herself to speak, her sweaty palm gripping the Chaos trap tightly. "What do you mean, Archon?"

"I speak of my hidden opponent. This invisible hand is reaching into Sol Polis, into our very center of operations, and is making tactical moves right beneath my nose."

The Archon's voice grew louder, carrying an edge of anger. The knuckles of the fist holding the sword turned white. "First, an assassin appears in my chamber and tries to murder me. Then, Dalwin Pretencia is freed from his cell and whisked away in the dark of the night. And, today, Sculdin tells me that somebody broke into his office and stole a map marked with key locations for our initial offensive assault."

That map lies hidden beneath my mattress.

Varius sneered. "This cannot continue! I'll not allow my plans to be thwarted!"

Quinn's mind raced. She wondered at what Iko had told his mother – what conclusions Varius might reach based on Quinn's history. *Does she suspect me? Does she know about Brandt? Does she know how to use a sword?* Her hand squeezed the bronze disk in her palm, preparing to press the switch and unleash the power inside. Somehow, Quinn was able to keep her voice steady as she spoke.

"Again, I ask what you wish of me."

Varius tilted her head, her tone softening as she lowered the sword. "You came here as a handmaid for Larrimor and soon shifted to the role of my handmaid."

She knows.

"Through a twist of fate, you then became my bodyguard."

She knows.

"You are in a unique position, Glynnis. You know the serving staff. You know many of the guards. You know every Council member and local official by sight, and you are able to move practically anywhere in the citadel with little challenge."

Oh, dear Issal, she knows. Quinn's thumb shifted to the release on the bottom of the Chaos trap, her finger on the trigger. The rapid thump of her pulse throbbed in her ear.

Varius eased closer and held the sword before Quinn while her other hand rested on Quinn's shoulder. Quinn's gaze shifted from the woman's hand to the sword, her breath caught in her throat.

"I want you to find this spy," Varius said in a hushed voice. "I will provide you the time and the liberty to search whenever and wherever the clues take you, but you must discover the spy and eliminate the threat." She grabbed Quinn's right hand, her empty hand, and placed the sword hilt in Quinn's palm. "The swords are for you, made by the finest weapon smith in Sol Polis. Proper weapons for a proper bodyguard. I recalled your mention of being a dual-wielder who prefers short swords and had the weapons commissioned for that purpose."

Quinn gazed upon the blade, sharp, balanced, and polished such that her own reflection stared back at her. She tested it, twisting her wrist. It was perfect. There was a letter engraved on the pommel, and Quinn held the hilt closer to examine it.

Varius said, "The pommel of each sword is engraved with a G for Glynnis. They were custom crafted for you, and for you alone."

Turning back to her desk, Varius picked up both scabbards, one of which was empty. Realizing the threat to her had passed, Quinn hastily stuffed the Chaos trap into the back of her breeches before the Archon turned back toward her.

"I knew I could count on you, Glynnis." Varius held the scabbards toward Quinn, who accepted them numbly. "You, my son, and Kardan are the only people in this world whom I wholly trust. Once the spy has been captured and my enemy outed, I will strike back. For, in Ratio Bellicus terms, it is time to execute an imperial gambit."

22

___

SERVANT

W aking, Brandt rubbed his eyes with his knuckles. The narrow window near the ceiling revealed the amber light of sunset outside. With a sigh, he stood, stretched, and padded over to his vanity. Splashing water on his face helped to wash away the lingering effects of his nap. He dried his face and wiped away the drops that had fallen on his shoulders and chest. Bending toward his mirror, he frowned. The mirror was subpar, its surface twisting his reflection and making it difficult to judge his appearance. After an unsuccessful attempt to tame his hair, he gave up with a shrug.

A knock at the door had him hoping it was not Master Sheen. He glanced toward his bare torso and considered donning a shirt before opening the door but chose a speedy response over his appearance. Sheen hated waiting.

Two strides took him across the tiny apartment. He opened the door and flinched in surprise.

"Qui…Glynnis." Leaning forward, he peered into the corridor and found it empty except for her. "What can I do for you?"

Quinn arched her brow, the bemused look on her face a contradiction to the firm manner in which she spoke, her voice projecting as if she were performing before a crowd. "Hello, Ebran. May I come in? I have some questions for you."

Brandt grinned and stepped back, playing along as he replied in a firm tone. "Please. Come in."

She slipped past him and he closed the door, his eyes drinking her in.

Quinn's golden hair was tied in a tail, her eyes blue and friendly. Dressed in her form-fitting black leathers, she projected an image that teetered between enticing and daunting. The combination stirred Brandt's blood. The short swords at her hips only enhanced the imagery.

"Nice swords," he said, his voice hushed.

Quinn looked down, caressing one of the golden-gilded pommels. "Varius gave them to me...as a gift. I still don't know what to think about the gesture."

"Her trust in you appears to run deep. You should consider that a good thing." His brow arched in question. "Other than to show off your new weapons, what is this about?"

She leered at his torso with a smirk on her face. "Is this how you greet all your female guests?"

He looked down at himself, then back at her. "Yes. Every one of them. Of course, you are the first since I've arrived here, but I'm hoping for future visits."

She ran a finger up his stomach and across his chest until she held his chin. "I wish I could visit more often...and that I could remain longer than a few minutes."

He took her hand from his chin and held it in both of his palms. "Is a few minutes all you have for me?"

"I'm afraid so. In reality, this visit is half for show."

He arched his brow again. "What is the other half for?"

Quinn's smirk returned. "For me." She leaned in and kissed him, but pushed him away when he tried to hold her. "No. We cannot afford to have anyone catch us. This must appear as part of my search and nothing more."

"Your search?"

"Yes. Varius is convinced there is a spy in our midst, and she assigned me the task of apprehending this invader."

"How ironic."

"I know, right?"

"So you came straight to me? Won't that arouse suspicion?"

"Not straight to you. In fact, I have already interviewed over half the citadel staff and a third of the guards."

His hands covered his heart. "It hurts deeply that I am so far down your list." Brandt did his best to appear forlorn. "Please don't tell me you kiss everyone you interrogate."

"Well...not *everyone*." Her eyes twinkled as she grinned.

He chuckled. *She is so easy for me to be with – to be myself.*

"Besides," Quinn said. "I thought it best to visit you later in the day to remove suspicion."

"Good idea." He had to admit, she was smart. And pretty. And brave. *Is this love?*

"I even had the chance to interview the jailor."

Anxiety quivered in Brandt's stomach. "What did he say?"

"The man insists he was beset by a squad of soldiers. Four or five men, all as big as him."

Brandt chuckled again. "It *was* dark."

"Not that dark. No, he is prideful and has created an impressive story to protect his job...and his image."

"You don't plan to tell Varius that."

"No. In fact, I plan to repeat the jailor's words exactly. It won't explain the missing map, but at least it clears suspicion of Pretencia's escape."

"Speaking of the map, they won't find it, will they?"

"I certainly hope not."

The thought triggered an idea. "Perhaps we should let them find it."

"What?"

"We could plant it somewhere to redirect suspicion."

Quinn frowned for a moment before a smile crossed her face. "Larrimor."

"You really don't like her, do you?"

Quinn's face darkened. "That woman is a bitter old hag. Besides, she has enough clout to weasel out of it, but proving her innocence will be a thorn for her to pick at until it's removed."

"And it will have them examining someone other than us. Anything that diverts their attention buys us more time."

166

"I agree." She looked toward the door. "I've been in here long enough. I should go...in case someone saw me enter."

When Quinn slid past him, toward the door, he grabbed her arm and spun her toward him.

Brandt wished she could remain. He imagined locking the door and the two of them just hiding in the room for the remainder of the day...and the night. There was so much more he wanted to say to her, but the only words he could muster were "Please, be careful."

A smile appeared on her face. "You care about me."

More than you know. "I have already admitted as much."

"True, but it's nice to hear it again." Her eyes – the color of the deep sea on a sunny day – stared into his. "Is there something else?"

He found himself scrambling to redirect the conversation. "What of the young men who arrived yesterday. People on the staff say that one of them is the Archon's son."

Quinn's smile melted. "Yes."

He saw conflict in her eyes, the azure shifting to gray. "There's something you aren't telling me."

She looked away, the mood broken – spoiled. "I need to go." She took a breath. "We can meet tonight. I'll tell you then."

"The tower?"

Wither her back to him, she nodded, opened the door and left the room.

Brandt stared at the door for a long moment and then suddenly remembered his job. He grabbed a white shirt from his chest and smelled it before sliding it over his head. He tucked it in, smoothed it, and donned his navy blue serving coat and rushed from his room. After locking the door, he hurried down the corridor and up the stairs. At the second level, he took a long corridor to the back of the complex and slowed as he reached a closed door. Muted noises carried through the door, the volume increasing tenfold when Brandt pushed it open.

The citadel kitchen was massive – with two oversized ovens at one end and four rows of counters where food was busily being prepared. A dozen kitchen workers in pale blue smocks toiled on the dinners that would soon be served. Six servers, including Brandt, were dressed in fine blue coats that were short of reaching their waists at the front but with split tails dangling past their rears at the back. Standing among the servers was a short woman who shouted commands, guiding the staff in a manner that would make the most seasoned ship captain proud.

"I need twelve plates of the baked fish ready for the Archon, her son, the Council, General Kardan, and Captain Sculdin. Don't let those vegetables steam too long and get soggy. Someone get the dessert into the ovens as soon as the dinners head out the door. We don't want to leave them waiting." Her demeanor was firm, demanding attention and instantly yielding a response.

As Brandt approached, she put her hands on her hips – hips that were difficult to miss. "You're late."

Brandt kneaded his hands, as if worried for his job. "I...I'm sorry, Mistress Harrington. I was answering questions posed by the Archon's bodyguard."

The blond woman's lips pressed together in a thin line. "That girl has been nosing about like a dog digging through the trash. I wish she would find what she is after and be done with it."

"Fish is ready," one of the cooks announced.

"Vegetables ready," another chimed.

"Bread is ready."

Harrington turned away from Brandt and resumed command. "Prepare the plates and begin loading the trays."

She then began barking out specific orders, citing which servers were assigned to each task. Once finished, and when all the other servers and stewards had assignments, she turned back toward Brandt.

"You are to serve Sculdin in his loft over the barracks. Bring him a plate and some wine. Be sure to mind yourself. If you cross him, he'll come complaining to me, and I don't need that."

As instructed, Brandt grabbed a carafe of wine, a goblet, a plate, and silverware. Once loaded, he strode to the door, backed through it, and headed down the hallway. He turned at the corner and strolled down another corridor to the stairs. One flight up, he approached a door at the end of a narrow hallway and knocked with his elbow.

"Come in," a man's voice called from inside.

Brandt frowned as he stared at the door, unsure of how to turn the knob with this hands full. *How do servants do this?* Finally, fearing that he would drop something, he gave up. "Can someone open the door?"

Footsteps approached. The door opened to reveal a face that was not Sculdin's. It was a female, not much older than Brandt. She had black hair and fair skin, her eyes a deep brown. He walked past her, noting the plain clothing and riding boots. *Messenger*, he thought.

Sculdin stood behind a table covered in maps and notes, busily writing a message. He looked up, and Brandt gave the man a slight bow.

"Where would you like your dinner, sir?"

After shuffling some papers to make space on the table, Sculdin said, "Set it here." He then returned to scrawling script on the paper.

Brandt set the plate and goblet in the open space. His gaze shifted to the map, but found it covered with paper, and he was unable to see the notations. After pouring a glass of wine, Brandt moved to the side of the room and waited.

Sculdin finished writing his note and walked toward the young woman, handing it to her. "Storms are common in the pass this time of year. Be careful or you won't reach Corvichi. This delivery is imperative. I need those weapons before spring hits."

"I understand, Captain. Jarlish will have this message in hand in two days' time."

"Good. You are dismissed, Dilynn."

The woman thumped her fist to her chest and headed out the door. Sculdin turned and frowned.

"I forgot you were here," the captain said.

Brandt gestured toward the table. "Your dinner, sir. I also filled the goblet with wine. Do you require anything else?"

Sculdin walked past Brandt, "No. That will be all. You can leave the carafe behind. This will be a long night, and I may need it."

"Very well, sir," Brandt bowed to the man and walked out the door only to collide with someone entering.

"You should watch where you are going," said a young man with dark hair and amber eyes.

With a barbed quip on his lips, ready to lash out, Brandt glared at the young man for a moment before he recalled his persona. Dropping his gaze toward the floor, he stepped back and allowed the young man inside. Brandt scrutinized the newcomer, who was tall, well dressed, and maintained a perfect posture. It was immediately apparent that this was somebody important.

"That will be all, Ebran," Sculdin said. Brandt bowed and stepped outside as Sculdin smiled. "Ikonis, what brings you here?"

"Hello, Scully," Ikonis replied. "I fear that I might lose my edge and wanted to arrange a few practice bouts with the guards, with your approval of..."

The words cut off as Brandt closed the door.

Ikonis. He's the one the serving maids have been gushing about – the Archon's son. He doesn't seem so special to me. Brandt then recalled the conversation he had overheard between Sculdin and the messenger. *Jarlish is in Corvichi!* With the revelation, puzzle pieces clicked into place.

He hurried along, eager to share his discovery with Quinn.

23

NEW OBJECTIVE

After standing guard while Varius ate dinner with Kardan and the Council members, Quinn escorted the Archon to her chamber and then left to get a meal for herself. She ate a bowl of beef stew, which had gone cold since dinner was hours past, along with a hard roll chewy enough to leave her jaw sore. Once finished, she headed up to her room.

The fifth-floor corridor was empty save for Ydith, who scowled at Quinn as she walked past. Seeing the guard made Quinn reconsider her plan with the map. *I wonder if I can get the map in her locker without notice. It would be nice to see Ydith squirm for once.*

Quinn drew the cord over her head and used her key to unlock the door. As she opened it, she heard footsteps down the corridor and found Iko approaching. She rushed into her room and heard him call out.

"Wait!"

She stared at the door, halfway closed, and considered closing it and locking him out. However, he had seen her enter the room. Such obvious avoidance might stir more trouble than facing him. With a sigh, she pulled the door open as he came into view.

"I would like to speak with you," Iko said as he came to a stop outside her room.

Quinn waved Iko in, closed the door, and turned to find him surveying her room.

"What is this about?" Quinn didn't attempt to disguise anger from her voice.

He turned toward her. "You still hate me." His tone carried a note of resignation. "I had hoped you had grown to understand."

"Understand?" She clenched her fists. "You killed two innocent girls and framed me for their murders."

"That was Percy's doing." He blurted before his voice softened. "Even then, it wasn't his intention to frame you. Percy merely spared you rather than killing you along with them. He saw it as a favor, not as an attack on you."

"Regardless, you knew the truth, but you said nothing." She wanted to punch him. Again. Beat him worse this time.

"I tried to convince Goren and Jasmine that you were innocent, that you would never commit such a crime, regardless of the lack of love you had toward Darnya." He shook his head. "Despite your situation, I could not betray Percy, nor the cause for which we fight."

Quinn pressed her lips together and glared at him.

Iko looked down and sighed. "I am truly sorry, Quinn. I care for you, despite our troubled past."

"I'm sorry as well, Iko. The moment has passed, the light of our relationship now forever tainted by shadow."

He looked at her, his amber eyes staring into hers, searching for something. A long moment of silence lingered, her dripping venom, him clearly wishing it were honey. Finally, he relented.

"Very well."

"If we are done, I would like to get some sleep." Quinn walked past him, sat on the edge of her bed, and began removing her boots. "I have more people to question tomorrow."

Iko did not leave, but instead he stared at her while she removed her boots. Quinn refused to look up and meet his gaze.

"Why are you here, Quinn?" He paused a beat, crossing his arms over his chest. "Or is it Glynnis?"

She set her left boot down and frowned in thought before replying.

"After you and Percy disappeared, I was removed from the academy. Two murdered cadets and two more gone missing, both occurrences tied to me...I lost their trust and was lucky to avoid prison. Instead, they expelled me, so I headed east to find a new life."

Quinn had run the lie through her head numerous times, hoping to construct something he might consider plausible. *The funny thing about lies,* Quinn thought, *When you commit to them utterly, you begin to believe them yourself.*

"I journeyed to Port Hurns and found my uncle Weldon. He helped me obtain a job working as a handmaid for a local merchant. A few months later, my uncle received a letter from Master Sheen, whom Weldon had known for many years. Sheen had an open position here, so I journeyed to Sol Polis and began working here as a handmaid.

"As for the name, I made the change because I thought it best if Jaquinn Gulagus disappeared, based on my recent history. My grandmother, Glynnis, was a handmaid for many years. Assuming her name seemed fitting."

Iko uncrossed his arms, his stance relaxing. "I find it odd that you ended up here, again with me." His amber eyes stared at her, and she feared that he saw beyond her charade. *But why does he not say something about it?*

She shook her head. "I had no idea you would come here...or that Meryl was your mother. How could I know?"

"And, yet, fate brought us back together." He moved closer, hope reflecting in his eyes. "Perhaps there is more to our story."

Quinn chose not to respond, instead proceeding to unbuckle her other boot.

"Mother told me you saved her from an assassin," Iko noted.

"Yes." She continued to loosen the boot straps, refusing to look back up at him.

"Sculdin claims the man was the best fighter among the palace guards. He called the man *a force of nature.*"

Quinn shrugged. "I got lucky." *I killed a man...a fellow warden. I'm sorry, Wyck.*

Iko snorted. "I know better than that. You may not be the best duelist, but you are tenacious. You are a survivor and have a determination others lack." He turned toward the door and stopped with his hand on the knob. "I hope you will forgive me one day, Quinn. I know you think I am not the person you had hoped I would be. Perhaps, one day, you will see that I *am* that person."

When the door closed behind him, Quinn stared at it for a long time. Her hatred for Iko was not as strong as she pretended. She had opened her heart to him and that had allowed him to hurt her more than she would admit. Time had healed that wound, and her feelings for Brandt had nurtured something else inside her, something that made her failed relationship with Iko seem inconsequential. Quinn admitted to herself that she had been attracted to Iko's handsome face and athletic build, but the connection between them had been little more than physical. With Brandt, she had found a kindred spirit and a friend who had grown into more than a friend. She was comfortable around him, yet when she looked in his eyes or felt his touch, her heart raced.

Recalling her agreed meeting with Brandt, Quinn looked at the window and found it dark. She didn't know how long it had been since the sun set, but she suspected she was late.

She scooped up her boots and slipped them back on, buckling them hurriedly before standing and shuffling to the door. After locking it, she opened the chest at the foot of her bed, dug out the rope and gloves she had buried at the bottom, and closed it quietly. The leather gloves were on in moments, giving her a layer of protection. Quinn's first trip out the window, weeks earlier, had taught her a valuable lesson about rope burns and thorns, leaving her hands sore for days afterward. Unlocking the window, she leaned forward to check her surroundings.

The air was cool, but not frigid, with an easy ocean breeze. The garden, five stories below, was dark, the trees and shrubs barely visible in the starlight. She listened and heard nothing but the soft breeze and distant noises of the city itself.

Quinn tied the rope to the leg of her bed before feeding the rope out the window. She then sat on the windowsill and swung one leg over, careful to place her foot on the ledge below it. With a firm grip on the rope, she pulled the other leg through, got her footing and began lowering herself down, hand over hand.

The rope was not long enough to reach the ground, but it did enable her to reach the ivy that grew up the west side of the castle.

With a good grip on the ivy, she released the rope. Her descent down the thorny ivy was slow and required care despite the leather protecting her hands and much of her body. The thorns were like small daggers, quick to draw blood. Twice she scraped her arm, and once she received a puncture in her thumb from the little buggers. When she finally reached the ground, she pulled the gloves off and sucked on her bleeding thumb while hurrying across the garden.

A guard patrolled the rear courtyard, strolling toward the barracks. Quinn timed her steps to match his as she crept toward the abandoned tower. The guard's back was still facing Quinn when she reached the tower, opened the door, and slipped inside.

Quinn climbed the stairs, careful to avoid the loose steps, and found Brandt waiting beside a small glowstone that illuminated the heart of the room and left the rest in shadow.

"I arrived here before you for once."

"I had a visitor who delayed me." Quinn's mood remained darkened by Iko's visit.

"It's not another boy, is it?" He stood and flashed a friendly smile.

Quinn stammered. "What…why would you say that?"

His smile faded. "Don't worry, I trust you."

He reached for her, his hands resting on her arms. She flinched when he touched her fresh scratches.

"Um…sorry." Brandt backed away as if he had been stung.

She followed him and put her hand to his cheek. "No. It's not you. I just scratched my arm on some thorns while climbing down from my room."

"Are you sure?" She saw doubt in his eyes. "You are acting a bit odd."

Quinn gripped his tunic at the front, leaned forward and kissed him. Her hands loosened their grip, her palms resting against his chest while his hands gripped her hips. When she pulled her lips away, she smiled and stared into his green eyes.

"It has nothing to do with you," she said in a soft voice. "I'm just experiencing a lot of stress. I feel like I'm constantly dodging traps and pitfalls with any misstep resulting in a dungeon cell or worse."

"I understand. My own situation feels stressful, and your role is twice as dangerous." He nodded, his hands shifting to her upper arms, gripping them softly. "I have news to share – news we also need to send to the Ward."

"Good." She nodded. "I have information to share with them as well." Quinn stared into his intense eyes. "Have you already contacted your sister?"

"Yes. I reached out to Cassie a few hours ago. She said she would gather the leaders and be ready after nightfall. They should be waiting for us." Brandt released her arms and settled on a pile of debris. "I'm going to talk to her now."

He closed his eyes for a long moment before speaking. "Cassie has everyone gathered. Nindlerod, Firellus, Goren, Ackerson, Alridge, and Delvin are all present, as is your brother. Kwai-Lan is away on a mission."

Quinn considered where to begin, choosing the bad news first. "Tell them that an Empire messenger arrived yesterday and reported that the Hipoint Garrison has been captured. The Empire now holds Hipoint, but Varius and Kardan remain unhappy. They consider the campaign a failure because it cost them too many soldiers with little gained."

She waited as Brandt shared the information. After a moment, he nodded. "What else have you discovered?"

"Well, it sounds like Sculdin is going to take over and lead a new offensive, but I have no details regarding his plans or resources."

Brandt opened his eyes. "I can add to that. I was in Sculdin's office today, where he was crafting a message for that Jarlish character. He sent a messenger with the note, requesting weapons." A grin spread across his face. "The messenger was heading to Corvichi."

Quinn's eyes grew wide as she connected the location with the man's name. "An abandoned castle? Corvichi is where they produce the weapons?"

Brandt nodded. "Yes. It makes sense, too. I bet they have been using it for years. Hidden away in the mountains, they could have been producing weapons long before they began their conquest of the eastern kingdoms, perhaps even before they murdered King Talvin of Vinacci."

Quinn found herself nodding in agreement. "True. And once they controlled Vinacci, they could add resources toward bolstering the production. They had flash bombs when they captured Cinti Mor, and that was over a year ago."

"Wait while I share this information with my sister."

While he closed his eyes and sent his message to Cassie, Quinn considered the situation and wondered what ICON might do with it. Her wait was long – minutes passing without any response. Finally, Brandt opened his eyes, and she found herself uneasy about the look he gave her.

"What is it? What's wrong?"

He rubbed his eyes and ran a hand through his hair, appearing weary. "We have a new objective. Elsewhere."

"What? But we just established ourselves here."

"Be that as it may, Delvin says it is time to leave Sol Polis."

Her brow furrowed. "And go where?"

"I'm sure you can guess."

Quinn took a deep breath, nodding. "Corvichi."

"Yes. We are to head to Castile Corvichi, but it will be dangerous." He stood and shifted closer, his hand gripping her shoulder. "Our mission is to sabotage their weapons supply by any means possible. We must destroy it all…at any cost. Until we limit the Empire's supply of flash powder, we remain at a disadvantage."

Quinn frowned. "After everything I have gone through to gain the Archon's trust, he wants me to leave? Why us? Why doesn't he send somebody else?"

"There is nobody else, Quinn. The others are all on assignment." He stared into her eyes and it seemed as if he gazed into her soul. "This falls on just you and me."

24

MISDIRECTION

Quinn finished writing the note, set the quill back into the inkwell, and folded the sheet of paper. Wax trailed down the shaft of the candle she had lit, solidifying as it cooled. She picked up the candle, tilted it, and the amber-tinted wax dripped onto the seam. Moving quickly, she pressed the pommel of her short sword into it, leaving an insignia of a stylized G. *Odd, but it looks more like a Q,* she thought. How ironic, considering the sword, and its twin, were gifts from Varius. *If she only knew the truth.*

After blowing out the candle, she opened the chest at the foot of her bed. She grabbed the rope and the pack that contained the supplies she had gathered over the past two days before closing the lid quietly. With the rope secured, she hung the pack out the window and began lowering it hand over hand. When she reached the end of the rope, Quinn leaned out the window and extended to the lowest point possible before letting go. A rustle and a thump came from below as the pack hit a shrub and landed on the lawn. She closed the window, walked to her desk to retrieve the sealed message, and glanced back at her room one last time.

Five weeks had passed since she began working for Varius. In that time, she had come to think of it as her room – her *own* room. Until coming to Sol Polis, she had never lived alone. At times, it was peaceful. At others, it was lonely. Despite the tension that had accompanied her stay and the lies she hid behind, she would miss it in an odd, almost sadistic way.

With a sigh that carried sentiments of resolve, she opened the door and left the room.

Hargrove was on guard duty, the man scarcely returning her nod as she walked by. Still, that was more than Ydith would have done to acknowledge Quinn. Thoughts of the vindictive woman left Quinn regretting her new plan for the stolen map. *It would have been a wonderful stroke of justice to pin that on her. Still, the new plan best resolves my situation.*

Quinn moved down the stairs at a brisk pace, eager to be away before she ran into Varius. Bumping into the Archon would destroy her story, the meager one she had assembled should she wish to return to Sol Polis once the mission was complete. She knew her chance of success was slim, her chance of survival even slimmer. Yet, she could do some good if she were able to return to her old role as the Archon's bodyguard – a role Quinn had sacrificed much to attain.

When Quinn reached the basement, she followed a corridor and stopped outside the door beside the room she had used upon her arrival at Sol Polis. She knocked firmly and waited, watching the hallway in case anyone else appeared. After a moment, the door opened and a young blond woman peeked out.

"Glynnis? What are you doing down here? This isn't about your search again, is it?"

"I'm afraid so, Jeshica. May I come in?" Quinn's tone made it clear that it wasn't a request.

Jeshica's eyes shifted, looking down the corridor in both directions before she nodded and pulled the door open. Quinn slipped inside to find a meager room, just big enough for a single bed, a chest, and a vanity. The room looked no different from Brandt's, or her old room next door.

A glowlamp upon the vanity painted the room in a faint, blue glow. A cloth lay beside it, likely removed after Quinn's knock woke the woman. When Quinn turned, she found Jeshica in her thin shift, the material doing little to hide the details of the curves beneath it. *Now, I know why she hid behind the door. If I had been a man...*

"Did you discover something about the spy?" Jeshica asked.

Quinn nodded, focusing on her mission. "Yes. While the search has been exhausting, requiring every bit of my attention the past couple days, I have uncovered several clues that converge on one person."

Jeshica's face paled. "Surely, you don't think I am a spy." Her voice grew frantic. "I would never betray the Archon." She bit her lip, her eyes on the verge of tears.

Quinn put her hand on Jeshica's arm. *Good grief. She has changed much after her time in the dungeon.* "Peace, Jeshica. It's not you. I am here because I *trust* you."

Relief was clear on Jeshica's face as she exhaled. "Thank Issal. Who, then?"

"He lives right down the hall from you." Quinn leaned toward her and whispered. "My investigation has led me to Ebran Pym."

"The steward?" Jeshica frowned. "He's new and mostly keeps to himself, but I wouldn't imagine him to be a spy. He's handsome, in a roguish way. But he's so…unassuming."

Somehow, Quinn was able to restrain her laughter. "That is even more reason to suspect him."

Jeshica's eyes bulged as she nodded. "Yes. Of course."

Quinn handed the note to Jeshica and looked her in the eye. "I need you to give this to Varius tomorrow after breakfast, but not before then."

Jeshica looked down at the seal on the note, her brow furrowed. "Why wait? Why can't you give it to her?"

"Because I need time, Jeshica. I am trying to capture the spy and expose the truth."

The doubtful expression on Jeshica's face forced Quinn to continue.

"After requesting that Sheen send Ebran to serve the Archon in her chamber, I left a note there that was intended to flush him out, and flush him it did. I knew she would not be there, and I suspected he would take the opportunity to read a note sitting out in the open. The way he hurried from Varius' chamber and headed straight for his room, I knew I had him hooked. Within minutes, he left the citadel while I trailed him discreetly.

"The young man is currently staying at a Downside inn, near the docks. I am heading there next. I expect him to catch a ship tomorrow morning, and I intend to follow him. Perhaps he will lead me to his superiors, and I can discover who was behind the assassination attempt. At worst, I have chased the spy out of the citadel." Quinn gestured toward the paper in Jeshica's hand. "My note explains this."

"But, why not just tell her yourself?"

"Because I am afraid she will stop me."

Jeshica nodded in agreement. "Yes. She likely would send another in your place."

"I believe I can best serve her and the Empire by following this spy and discovering the truth."

The woman's face contorted as she chewed on her lip. Finally, she took a deep breath and nodded. "All right. I'll help you."

Quinn smiled and hugged her. "Thank you, Jeshica. I knew I could count on you." She released Jeshica, but held her hand while she spoke, seeking to reassure her. "When I return, should Issal wish it to be so, I will be sure that you are credited for helping me in this endeavor."

"When I give her the note...won't Varius be angry with me?"

"I suspect she will be angry, but not at you. At me." She squeezed Jeshica's hand. "Claim to know nothing other than I left you this note you did not find until you returned to your room after breakfast."

Quinn turned toward the door. "Be well, Jeshica. I hope to return soon."

Without another word, Quinn stepped out and closed the door. She then walked deeper into the basement, past the double doors that led to the old section of the building, and down a long, dark corridor lit only by dormant glowlamps positioned at each end. She then took the stairs to the main level and slipped out the side door.

She paused for a moment, listening. A dog barked somewhere in the distance, and the crunch of footsteps came from around the corner, beyond the guard barracks. Hurrying, she ran along the side of the building and ducked around another corner just as the approaching guard came into view. She pressed her back against the wall and listened over the rasping of her breath. *No alarm. He didn't see me.*

Turning, Quinn scurried around the shrubs growing along the castle wall. When she neared the far end of the wall, she slowed and began searching the ground and the shrubs. Finding nothing, she looked up and located her window. *Where is it?* She began to panic, thinking someone had found her pack.

"Psst."

The sound came from the shadow-filled garden behind her.

"Over here."

Quinn slipped through the shrubs along the path and found Brandt waiting in the shadows, his silhouette barely visible.

"I have your pack," he said in a hushed voice.

"Thank Issal," she whispered. "I feared that someone had found it and taken it."

"Someone did." The white of his teeth revealed his grin.

She smiled and shook her head. *He has a way of dispelling my tension.* "Are you ready?"

"Yes. After I found your pack, I gave myself an augmentation."

He bent over and scooped her up. The way he squeezed her – with her arms crushed against her chest – made her grunt and left her fighting for breath.

"Sorry," he said as his grip loosened. "How's this?"

She breathed deeply and freed an arm to grip his wrist. "Yes. Much better."

"Well, I don't want to drop you, nor do I wish to crush you. It's no simple feat to judge my strength when filled with Power."

"Yes. I know, remember?" she replied, her tone sardonic.

He chuckled. "Yeah. Right."

With a pack over each shoulder, he ducked beneath a branch and walked toward the outer wall.

"Did you get the map?" she asked.

"Yes. I took it from the tower and hid it in my room as we discussed. To add some spice, I made a few notes on the map that might give them pause." He chuckled at his own statement.

"Brandt..." Her tone was one of warning. "That wasn't the plan."

"Funny. I have never painted outside the lines before. How odd of me." He stopped in an open area, twenty feet from the wall.

"Sarcasm? Now? You know this is a serious matter?" She couldn't stop grinning.

He smiled at her. "All the more reason for it."

"You are incorrigible," she laughed.

"Isn't that part of my appeal?" He looked up, his humor falling away as he focused on the wall. "Now, hold on."

With two running steps, he leaped. The force of their upward acceleration drove Quinn's body against his chest. They easily cleared the thirty-foot wall before they began to fall. Quinn closed her eyes, fearing what might wait below while her stomach fluttered from the rapid descent.

The landing again drove her body hard against his arms, arms hardened like steel. She grunted at the force and opened her eyes to find they had landed in a quiet plaza, at the midpoint between glowlamps lighting the corners. Brandt twisted, tipped her up, and set her feet on the cobblestone-covered ground. Quinn stood, stretched, and worked the kinks out of her neck.

"Are you all right?"

She smiled at the concern in his voice. "I'll live. Let's go."

They headed east, away from the harbor. The city gates would be closed for the night, but that wall was no taller than the citadel wall. Once beyond it, they would get far from the city and find a quiet place to sleep. Tomorrow would be a long day.

25

THIEF OF HEARTS

Brandt opened his eyes to the pale light of breaking dawn. Hair of gold lay before him. He craned his neck and sniffed, the hair smelling of flowers and spice, like its owner's enticing appearance and contrasting spitfire personality.

Quinn's back was facing him, his arm wrapped about her midriff. Her cloak covered them while his lay between them and the forest floor. The warmth from Quinn warded off the damp chill of the morning air. Despite all that was wrong with the world, nothing had ever seemed so right. Waking with her beside him made the dangerous nature of their mission worth it, even if just for this moment. Brandt didn't want to move for fear of waking her and ending the perfection.

The squawking of a nearby bird broke the spell, causing Quinn to stir. She opened her eyes, blinking away lingering sleep.

She looked at him and frowned. "Why are you staring at me with a smile on your face? Do I look horrible?"

He chuckled and kissed her cheek. "Anything but."

"The sun is rising. We should pack up and get started."

She stood and dumped her cloak over his head. He pulled it away and watched her as she stretched. Dressed all in black with leather padding on her torso and shoulders, forearms covered by plated bracers, she appeared almost as tough as she was in reality. Tight breeches and tall boots highlighted her lean, athletic figure. He continued to watch her as she squatted, scooped up her swords, and belted them to her waist.

Quinn looked down at him with narrowed eyes. "Are you watching me?"

He flashed her a smile. "Guilty."

"Well…it's kind of creepy."

"What's creepy about it?" He was incredulous. "Is it so wrong to admire beauty?"

"I don't know." She wore a half smirk while she looked at him. "It kind of makes me feel like a wench in a tavern doing a dance for the men in the room."

He rose to his feet, collected his cloak, and held the other cloak out toward her. "What's wrong with that?"

Quinn glared at him as she snatched the cloak away.

He raised his hands in surrender. "I'm not saying you're a tavern wench or anything. I just don't see anything wrong with appreciating the appearance of another person…especially someone who has stolen your heart."

Her gray eyes softened to blue as she stared at him, her hard shell falling away. "Your heart?"

He shrugged. "It feels that way."

She slid in closer, her eyelids at half-mast, biting her lip as she smirked. "So, am I a thief of hearts, now?"

His arms slipped around Quinn, and her lips met his. He fell into the kiss, reveling in the moment while embracing the girl in his arms. The thumping of his heart was a drum in his ears, and the world was perfect again. Too soon, she slipped away, leaving Brandt to deal with the storm of emotion raging inside him.

"Since I have stolen your heart," she said as she gathered her pack and water skin, "you had better follow along. You don't want me selling it to the first woman I see."

She turned and walked toward the fields to the south.

"What?" He stuffed his cloak into his pack, tossed the pack and his water skin over his shoulder, and scrambled after her. "Why would you say such a thing?"

Quinn chuckled as he caught up to her. "You know me better than that. I am far too loyal to sell your heart."

He released an exaggerated sigh as he played along. "Thank Issal."

They left the shadows of the trees and entered a field of yellowed, knee-high grass before turning east. The sun, edging over the hills at the horizon, forced Brandt to squint.

"No." Quinn said, her tone wistful. "If I decide I am through with your heart, I'll just smash it to bits and throw it into the sea."

Alarmed, he turned toward her and found her expression lacking any semblance of humor.

—◆—

Air bubbles arose from the river as Brandt filled his waterskin. Once full, he stood, capped the waterskin, and climbed the riverbank to join Quinn beside the road.

"I would like to know how long it will be before we reach Vinata," she said as she stared toward the northeast.

Brandt swung his pack around, dug inside, and pulled out a folded piece of paper. With a furrowed brow, she watched as he unfolded it. "What's that?"

"A map. I copied it from the one you stole. Of course, I only copied the area north of Sol Polis, so it's much smaller in scale."

She leaned close, examining it. "This is pretty decent. You have some skill in this area."

He snorted. "Blame Master Padia. Among other things, she taught me, my sister, and my brother cartography."

"Maps." She gave him a sidelong look. "You know how to draw maps?"

"Don't look so surprised. I *did* have an extensive education. I'm a prince, remember?"

"Shh." Quinn looked around, obviously finding nobody listening. They were in the middle of nowhere.

"I think we are pretty safe from prying ears, you know."

"You can't be too careful." She leaned close. "Where are we now?"

He pointed toward where the road and river intersected. "We are here, roughly a quarter the way between Sol Polis and Vinata. We walked for an hour last night to our camp." His finger traced their route as he spoke. "We've been on the road another two hours this morning. If it took three hours to get this far, it will likely take another nine hours to reach Vinata."

Quinn's lips pressed together and nodded while staring at the map. She then pointed toward an area northwest of Vinata. "What's this?"

"I think it's a road, one not shown on other maps." Brandt recalled tracing that particular element very carefully. "We need to find it and follow it to a castle in the mountains between Vinata and Yarth."

"Well, let's get moving. It gets dark early now, and the sun will have set by the time we reach Vinata." She turned and began walking at a fast clip. "I don't know about you, but I didn't care for our late stroll last night. We were lucky we didn't get injured or lost in the dark woods."

He caught up to her. "I could always heal you if something happened."

"And what about you?" She slowed, glaring at him. "You can't heal yourself, and I certainly can't do it."

She's too smart sometimes. "True." His stomach rumbled, unsatisfied by the hard rolls and cold sausage he had eaten for breakfast. "Nine hours is a long time yet. Although a soft bed sounds wonderful, I can't wait for a good, hot meal. The rations I packed aren't exactly food fit for a prince."

She chuckled. "Careful. If you continue whining, Jonah is going to think you're after his crown as the King of Complaints."

He glared at her subtle smirk. "Do you lack sympathy for everyone, or just for me?"

She patted his cheek. "Only for you, my Prince."

He shook his head but was unable to restrain a grin. "I find it quite unfair that Issal saw fit to make us men desire you women so, only to have you constantly confusing us and leaving us wondering why you make us suffer."

Quinn laughed. "Suffering and love, love and suffering. All the best stories connect one to the other."

His smile faltered, something more serious forcing it away. "Is that what this is? Between us?" Brandt watched for her response. "Love?"

She gave him a sidelong look. "I am no expert, so I'll not

comment…at least not yet." Her grin reappeared. "Still, you could use a bit of suffering. It builds character."

Brandt escorted Quinn through the streets of Vinata, glowlamps at the intersections lighting their way. They passed foot traffic while shops were closing their doors for the night. At the fifth intersection, Quinn turned and led him up the hill of a quiet side street.

"That guard at the gate deserves a good beating," Quinn grumbled.

Brandt sighed. "Sometimes, it's better to sweeten people up rather than dress them down. You can't expect everyone to bend to your will, Quinn."

She stopped and glared at him, her lips pressed tightly together. "Those men saw us coming." Her arm extended, her finger pointing back toward the gate. "We were no more than a hundred feet away when they closed the gates."

The fire in her eyes made him smile. He found her spirit and her unbending sense of justice endearing.

"I don't disagree. I also understand why you see it as a spiteful act, but they may have just been obeying orders." He shrugged. "Then again, they may have thought it fun to make us squirm before letting us in."

Quinn snorted. "If I see that smart-mouthed guard again, he will be the one squirming – squirming on the ground in pain."

He chuckled. "Well, they *did* let us in after I appealed to their better nature. Perhaps you should try that next time, rather than shouting and cursing."

Her eyes narrowed as she stared at him for a long, quiet moment. She then sighed, "Perhaps my temper did get the better of me." He heard an ache in her voice, as if admitting wrong caused her physical pain. "Still, that man is lucky he didn't receive a throat punch."

She turned and resumed the uphill climb, forcing him to hurry to catch her. Atop the rise, the couple turned into an alley that led to a courtyard.

"This is it. Pintalli's Inn." Quinn said as she headed toward the back door. "Let me do the talking."

"Well, I hope you intend to treat the owner better than the guard back there. I doubt a throat punch will get us a meal or a room for the night." He could not restrain his grin, despite the glare she gave him.

When Quinn opened the door, the inn greeted them with noisy chatter and the aroma of grilled fish. While it wasn't his favorite meal, Brandt's stomach growled and his mouth watered in anticipation.

They stepped into a busy taproom with only a few tables unoccupied. The bar stood directly to their left, and Quinn went straight for it, pulling up a stool. Brandt did likewise as he removed his pack and cloak. With the cloak piled atop the pack, Brandt leaned on his elbows and eyed a waitress who passed by with two steaming plates of food.

The middle-aged man behind the bar was short, with black hair and a black mustache, waxed and curled in typical Vinacci fashion. After refilling two goblets of wine, the barkeep pocketed the coppers pushed toward him and looked in Quinn's direction. His eyes widened, and he put on a smile while bustling over.

"I never forget a pretty face," the barkeep crooned. "You were here a number of weeks back."

Quinn flashed a friendly smile. "Hello, Pintalli. Yes, I stopped by here on my way to Sol Polis. At the time, I was accompanied by a quite *iconic* companion whom I believe you know."

The man dipped his head in acknowledgement, his eyes shifting toward Brandt. "Yes. I recall. What brings you back? Is all well?"

Quinn gazed at Brandt as she replied, "This is my friend...my boyfriend. He and I are taking a trip together."

Pintalli grinned at Brandt. "Boyfriend, eh?" He leaned closer. "Good luck. I hear she's a feisty one."

Brandt chuckled. "You have no idea."

Pintalli shifted his focus back to Quinn. "Judging by your outfit, your trip appears...dangerous."

"Well...this is a bit of a hunting trip. In fact, we plan to purchase a few items before we leave Vinacci."

"I know a few shops who owe me a favor or two. I bet I could get you a good price."

Quinn smiled. "I knew I came to the right place."

Pintalli smiled in return. "Glad to help. Now, speaking of business, would you be interested in a room, dinner, or drinks?"

Brandt interjected, slapping the bar. "Yes! All of the above, my good man."

Quinn scowled at him, and Pintalli laughed.

"All right." Pintalli said with a smile. "After I pour you each a glass from my favorite vineyard, I'll order two plates from the kitchen." He leaned over the bar, his voice dropping to a hushed tone. "You're in luck. I happen to have the best cook in Vinacci, but don't tell her that. She might ask for more money."

Brandt's brow furrowed. "If she's so wonderful, why not just pay her more?"

"Because," he grinned broadly, "she's my wife."

26

MISSIVE

Iko kept his stance balanced, shield in position, sword ready to respond. His opponents eyed him, likely searching for a weakness to exploit. They would find none.

Ydith lunged with a thrust Iko redirected with a twist of his sword. She was quick, but so was he. As expected, Berd attacked the moment Ydith engaged. Iko blocked the big man's swing with his shield and grunted from the impact. Spinning away, Iko brought his sword around in an arc to keep either guard from advancing.

In a bold move, Ydith drove forward with a thrust before Iko's shield could come around. He twisted and hacked at her hand, striking it hard. Her wooden sword fell to the dirt as she cried out in pain. Berd then barreled toward Iko, his sword flashing side to side, forcing Iko backward in a series of rapid, jarring blocks.

After four steps, Iko smacked the man's sword aside with his shield, spun in a crouch so the return strike flew over him, and swung low at his opponent. The wooden sword struck Berd's ankle. Hard. Berd roared in pain and hobbled backward. Iko charged at Berd, going for the kill.

Berd blocked the first swing and the second, but he doubled over when a thrust slipped through his defense and Iko's sword buried itself in his abdomen. The man stumbled backward and fell to one knee, coughing.

Iko lowered his sword and glanced toward Ydith, who had moved to the side of the floor. The scowl and narrowed eyes she directed toward Iko were expected. The woman did not like to lose. A healer walked in and approached Berd, but the man waved her off.

"No. A little pain will do me good." Berd growled. He held one hand to his stomach, wincing as he limped toward Iko. Extending a thick hand, Berd gave Iko a nod. "You have skill, Ikonis. If they ever resurrect the dueling championships, you might consider entering."

Iko shook the man's hand. "Thank you, Berd. And thanks for the duel as well. It's good to remain in practice. Besides, sitting around in this palace is agonizing. A bit of action to keep me occupied is much appreciated." Iko turned toward Ydith, "Thank you as well, Ydith. Sorry about your hand."

The woman turned away and muttered. "Sure. Anytime."

Berd limped over to her, clapping her on the shoulder. "Come on, girl. You can't win every time. Besides, losing to someone as skilled as young Ikonis is no slight." The man leaned close to her and whispered, just loud enough for Iko to hear. "I doubt the Archon would be happy if we hurt him anyway."

Ydith grunted and headed toward the door to the barracks.

Iko approached the weapon rack and returned the wooden sword and shield. He then bent, picked up his scabbard, and began belting it back into place.

During his stay at Kantar, he had grown used to wearing a sword. Accordingly, he had acquired one from the Sol Polis armory the day after his arrival. He paused, frowning as thoughts of Broland returned. Those memories, once something he had legitimately held dear, now only brought pain.

"Good show, Ikonis."

Iko looked up and found Captain Sculdin leaning over the rail of the loft that overlooked the sparring yard.

"Good morning, Scully. How long have you been watching?"

"Most of the bout. It's not every day I get to watch someone duel multiple opponents. The last guard I had who could manage it ended up dead."

"Yes. So I've heard," Iko replied. "As for me, I thought it a good test. With war on the horizon, experience facing two opponents might be a skill that saves my life."

"True." The pleasantness had left Sculdin's voice. "Why don't you come up, and we can talk for a bit."

Iko finished buckling his sword belt with a nod. "I'll be right up."

He left the room and climbed the stairs to Sculdin's loft. The man was alone in the room and had shifted to stand over a table covered by maps and notes. He bent and jotted something down on a list before glancing up at Iko.

"You appear busy, Scully."

"War requires detailed planning. Soldiers can die of malnourishment, dysentery, or extreme weather conditions as easily as they can by a sword."

Iko's gaze fell on the map, and he found areas circled with numerous lines converging on Yarth. Some by sea, others by land.

"It will come to war, then?"

Sculdin moved away from the table, nodding. "It appears so. Kardan has assigned me with logistics planning. I have already sent couriers across the Empire to secure what is required. I'm moving livestock and fall crops to Yarth and have already placed orders for winter crops grown in south Kalimar. I may even claim a portion of the spring crops grown from here to Vingarri. I'm building a storage center north of Yarth just for this effort and will have fifty wagons dedicated to moving food and supplies for the Imperial Army alone."

Iko blinked at the breadth of it all. "I knew that logistics were important to feed an army, but I didn't realize it was so complex."

"Battle tactics are not the only key to a successful war campaign. Soldiers are assets who must be cultivated or they will wilt and die faster than any untended crop."

"How long will it take to orchestrate all this?"

"Thankfully, Kardan and your mother have agreed to hold our ground until spring. That gives me at least eight weeks, ten at most, before we advance beyond Hipoint...assuming that idiot Mollis can hold the garrison until I arrive."

Iko snorted. "I met Mollis a few months back. He seemed...pig-headed."

Sculdin grinned. "Good description. He can execute orders and motivate his soldiers, but he lacks creative thinking. Surprises don't go over well with Mollis."

"He sounds like a poor Ratio Bellicus player."

"I suspect he is." Sculdin circled back around his table and gave Iko a sidelong look. There was a contemplative glint in the man's eyes as he spoke. "You have always shown a creative flair. You know how to use a sword well, and you possess some military training."

Iko frowned. "Yes. So?"

"So, when I leave this spring, I could use a lieutenant I trust by my side."

"Lieutenant? Me?"

"Think on it. If you are interested, I'll put a request in with Kardan. You may have to convince your mother, but I think you'd be a solid second-in-command."

Iko's gaze shifted to the floor, but in truth, he was staring at nothing. The idea of commanding troops was something he had never considered. At the same time, his path was uncharted, and he didn't know where his life would lead. His gaze shifted back toward Sculdin and found the captain staring at him.

"I guess I never considered myself an officer," Iko said. "How many soldiers are you talking about?"

"While the core of our troops are already stationed outside of Yarth, I have sent the call out to drain the other cities. By the time we march, we should have close to ten thousand armed soldiers. While the platoon from each city has its sergeant, and I have Rorrick to lean on, a force of that size is too much for two men to manage." He put his hand on Iko's shoulder. "I could honestly use your help. Besides," he grinned, "we have flash powder on our side."

When Iko reached the top floor, he heard shouts ahead. At the far end of the corridor, a guard leaned against the wall, showing no interest in investigating the ruckus. A blond woman in a dark blue dress rushed out of the Archon's chamber and closed the door. She hurried in Iko's direction, visibly shaken.

"It's Jeshica, I believe?" He altered his path to intercept her. "Are you all right?"

The woman stopped short of him. "Yes. I'm fine." Jeshica looked back at the door. "She's upset about some news I had to deliver."

Iko knew that side of his mother well. He also knew that it was best not to be the target of her anger. He gave Jeshica a smile.

"You appear to have escaped unscathed. My mother runs hot when she hears bad news, but she also tends to cool quickly." He tried to sound reassuring. "I can't remember her ever being angry for more than an hour or two. After that, well, let's just say she focuses on retribution."

"I have...some experience in that area." Her gaze shifted to the floor as she circled around him and headed toward the stairs. "I wouldn't want to be in Glynnis' position when she returns."

Iko spun around, facing her. "Wait. Glynnis? Returns from where?"

Jeshica glanced back and shook her head. "You had best ask your mother." She then bustled down the stairs and faded from view.

Concern for Quinn left Iko considering how to broach the subject. Saying the wrong thing could result in his mother's anger redirecting toward him. However, he had to know.

He knocked on the door and listened.

"I told you I didn't want to be disturbed," his mother said in short, clipped words, each filled with a note of anger.

Swallowing a deep breath of courage, Iko turned the knob and strode inside. "It's me, Mother. I heard shouting. Are you all right?"

His mother was standing with her arms crossed over her chest while facing the window. She spun around, stomped to her desk, and lifted a crumpled piece of paper. "She left. Without a word, she just up and left me."

He chose to play dumb. "Who left you?"

"Glynnis," she snarled and held the paper toward him.

Iko moved closer and accepted it. His mother turned back toward the window, her face in a scowl. He pulled the letter open, smoothed the wrinkles a bit, and began reading in silence.

Meryl,

.   .   .

As you requested, I have made a focused effort to uncover the spy in our midst. At first, there was little to report as everyone I questioned appeared innocent and lacking motive. I then shifted my focus to newly hired staff members. Among that small group, I found a pattern that led me to a wine steward named Ebran Pym. Suspecting him, I set a trap to discover if he is the vermin I seek.

I wrote a false letter to you, confirming the presence of a spy in the palace, and I knew how to prove him guilty. Without naming him, the note suggested that you sanction the arrest of a person on the serving staff. In the note, I promised to have him in shackles by morning and to have him hanged by nightfall.

I then requested that Sheen send Ebran to serve you and Kardan in your chamber. Since I knew you two would still be in Kardan's office, your room would be unoccupied. I placed the folded note on your desk and waited in my room. Sure enough, our little rat took the bait.

The moment I heard him leave, I entered the room and found the note unfolded and resting beside a carafe of wine and two glasses.

I later caught up to Ebran outside his room where I heard him busily packing things. I followed him to an inn near the docks, and I believe he will board a ship first thing in the morning. When the spy leaves Sol Polis, I intend to follow him in hope of discovering his contacts. Perhaps it will reveal whose unseen hand is moving the game pieces against us.

Don't blame Jeshica. She knows nothing and is only a convenient messenger. I will return soon, and I hope to have answers.

-Glynnis Mor

A conflict of emotions battered Iko as he thought about Quinn. Concern. Relief. Regret. He wondered at the sincerity of her letter... and if her disappearance had something to do with him. She had named Ebran as the spy, a name Iko recalled. *I ran into him in Sculdin's office just before the map was stolen.*

He flipped the paper over and found the words *Deliver to Archon*

Varius written beside a broken wax seal. He lowered the note and looked at his mother. "What does your handmaid have to do with this?"

His mother continued staring out the window. "Jeshica discovered the note on her floor when she woke this morning. Apparently, Glynnis had slipped it under her door while she was sleeping."

"So...you're angry at Glynnis, not at Jeshica."

She sighed. "Yes. I'm angry that she didn't discuss this with me first."

The sigh was a sign of her calming. He considered what he might say to further diffuse her anger. "Your bodyguard seems quite... resourceful. Perhaps her mission will yield something useful."

Turning from the window, she strolled to her desk and sat. "True, but I now find myself without a bodyguard. What if there is another attempt on my life?"

An idea struck him – one that would solve his own problem while helping to ease his mother's anger. "Well, I am here, and I know how to use this." He patted the sword at his hip. "Besides, I have been... bored since I arrived. Now that Percy is gone, I don't even have him to occupy my time."

She stared at him for a long moment before nodding. "Very well. I trust you, and that is more than half my concern toward anyone who spends time alone with me...especially if they are armed."

Iko exhaled a breath of relief. *Her anger has passed, and she is now moving forward.* His immediate future had an objective, but his longer path remained undefined. The thought reminded him of his conversation with Sculdin.

"I stopped by Sculdin's office after my morning duel." Iko sat across from his mother and crossed his legs, one hand going to his knee, tapping it as he spoke. "We had a brief discussion about the coming war and the logistical complications of feeding so many soldiers."

"Yes. It's not a trivial concern." Mirroring him, she crossed her legs and nodded. "Our recruitment and training efforts have been underway for some time now, but having command over such a large army does little good if they lack the supplies to survive."

Her mind is on the problem, a cause she believes in. I need to do it now.

"Scully also said he needs officers, people he can trust." Thoughts of Quinn's steely gray eyes arose in his head, galvanizing his resolve. "He asked me to be his second-in-command."

She stared at him, unmoving for a long, quiet, uncomfortable moment. Finally, her eyes lowered, her face taking on a contemplative expression. "After I sent you off to train with Rhone and his guards, I often wondered where it might lead. I only knew that the world was a cruel, hard place, and you needed the tools required to defend yourself.

"When Kardan came to me with the plan to send you to the military academy in Fallbrandt, both to learn and to spy, that plan seemed a natural next step in your progression. When you and Percy returned, I was happy to have you back and thought it might be the end of your time away. That is, until I decided to send you to Kantar. It was a risky plan – one of great import. To work, it required just the right individual. Kardan convinced me that you were our only choice. I hated sending you, but I also had faith in your abilities. In the end, it worked out quite well, and you returned safe."

She held her hand over her eyes, as if wearied by the decision he had forced upon her. "You must know that war is trouble of a different nature." She dropped her hand and looked into his eyes. "Despite sound strategy and detailed planning, anything can happen. I am reluctant to place you in a position of such danger. There is nothing in this world I cherish more than you, Ikonis. I don't know if I can bear losing you.

"However, I also realize that our fight, our ideals, are more important than my own selfish desires. If this is something you want, I will support Sculdin's request, but you must honor your agreement to guard me in the interim…at least until Glynnis returns."

Iko blinked in disbelief. *She said yes?* More than his victory earlier in the sparring yard, perhaps more than any success he had ever achieved, convincing his mother to agree to his request was a major coup.

Restraining a grin, he replied in an even tone, "Thank you, Mother."

She pulled her chair in and picked up a message that lay on her desk. "You may go. Be sure to return for the mid-day meal. You can dine with me and then escort me to the Council chambers. Kardan and I are meeting with the Council this afternoon."

27

SURVIVAL

A bell rang in the heart of the city, a greeting to the morning sun as it edged over the horizon. In response to the bell, some guards began cranking a wheel with long wooden handles, raising the gate. Quinn squinted at the light, her head still pounding from the wine she had consumed the prior evening. Although she wanted to blame Brandt...or Pintalli, she had to admit it had been her own doing. *At least it was a fun evening*, she thought. In fact, the entire stay at Vinata had been enjoyable.

She and Brandt had spent the prior day visiting shops in the city, purchasing the supplies required for their mission. Thanks to Pintalli and his connections, the cost was a fraction of what it would have been otherwise.

Brandt stood beside her, wearing a dark gray travel cloak over an all-black outfit, similar to her own. Quinn had to admit that Brandt cut a dashing figure, the way his leather-padded coat fit his lean, muscular torso. Somehow, the tailor was able to measure him and make the necessary adjustments to the new coat and breeches in less than a day.

A sense of pride arose as Quinn stared at him – his handsome face, his regal bearing. He was like her in many ways, but different enough that his strengths balanced her weaknesses. Feelings toward him welled up inside her, and she grabbed his hand, giving it a squeeze. He looked at her with a smile that she returned.

A wry expression appeared on his face. "Are you sure we can't go purchase a nice, sturdy quarterstaff for me to use?" His tone was smooth, an attempt to sound convincing. "Wouldn't you feel safer if I were armed?"

"For this mission, we agreed that stealth was our best approach. How are you supposed to hide something as long as a quarterstaff?"

His brow furrowed. "I know, but what if we get into a physical confrontation?"

Quinn gripped the hilt of the sword on her hip. "I do know how to use these, you know."

"Yes, but what about me?"

She patted his cheek, grinning. "Don't worry. I'll protect you."

"Why do I get the feeling that you enjoy having the advantage?"

"Perhaps...because I do."

Brandt grimaced and she laughed.

His laughter joined hers, and he shook his head. "And you call *me* incorrigible."

The portcullis finished rising, a guard beside the gate shouted, and the small crowd that had gathered began to filter out.

Quinn hefted her pack over her shoulder. "Let's go."

As they melted into the caravan of people and wagons passing through the gate, Quinn watched the guards posted there. Dressed in chain mail and white tabards marked with a blue Order rune, the Imperial soldiers intently surveyed the people and wagons entering the city. In contrast, the guards appeared to ignore those who were leaving.

They walked down the slope toward the river. To the southeast, a road ran between the river and the city wall, toward the harbor where Quinn had arrived weeks earlier – a time that had both gone by quickly, yet seemed so long ago. Thoughts of the sea voyage stirred memories of the Razor and the damage the ship had taken from the Empire flash cannons. The threat of those cannons, along with flash bombs and Issal-knows-what other weapons, were the motivation behind her and Brandt's mission. Somehow, the two of them needed to prevent any further weapon production. Somehow.

The road leveled as it approached River Iglesia, named after some long-dead Vinaccian queen. They strolled onto a wooden bridge with rails on both sides. A wagon rumbled past them, the bridge large enough for traffic to flow in both directions. Ten feet below, slow-moving waters flowed toward the bay. Rowboats with long fishing poles mounted to the stern were anchored at the mouth of the river while larger ships occupied the harbor further out. The bridge ended and became gravel again as they crossed a small island to another bridge. Two more islands and two more bridge spans led them to the north bank, a half mile from the city.

Mirroring the rolling hills south of Vinata, the hillsides around them were covered in vines that grew along man-made trellises. This stretch of land grew the grapes used to make Vinaccian wine, the most renowned wine in Issalia. Quinn wryly recalled the prior evening when Pintalli eagerly had her and Brandt sample various bottles from his favorite vineyard. The drink was fruity and flavorful, neither too bitter nor overly sweet. She soon grew to enjoy the beverage, perhaps a bit too much. Her headache still lingered.

Beyond the next rise, they discovered rolling hills that ran north along the coast, all occupied by vineyards. At the bottom of the hill before them, a narrow gravel road turned inland. Yellowed grass growing between the narrow wagon ruts that defined the road marked it as a lightly traveled route. Brandt stopped, pulled his map from his pack, and unfolded it.

He pointed toward the narrow road. "That must be the route to Castile Corvichi."

Quinn looked toward it as the wagon ahead of them continued past the intersection and continued north, toward Vingarri. "While it's not a primary road, it *does* appear recently used." She looked down at the map following the curled line that ran from Vinata to their destination. "The route to Corvichi appears to be as long as our trip was from Sol Polis to Vinata."

"Yes." Brandt folded the map. "Worse, this one leads into the mountains, not through an easy pass like our journey here."

With a sigh, she headed down the hill with him at her side. "Best to get going. We have many miles ahead of us, and we'll want to find a safe spot to camp for the night."

"I agree," Brandt said, each footstep heavy as he tromped downhill. "Tomorrow, we can scout the area, watch for patterns, and come up with a plan."

The clouds rolled in, growing thicker and darker as the day dragged on. By mid-afternoon, the threat of rain became apparent, if not imminent as thunder rolled in the distance. The open view of the surrounding hills had long faded, now obscured by wooded hillsides that enveloped the narrow road. Worse, the wind had increased from a breeze to gusts that would, at times, howl through the surrounding forest. Quinn began to realize why this castle in the mountains might have been abandoned. The distance from the shore and the lack of surrounding civilization left her wondering why Corvichi had chosen such a remote location in the first place.

Brandt stopped, frowning as thunder rumbled.

She turned toward him "What is..."

He held his open palm up, stopping her in mid-sentence. Then, beyond the howling wind, she heard it – a deep rumble coming from the road ahead, the sound drawing closer. It wasn't thunder.

"Quick. Hide!" He scrambled off the road, squeezing through the brush.

Quinn scurried after him, looking toward the bend in the road with trepidation. She passed beyond the outer layer of shrubs and ducked beside him as a wagon rounded the bend.

Drawn by two workhorses and driven by a young man with a soldier seated to each side of him, the wagon rolled past, the trio oblivious of her or Brandt. After the wagon passed by, she stood and spied the barrel of a flash cannon poking out from beneath a tarp in the wagon bed. Judging by the size and shape of the object beside it, she assumed it was two cannons. The wagon faded from view, leaving only the dust stirred by its passing. The forest fell quiet, the blowing wind now joined by the soft patter of raindrops.

Brandt looked up with a grimace. "I hope it doesn't rain any harder or this trip is going to be a slog through mud."

She pushed her way through the brush. "At least we now know we took the correct route."

He returned to the road, brushed some burrs from his cloak, and raised his hood as they resumed their journey. "True. Yet, rather than being reassured, I now have a bad feeling about this mission."

Lightning struck, a strobe of flickering light joined by a teeth-rattling rumble of thunder. The sky opened and the sprinkling rain became a downpour.

Quinn was wet. Everywhere. Wet and cold. The combination made her grumpy – angry that she had no choice but to endure the suffering. Brandt squatted beside her, the two of them peering over a gray rock atop a saddle between two peaks. Despite the lessening rain and the dimming light, their position made it possible to see their destination.

A valley lay before them, surrounded by mountain peaks, the modest peak in the center topped by a pale castle. The brown strip of a single road ran up to the castle, winding through the dark green trees that surrounded it. At the valley floor, the road intersected with another that ran in the opposite direction and then faded from view.

"That other road appears to head west," Brandt noted. "I'll bet it leads to Yarth,"

"This is stupid." Quinn wanted to scream at someone. She hated being wet and cold. "How do we get up there without being seen? Do we do it at night? Can we make it in without being heard or injured or worse?"

Brandt shook his head. "Not tonight, we don't. I'm freezing and exhausted." He looked at her, his eyes widening when he saw her glaring back. "I'm sorry. I'm sure you feel the same way. We both need to warm up and get some rest. That will give us time to think"

She held her hand out, sprinkles striking her palm – much better than the flood of drops that had doused her for the previous three hours. "The rain is dying out and should end soon."

"I agree," he said. "It'll also be dark inside the hour. Let's move farther away from the road and find a low area to camp, hidden where they won't spot a fire. We'll wait until dark so they can't follow the smoke."

He turned and began weaving his way through the forest. She followed, ducking beneath branches and twisting around a thorn-covered thicket. The undergrowth, and everything else, was wet. Each brush up against leaves added to the wetness that already covered her clothes.

"How are you going to start a fire?" She grumbled. "Everything is soaking wet."

Pausing, he turned toward her with a small smile on his face. "You sound awfully grumpy. Admittedly, I found rain unfortunate, but you downright despise being wet, don't you?"

She glared at him. "What's your point?"

"Wouldn't you like to be warm and dry?"

"Of course, but we are alone in a forest that is as soaked as we are. Wishing for it won't change a thing."

"Oh, how easily you forget. You are with me." His grin widened. "I can do magic that will make your wishes come true."

For some reason, his glib attitude stirred the testy beast inside her. "Get moving, or I'll wipe that smile off your face with my fist."

"Wow." His smile slid away. "Sorry."

Quinn sighed. "No." She grabbed his arm before he could turn away. "Don't be sorry. That was…unfair. I'm just irritated about being cold and wet and hungry."

"Apology accepted…and noted." The corner of his lip turned up in a smirk. "I was wondering if it were even possible for you to admit you were wrong."

"Don't test me, Brandt," she growled.

"Um. Never mind."

He turned and resumed his route down the hill, through a copse of tall pines, and into a sheltered clearing with a boulder at the center, joined by a lonely tree, nearly bereft of leaves.

Brandt pulled his hood back and surveyed the area, nodding as he spun about. "This is perfect."

She scrutinized the clearing, turning his statement over in her head. Knee-high grass and brush surrounded them, the bare tree leaning away from the boulder as if it feared the thing. The boulder itself was nothing special – an ordinary chunk of gray rock that stood chest-high and had a similar diameter.

"Why is it perfect?"

"You'll see." He turned and walked toward a fallen tree, fifty feet away. "Look around and find branches and loose wood we can use for a fire."

After a moment of consideration, Quinn did as requested, heading back into the trees. She spent the next few minutes collecting an armload of sticks and branches that dotted the forest floor. By the time she returned to the campsite, he had a pile as well, and nightfall was upon them.

"Throw yours beside mine," Brandt said, pointing toward the pile beyond the tree. "That should be far enough away."

After throwing her collected wood atop his, Quinn pulled her hood down and realized that the rain had stopped. Turning, she found Brandt kneeling beside the boulder, drawing a symbol with a chunk of glowstone. The pale blue lines glowed in the dimming twilight. Quinn recognized the rune and realized what he intended. *I should have thought of that.*

He stood back, closed his eyes for a long moment, and opened them to reveal crackling red sparks. The rune bloomed with a crimson hue and Brandt backed away, pulling Quinn with him. When the glow settled, the rock burst into flames, flaring white-orange with an inferno that burned fifteen feet high. Even standing ten strides away, Quinn felt the heat from the intense blaze. Brandt took his cloak off and hung it from a bare branch of the tree beside them.

Quinn frowned when he began to undo the buttons of his coat. "What are you doing?"

He looked toward her as he continued to undress. "We need to get dry. We are in the mountains and far from the sea. It will get cold tonight – cold enough to see our breath. Believe it or not, we could die if we can't stay warm."

"Okay. I'm with you so far." She undid her cloak and lifted it toward a branch, flinching from the heat when it forced her to move closer to the fire.

"The fire's intensity will last an hour before it begins to fade.

Drying our clothes now will allow us to wear them when we sleep, when the fire is far smaller and much cooler."

"You want me to take my clothes off?"

He pulled his coat off, revealing the thin tunic beneath. A grin crossed his face. "While I can't deny that it aligns with my personal desires, this is for your own good – your survival. It's not exactly the romantic moment I might have wished for, but yes, I want you to take your clothes off."

She stared at him as he pulled his tunic over his head and turned toward the tree, the ripples of his damp torso glistening in the firelight. He then leaned against the tree for support while he unbuckled his boots.

Shrugging to herself, Quinn began unbuttoning her leather jerkin. She found herself wondering if Brandt had somehow planned the whole scenario with this end in mind. Surprisingly, she realized that it didn't bother her either way.

28

SURRENDER

"Thank you, Master Beldon," Ashland said, dismissing the minister.

Beldon bowed his head. "Until next time, my Queen."

The man turned and ambled down the throne room aisle with Wharton as his escort. The door opened, and both men faded from view. Ashland glanced toward the door at the side of the room, her gaze briefly meeting the blue eyes of Ran, the latest elite guard recruit.

Tall, muscular, and tanned, Ran was undoubtedly the youngest of her guards and likely among the youngest recruits ever to accept the position. Her gaze shifted to the markings that graced the exposed portion of his arms, between the metal bracers on his forearms and the rounded plate that covered his thick shoulder. Body art was a rarity outside of vocation runes. The symbols marking him were even more atypical.

I see much of his parents in him, Ashland thought. *The calm demeanor, his quiet manner. The unspoken threat of violence, should the situation demand it.*

The door opened, and Wharton entered with a young woman trailing him. Her blond hair was tied back in a tail, her plain clothing covered by a long, dark cloak. Wharton stopped five strides before the throne and gave Ashland a shallow bow. The woman beside him mirrored his action.

"Sorry to disturb you, Your Highness. A messenger just arrived, and I thought it best if you heard her report yourself, should you have any questions." Wharton moved aside and gestured for the young woman to take over.

She shuffled forward, her downcast eyes flicked up, met Ashland's gaze for a moment, and then returned to stare at the dais. The woman could be no older than twenty-five summers. A Cognitio rune graced her forehead, marking her old vocation path as someone who sought knowledge.

The messenger cleared her throat and spoke in a quiet voice. "I just heard about what happened...I am so sorry about your husband and son."

"I appreciate your concern," Ashland said. "However, I must set my grieving aside, for I have a kingdom to manage and citizens to protect. I assume you have a name and you are here for reasons beyond offering condolences."

"Yes. Of course. My name is Samantha, Samantha Brine. I was assigned the role of recorder and messenger for Captain Marcella. I have spent the past four months with her at the Hipoint Garrison."

The messenger paused and glanced toward Wharton, who nodded for her to continue.

"We spent the bulk of that time repairing and fortifying the garrison while the miners with us dug an escape tunnel. A few weeks back, we were joined by a small party of special fighters who had come from Fallbrandt."

Samantha paused while staring at Ashland, who nodded that she understood. *Wardens.*

The woman took a deep breath and continued.

"When we learned that an enemy attack was imminent, we evacuated the village and prepared for battle. All that remained were five hundred soldiers in the garrison, a single ship, and Baron Rhone, himself. The baron refused to leave his manor, despite our pleas.

"On the day of the battle, Marcella sent me with this note and bade me to wait upon the ship until the last possible moment. The battle began mid-day. When the enemy drew close, we crushed two of their catapults with an incredible landslide. Even that event was nothing but a delay for the inevitable.

"Night fell, and my ability to monitor what transpired grew limited. Yet, I waited in hope of a miracle that would not come. When green flames and explosions lit the night, it soon became obvious that the garrison would fall. Upon the cliffside, orange fires burned, providing light for the horror to come.

"Fearing my message would not reach you should they attack our ship, I gave the command to set sail. Even as the ship drifted out to sea, I watched thousands of Imperial soldiers storm the breached garrison walls. There were shouts and screams and cries of people dying in the fracas. As we reached the breakers, another explosion, this one appearing as if red lightning had struck, blasted the garrison walls away and everything on the coast fell black."

Samantha leaned forward and held a message out toward Ashland. She accepted it, unfolded the note, and read in silence.

King Brock,

You assigned me the task of reclaiming the Hipoint Garrison and restoring it to the best of my abilities. With the soldiers I was promised, exceeding thirteen hundred in total, I was to hold the garrison and prevent our enemies from advancing up the coast. After pouring every bit of our energy into preparation for an attack, I now realize that we cannot prevent the inevitable.

We face a far superior army, for the reinforcements Duke Chadwick was to send never arrived. Instead, a force of five-hundred Kantarian soldiers will confront an army of thousands. Worse, our enemy is armed with explosives and weapons unlike any we have ever seen. Rather than sacrifice hundreds in a fruitless pursuit, we intend to make them pay deeply for the ground we give.

By now, the garrison has inevitably fallen. If our tactics play out as hoped, a significant portion of the enemy army has fallen as well. I only pray that the price was high enough to make them cautious to advance further.

We plan to regroup and will again face them at the Kantarian border. Please send additional troops, for I fear an attack on Wayport is imminent.

Honor, always,

Captain Marcella Urig

. . .

Ashland lowered the note, her gaze shifting first to the messenger, and then to Wharton.

"We have lost Hipoint." The words came out of Ashland's mouth as a statement.

The captain of the guard nodded.

Ashland sighed. "While that is regretful, it is not the worst thing to occur. Until recently, the village, and the garrison, had been on Kalimar land. The advance removes another port from our cause, but it was a minor port at best.

"I am more concerned about the reason behind Chadwick's forces not arriving at the garrison as planned."

The door burst open and Magistrate Filbert strutted into the room. His arms were crossed over his chest, his black robe flowing behind him as he strode down the aisle.

"What is the meaning of this?" Ashland demanded.

Filbert stopped and raised his brow at the messenger before glancing toward Wharton.

"I thought it best to inform Your Highness that there is an angry mob out in the receiving hall."

Wharton's brow furrowed. "What are you going on about, old man?"

"Don't believe me? Go on and see for yourself."

Shouts came from beyond the closed doors, trailed by the distinctive clang of steel on steel. Wharton drew his sword and started down the aisle when the doors burst open and Nels staggered in. The man was covered in blood, holding the side of his neck with one hand, the gruesome remainder of his other arm dangling as blood dripped on the floor. He fell to his knees and choked before falling face first. Dead.

Soldiers, all dressed in the black, red, and gold of Kantaria, ran into the room, stepping on and over the dead guard. With weapons drawn – some of which were covered in blood – the guards fanned out, raised their shields and faced Wharton from across the room.

During this process, Filbert had climbed upon the dais and stood to Ashland's left.

"Stop!" Filbert bellowed. Everyone froze.

When the magistrate turned toward Ashland, he wore a grin upon his face – a smile bereft of humor.

"Queen Ashland, as Chief Magistrate of Kantaria, I find you unfit to rule." Filbert's voice was firm, as if he were presiding over his court. "You face a decision. Surrender, abdicate the throne, comply with my will, and you will depart this room alive. Any action contrary to this demand will result in your death in addition to those who choose to support you."

Ashland glared at Filbert while she considered his words. Her gaze shifted to Wharton, who stood at the midpoint between her and more than twenty guards. Wharton held his blade steady, his gaze affixed on her as he waited for her orders.

"Well," Filbert said, "what will it be, my *Queen?*" He sneered, the last word thick with contempt.

The study of lore had been an area of interest to Ashland. She knew the course of history often teetered upon decisions such as the one she faced. One choice might yield years, or decades, of tyranny and oppression. The other choice might be even worse. Then, again, sometimes, one finds a third path.

Her gaze shifted to the messenger, the girl's eyes bulging with fear – the same fear clawing at Ashland, demanding her surrender. *Surrender,* she told herself. *Yes. I must surrender to my fear.*

Ashland closed her eyes and used her fear as a conduit, drawing in the surrounding Chaos. Raw, angry power surged through her. She turned away from Filbert, opened her eyes and released the stored Chaos into the rune marked upon Ran's arm. It began to glow. She turned toward Wharton, their gazes locking.

"I will never surrender to you," Ashland growled.

Filbert screamed. "Kill them!"

—✧—

Curan remained calm…waiting.

He counted twenty-six guards at the back of the throne room, Wharton standing in the center, the messenger backing toward the opposite side, the magistrate upon the dais, and Queen Ashland seated on her throne. Flexing his left arm, Curan felt tension against the tight straps of the shield strapped to it. He twisted his body, so his right side faced the queen and waited to see if she would surrender. When the Power rune on his right bicep began to glow, he knew the answer.

An enormous surge of energy ran through him, hot and powerful and angry. White spots danced before his eyes, and he staggered as the power overwhelmed him. Now familiar with the feeling, he waited for it to pass.

"Kill them!" Filbert screamed.

The guards attacked.

Soldiers with weapons drawn spilled down the center aisle. Two standing near the end of the line fired crossbows at Curan. He twisted, dodging the first bolt and blocked the other with his shield. Lunging forward, he grabbed the nearest bench – twenty feet long and weighing hundreds of pounds – and launched it at the guards as if it weighed nothing. One guard dove out of the way, but the two holding crossbows and the four guards standing beside them were not so lucky. The bench crashed into them and drove them into the wall in a collision of crushed armor, broken bones, and blood. Splinters from the shattered bench were still tumbling down when Curan leapt. He arced high, nearly colliding with the domed ceiling three stories above, before landing at the far side of the room, eighty feet away. As he spun around, the guards at the fore attacked Wharton, the man's blade a flurry as he tried to fend off three foes at once.

Curan slid two more benches forward, driving them through the heart of the attackers and sending two guards through the air screaming, bones broken. The benches collided with those on the opposite side of the room and settled to block the center aisle, dividing the enemy into two groups. Five guards stood to one side of the bench, three of whom were heavily engaged with Wharton. The thirteen other remaining guards turned to face Curan.

Gripping the hilt, Curan drew his sword and moved toward his enemy, down the path created by the displaced benches. He suspected they had never witnessed a fighter charged by a Power rune. If so, they likely would have run rather than attempt to face him.

With a lunge and the sweep of his arm, his Elastic-infused blade hammered through five extended swords, the force of the impact pushing them aside like blades of grass bending to the wind. Three of the five swordsmen lost their grips, and their weapons went spinning away. All five cried out in pain, and a few gripped their stinging hands.

Lowering himself to a crouch, Curan's back-hand swing brought his sword across the legs of those same men, slicing through leather and flesh with ease. Screams filled the air as they spilled to the floor.

A female assailant to Curan's left threw a knife, and he hastily lifted his shield to redirect the throw. Another blade appeared and sailed toward him, burying deep into his thigh. He cried out, but the Power surging through him carried an adrenaline that drowned out most of the pain.

He backed away two steps and gripped the hilt with his shield hand. A guttural growl slipped out as he pulled the dagger free and tossed it aside. Testing his leg, he found it still strong enough to support him, and he refocused on the enemy.

Four guards moved past their downed comrades and advanced warily while the other four circled around the benches to come at Curan from his left, down the outside aisle. Curan backed away and considered his options.

Rather than face two clusters attacking from different directions, he turned, jumped over five benches, ran along one, and leapt across the aisle, slicing the heads off two of the men attacking Wharton. Their bodies crumpled to the floor as Wharton ran the third man through.

Landing on a bench on the other side of the aisle, Curan lost his footing, stumbled, and banged his head against a bench. Everything went black.

—◆—

Exhausted from her use of Chaos, Ashland slumped back in her throne. Sweat tracked down her temple as she watched the guards rush forward to attack Wharton. To her right, Curan burst into action, tossing a bench into some of the attackers before leaping across the room.

Magistrate Filbert suddenly obscured her view, the man scowling as he menaced over her.

"I knew you would not surrender. Neither you, nor your departed husband knew when to accept reality." He sneered. "You'll no longer hold your magic over us as a threat. It is time to be rid of you and your filthy Unchosen. They should have never been allowed out of the gutter."

She glared back at him. "After all this time, you still cannot accept the Choosing Ceremony as a lie, that it was merely the Ministry attempting to weed out Chaos?"

"Oh, I know the truth of it all. The truth is that the Choosing Ceremony was too lenient. Rather than allowing those children to live as Unchosen, we should have just killed them and have been done with it."

"You would murder innocent babes just to suit your agenda?"

"No. I would do it to suit Issal's agenda."

A knife appeared in Filbert's hand, the blade wet, glazed glossy black. Terror gripped Ashland. One touch of that poison would kill in seconds. Trapped in her throne and weaponless, she froze.

He grinned. "Your magic cannot save you this time. You didn't think I would know, but I do. You already wasted your power on that guard. Now, you die."

Filbert raised the blade and paused. His jaw fell open, the whites of his eyes flaring as they bulged. Ashland made a desperate twist and rolled over the arm of the throne, landing rear-first on the floor with a grunt. The magistrate fell forward into the throne, his poisoned blade stabbing the padding, tearing down the back as he fell to his knees. His hand released the hilt, falling to settle lifelessly beside his head on the seat of the throne. The hilt of a dagger was sticking out from the back of the man's neck. The messenger, Samantha, stood over him with tears in her eyes, her hands covering her mouth.

"I'm sorry...I had to do it." She shook her head, crying. "I...I couldn't let him kill my queen."

"Thank you," Ashland said as she scrambled to her feet.

She turned and found Wharton facing a swordsman. Wharton's left side was covered in blood, yet he held his sword ready as the opponent advanced. Blood and bodies covered the floor before him.

Ashland searched the room for Curan. Eight attackers remained, circling the far end of the room with caution. Her gaze swept past the dead soldiers, past the broken mess of benches, and she found Curan lying on the floor, not far from his original post.

She scrambled off the dais, around the front benches, and knelt beside him. Blood ran down his forehead, his helmet lying on the floor beside him. With her hand on his cheek, she closed her eyes, and found her center. Extending her awareness, she coaxed his source of Order to heal him. He shuddered and came awake with a jerk. Opening her eyes, she looked up to find guards rushing down the outer aisle toward them.

"Hurry!" Ashland squealed as she scrambled backward.

Still lying on the floor, Curan grabbed the bench beside him and flung it away. It collided with the next bench, spun over it, and struck the three guards in the lead. The column behind them came to a halt as Curan rose to his feet.

Blood covered the side of his head and most of his sword arm. Tall, powered by Chaos, and wearing a grim expression, he appeared like death walking. When his gaze met Ashland's, she gave him a grim nod.

"End this." The command carried a determined finality.

Curan bent, picked up his sword, and turned back to the assailants.

The remaining four guards shuffled past the broken bench, then advanced with their swords ready. Curan crouched and waved toward them with his shield. The four soldiers took a step, and then another. Curan reached down and grabbed his helmet with his shield hand. Rather than put it on, he flung it with a backhand flick. The helmet smashed into one man's face, the force lifting him off his feet and sending him crashing into the mess of benches. His body settled and did not move.

Three men remained. As one, those three men attacked.

Curan blocked one strike with his shield, another with his sword, but the third caught his shield-side shoulder, slicing it open. He staggered back, holding his arm to his side. The men attacked again, but he shuffled backward, forcing Ashland to dart out the side door into the antechamber. Curan turned and followed, stopping just inside the room with his back to the wall. When the first man crossed the threshold, Curan ran him through. The guard fell to his knees and tipped forward in a pool of blood.

The other two guards backed away and then disappeared. Ashland waited for two panting breaths, and saw nothing, heard nothing.

"I can't see them," she said to Curan, who still had his back to the wall.

"I'll go," he said, his face twisted in a grimace.

Her gaze went to his bloody shoulder. "Let me heal you, first."

"Sorry. Can't wait."

He spun, dove through the door, and rolled to his feet, ready for an attack.

"They're running for the door," he said.

Hearing that, Ashland ran back into the room. "Let them go. We must help Wharton."

She rushed past the benches and found Wharton lying face-down in the center aisle, amidst seven dead guards. Squatting, she rolled him over. His face was streaked red, his side wet with blood. When she put her hand on his head and extended herself, she found his life force dim and weak. Gently, she coaxed his source of Order to heal the wound in his side but was forced to stop before she pushed him too far.

The throne room was quiet – eerily silent until Samantha spoke.

"Is he dead?" she asked with tears in her voice.

"No. Not yet, at least." Ashland stood and turned to Curan. "This time, you will remain until I heal you." She put her hand on his arm. "That's an order."

A shiver ran through him as the healing completed. Opening her eyes, Ashland looked up and found Curan's eyes glazed over, staring into nothing. His stomach growled noisily, demanding food to compensate for the healing.

"Are you all right?" Ashland asked with a soft voice.

Curan blinked and looked down at her. "The stories my father told me about his battles against the Horde – they had always seemed so glorious, heroic. It was what I imagined when I left Mondomi to join ICON." He shook his head and a tear tracked down his cheek. "But this…this is horrible. Killing men…women. The fighting, the dying, all for what? Power? Conflicting beliefs?" He shook his head. "I don't understand. There has to be a better way."

Ashland leaned forward and hugged the young man who reminded her so much of his father.

"I'm sorry, Curan. While we didn't make the world the way it is, we can still try to make it better." Her voice fell to a whisper. "I pray that one day, we will again find peace without abandoning our freedom."

29

A FLASH

The sun hung low in the west, hidden somewhere behind the castle-topped peak above the valley where Brandt and Quinn waited. Through a narrow gap in the trees, Brandt spotted guards patrolling the distant parapets, holding weapons that might be cross-bows. The surrounding forest was quiet. Too quiet. It left him feeling as if someone were watching, just beyond his view. Quinn's hushed voice came from above him, disturbing the silence.

"I see a wagon coming."

She began a careful descent down the thickly branched pine she had used for her perch. When she reached the bottom branch, she hung for a moment while he wrapped his arms about her legs and then lowered her down.

"The wagon is still on the downslope, so we have few minutes before it arrives." Quinn looked at her hands, covered in dark splotches. "Ugh. Sap. Now, my hands are going to be sticky the rest of the night."

"You can worry about that later." He glanced toward the cluster of rumberry bushes where they had hidden their packs. If he stared hard, he could see the straps of the packs, the leather of the water skins. *Unless someone comes in here, knowing where to look, they'll never find them.*

Brandt waved for Quinn to follow. "Come on. Let's get the tree in place before they reach us." He hurried to the thick end of the downed tree, the roots raw and frayed from Quinn hacking at them with her sword. "Grab the other end of the tree so we are ready before they reach us."

Quinn moved beside the tree, gripping the trunk three quarters of the way up. "Ready and...lift."

Brandt grunted from the weight, gripping two thick roots tightly as he waddled, following Quinn as she crossed the road. When he reached the hole they had dug, he let the trunk fall, the thud of the landing tree joined by a grunt of relief from his lips. As Quinn set her end down at the other side of the road, Brandt scooped some damp soil from the hole and squeezed it against the frayed roots to hide them. Stepping back, he nodded, happy with his work.

"Looks good." Quinn noted as she settled beside him. "They'll think it just toppled during the storm."

He dusted his hands off and showed them to her. "See. You're not the only one with dirty hands."

"Yeah, but yours aren't sticky."

"I prefer to keep it that way." He spun about. "Come on. Let's get into position."

They walked through the woods, moving further downhill, and the road soon reappeared. Brandt reached the forest edge and peeked out to verify that the downed tree remained hidden around the bend in the road. He then joined Quinn, both of them squatting behind a clump of shrubs. After withdrawing a chunk of glowstone, he traced a symbol on his hand before turning to Quinn.

"Give me your hand."

Her hand went to her chest, her face appearing shocked. "You're asking for my hand already?" A devious smile bloomed on her face. "My, you are an eager one, aren't you?"

"How droll." He shook his head. "You know what I mean."

She held her hand out to him, palm down. He drew the same rune on her and pocketed the stone. Closing his eyes, he grappled for Chaos and latched on, drawing in as much as he could handle. He then poured a portion of the Chaos into his own rune before shifting to the symbol on Quinn's hand. The remainder of the Chaos rushed out, and her rune began to glow while his pulsed and faded. Exhaustion hit him and left him weak. His stomach flipped as gravity's hold loosened – an effect of the augmentation.

A rumble arose from the forest, joined by the clopping of hooves and the squeak of wheels. The wagon rolled into view. Brandt and Quinn watched it through gaps in the shrubs as it rolled past them. Two Empire guards, a man and a woman, flanked the wagon driver. As the wagon rounded the corner and the obstacle came into view, the driver pulled the reins and drew the horses to a stop.

"Downed tree," the driver said.

"I can see that. I'm not blind," the female guard quipped.

The male guard added, "Must have fallen during yesterday's storm."

"Well," the driver said, "are you two going down there to move it, or are we sitting here all night?"

With some grumbling, the two guards climbed out of the wagon and walked toward the tree. Brandt tugged on Quinn's hand and gave her a nod. The two crept around the shrubs, through the long grass beside the road, and scurried to crouch behind the wagon before the guards reached the tree.

Sitting, they each pulled themselves beneath the wagon. Brandt then hooked his feet over the front axle, gripped the rear axle tightly, and lifted himself off the ground. With his weight drastically reduced, it took little effort. Glancing to his right, he found Quinn in a similar position – off the ground and ready.

The guards returned and climbed into the wagon, causing it to wobble and shake. Moments later, they were moving, the ground rolling past just inches below Brandt and Quinn.

With gravity's pull a fraction of what was normal, Brandt was able to support himself with little effort. Twice, they came across rocks that jutted above the road's surface and scraped his backside, causing him to wince and nearly let go. Minutes passed, and, even at his reduced weight, he began to tire. By the time the wagon reached the mountain-top, his muscles were cramping, his arms shaking at the effort.

Brandt watched the outer wall roll past as the wagon entered the castle grounds. Within, he found an open dirt courtyard with hay bales lined along one wall. Holes dotted the white and red targets secured to the hay. Soldiers moved about the space, some in rank, others strolling about freely. The wagon circled to the side and entered an outbuilding before the driver pulled the reins.

"Whoa. Easy, now," he crooned as the workhorses drew to a stop.

The two soldiers climbed out. "That's it for us. We're off for the night, Dillard. We'll see you next time we draw escort duty."

"Have a good night, Jira. Seward."

The guards walked away as the driver climbed down and began to unhook his team. With the first horse free, the man led it further into the massive stable. Brandt relaxed his arms and let out a sigh as he lay on the dirt floor.

Quinn elbowed him. "Come on. We need to hurry."

Obeying, Brandt rolled out from beneath the wagon and surveyed his surroundings.

Another half-dozen wagons waited nearby, all empty and lacking horses. Carts lined another wall, some of which held metal parts, some held tools, others stood empty.

Brandt scurried around a neighboring wagon and ducked down while Quinn settled beside him. He then noticed a small storage closet, the door halfway open. Through the doorway, he could see a pitchfork, a pair of shovels, and enough space for him and Quinn. Slinking in, he waited for Quinn to join him, and then he closed the door, leaving it open just a sliver.

"What do we do now?" she asked, her voice a whisper in the dark.

"How should I know?"

"This was your plan."

"My plan only involved our getting onto the castle grounds. The rest...well...we will just have to improvise."

"Suggestions?"

He considered the original plan to make their move at night. It was still the best idea he had to offer. "It will be nightfall soon. Whatever we do, it will be easier to move about without notice when it's dark. Besides, I need time to recover. I suspect we'll need magic to pull this off."

"Fine. We'll wait, then." She nudged him in the stomach. "Was that so difficult?"

"You know, you can be awfully frustrating sometimes."

"I'm a female."

"What's that supposed to mean?"

"It means I am supposed to be mysterious and bewildering to boys like you."

He snorted. "Well, you are doing a stellar job of it."

"Thank you."

"That wasn't a compliment."

She elbowed him again, this time driving the air from his lungs and ending the conversation.

—⊶ ⏀ ⊷—

From the barn interior, Brandt peeked around the doorframe and found it dark outside. Glowlamps mounted atop the exterior wall shone in the night and offered enough light to navigate the castle grounds. The courtyard appeared empty save for a cluster of guards near the gate, deep in conversation. Movement upon the wall drew Brandt's attention as a patrolling guard eclipsed one of the glowlamps. If there were one guard up there, he expected there were others.

"Is it clear?" Quinn whispered from behind him.

"Yeah." He gave her hand a tug. "Let's go."

He slipped around the corner and hurried along the wall, feeling very much exposed. At the first corner, he turned and melted into the shadows with Quinn a step behind. A path between the stables and the castle led to an open stairwell. Brandt crept up it with Quinn following, both crouching low during the ascent and slowing as they reached the top. A brief peek over the wall revealed a rooftop patio with a fire pit at the center. Chairs surrounded the pit, and all were empty as was the patio. A waist-high wall with crumbling sections surrounded the patio.

He climbed the last few steps and padded toward a pair of glass-paned doors. The curtains inside were open, the room dark.

Brandt tested the door. "Locked. Give me your knife, and I'll break the window."

"That won't be necessary."

He turned toward her. "What else do you suggest?"

Step aside," Quinn slid past and knelt before the lock.

He watched in curiosity as she produced a pair of needles and inserted the first into the lock. Her focus was intense, her movements careful and slight until a faint click came from the lock. She slid another needle into the lock while holding the first in place. Again, she focused, shifted a fraction, and produced a click. She hefted her dagger, the tip sliding into the slot and turning the lock a half rotation. With the dagger and needles returned to the sheath strapped to her leg, Quinn turned the handle.

"Who knew you were such a rogue?" he said.

Quinn smiled, her teeth tinted blue in the light of the distant glowlamps, her voice a whisper. "There is much you have yet to learn about me, my Prince." She then opened the door and slid inside.

Brandt gently closed the door and surveyed the dark, quiet room. Praying they had not stumbled into an occupied bedroom, he dug out his chunk of glowstone, the pale light giving shape to their surroundings.

It was a spacious chamber, expansive enough for royalty. Six tables occupied the room, each covered in sheets of paper. Upon closer inspection, Brandt found drawings of various contraptions on the nearest tables. Each drawing contained notations, many with numbers and calculations that made his head hurt when he tried to follow them.

Deciding he wouldn't learn anything from the diagrams, he looked up and found Quinn with her ear to the door. As he crossed the room, she cracked it open. A sliver of blue light streamed through the opening, growing brighter as she eased the door wider. She peeked out briefly before closing it and turning toward him.

"The corridor is empty. Let's go."

Brandt trailed her through the door into a narrow corridor. A glowlamp on the opposite wall lit the center while the corners where the hallway turned remained dark. The smell of burnt metal hung in the air, reminding him of the Forge back in the Arcane Ward. He pocketed the glowstone and considered their next step.

"Which way?" she whispered.

He gestured to his left. "That way goes deeper into the castle."

Quinn crept down the hallway, put her back against the wall, and peeked around the corner. She then slipped around it with Brandt following close behind.

This corridor was far longer than the first, with evenly spaced doors lining one wall. The other wall ended after a few strides before it became a waist-high railing. Quinn moved to the railing and ducked to peer between the balusters. When Brandt joined her, he discovered where the scent of burnt metal originated.

Before him was an expansive courtyard, open to the night sky. A hundred feet across from him, two levels of open corridors mirrored the one where they crouched. The wood along both terraces appeared newly replaced, far newer than the castle itself.

The courtyard was filled with metal workings in various states. In the center of the room were a pair of massive forges, their coals glowing orange and heating the area despite the chilly evening air. A pile of rectangular iron ingots and bins of black coal stood along the wall beyond the forges. Casting blocks of various sizes were stacked beside the coal bins. Four massive anvils stood beside the forges, surrounded by worktables – all filled with metalworking tools. Three flash cannons, each in a different state of assembly, rested atop carts positioned beside the workstations.

A dozen men worked below, busily securing narrow metal tubes to odd wooden handle assemblies, forming a weapon Brandt had never before seen. They all wore leather aprons over stained, blue tunics. Black soot and burn scars marked the men's arms and faces.

A short, portly man with a balding head of dark hair strolled in. He wore a stained white smock with an Order rune on his left breast. The man in white stopped and spoke to the workers, his voice only just audible.

"...enough for the day. Get yourself some food, and I'll see you in the morning."

A few of the men nodded, set their half-assembled weapons down, and strolled out of view. The others continued working for another minute, finishing their assemblies before following the first group out the door. The portly man in white remained, inspecting completed weapons and jotting down notations on a tablet he carried. He set the tablet on the table and collected a handful of small metallic objects from a workbench before turning toward the door. When he faded from view, Quinn leaned close to Brandt.

"How do we destroy all of this?" she whispered.

"I don't know. I see a LOT of metal. It will take something impressive...and a lot of heat."

"Well, let's go."

"Go where?"

She looked at him, her eyes as hard as steel. "Down there."

He wanted to ask her if she was crazy, if there was some other plan they might try, but he saw her determination and knew there was no talking her out of it. Restraining his sigh, he nodded.

Quinn scurried over to the brick column that supported the ceiling above them. She climbed over the rail and began lowering herself down the column to the terrace below. He looked down with a grimace. *This would be easier if the Reduce Gravity augmentation was still in effect. However, I might need my magic for something else soon...something more desperate.*

Having no other option, he climbed over the rail, lowered himself until he was hanging by his hands, and wrapped his legs around the column before shimmying down. By the time he was on the second floor, she was already dropping to the courtyard below. Likewise, he lowered himself until he was hanging by his hands, and he let go.

Despite his attempt to land lightly, the thud of his boots striking the stones of the courtyard floor made him wince. She held her finger to her lips, and he shrugged in response. He spotted a wooden barrel in the corner that had been hidden from view when they were on the terrace above. The barrel lid was painted bright red. Beside it were shelves lined with unfamiliar metal and wood weapons.

In the direction where the Imperial workers had headed was an open door, painted green. Shelves stood beside the door, most of which were filled with bronze-capped glass jars arranged in padded wicker baskets. The only other visible doors stood at the opposite end of the courtyard, both painted red.

Quinn moved beside a table, peering closely at the items that lay upon it. Four glass jars and cast bronze components rested there. Some of the bronze parts were smaller than one of her lock picks. Others matched the diameter of the jars. A basket with eight woven pockets, each the right size to hold a jar, rested on a cart beside the workbench.

A noise came from beyond the open door, and they both ducked, hiding behind the nearest workbench. From his position near the floor,

Brandt watched a pair of feet bustle across the room, straight toward them. The man paused just to the other side of the bench.

"Oh, there it is," the man mumbled.

Circling the bench, he picked up the tablet and his eyes widened – beady eyes behind rounded spectacles. Those eyes locked with Brandt's. The man and Brandt both froze.

In a flash, Quinn lunged past Brandt, her fist striking the man in the throat. He dropped the tablet and staggered backward with his hands around his neck, choking. A roundhouse kick followed. The heel of her boot struck the man's head and sent his spectacles spinning to the floor, broken glass shards scattering. The force of her kick spun him around a full circle. He staggered, collapsed, and splayed out on the floor. There, he remained, unmoving.

"Run!" she said.

Panicked, they bolted past the forges and toward the red doors at the far end of the room. Reaching one, Quinn eased the door open to reveal a dark room beyond. From that narrow opening came an unsavory smell that reminded Brandt of rotten eggs. She opened the door further, the orange light from the forges illuminating the room to reveal more barrels, both large and small. Beside the barrels were two wagons, both containing broken chunks of rock.

Curious, Brandt moved closer to the wagons. Something in the rocks sparkled, reflecting light as if filled with bits of metal. His eyes narrowed in thought as he turned toward the barrels, the lids painted red.

"This is it," Brandt said, nodding.

"This is what?"

Brandt pointed at the wagon before him. "The sparkling rock. It's what they use to make flash powder." He shook his head in disbelief. "We found their supply. I bet the barrels are filled with it as well."

Quinn's gaze swept the room. "There is no way out of here. We either have to climb up and leave the way we came in, or we need to go out the green doors."

Brandt's mind raced as he considered their options. They needed to destroy this place, but he didn't wish to die in the process. More importantly, he wanted to keep Quinn safe. His gaze landed upon the barrels and a plan coalesced.

"I have an idea. It's risky, but it might buy us enough time to escape." He held his open hand toward her. "Give me your knife."

Quinn drew the knife and set it in his palm. He moved close to one of the smaller barrels, lifted the knife high and thrust it down, the tip burying in the lid with a thud. Three more times, he struck the lid, each strike stinging his wrist. The result created splintered slots in a narrow area.

"What are you doing?" Quinn demanded in a hushed voice.

"Breaking this barrel open."

Again, he jammed the knife into the lid, cracking it. Another strike sent splinters and a thin puff of dark powder into the air. With the knife wedged in the hole, he rocked it back and forth, opening the hole wider before returning it. He then shifted behind the barrel and put his boot heel against it. A shove rocked the barrel. Another shove, timed properly, tipped it over. Dark powder spilled out on the floor as the barrel rocked and settled.

"Now what?" Quinn asked.

"Now, you help me roll this across the room out there."

Shrugging she shifted behind the barrel, the two of them rolling it out the door. It rumbled as it rolled, making more noise than Brandt intended, but he had no better ideas. As they rolled it past the iron ingots and bins of coal, dark powder continued to leak from the hole in the lid, leaving a trail to the storage room behind them. They steered clear of the forges, keeping the barrel and the trail of flash powder as far from the fire as possible. Brandt imagined a spark from a popping coal falling into the flash powder, the blast taking them and everything else with it. That thought was running through his mind when Quinn abruptly stopped the barrel.

"Where is he?" Quinn's voice was thick with panic.

"What? Who?"

"What do you mean, who?"

Before he could reply, a staccato of hurried footsteps came from beyond the open door ahead.

Three soldiers ran into the courtyard with swords brandished. They raced past the workbenches as Quinn drew her swords, the ring of her weapons like an answer to a challenge. She leaped over the barrel to meet them, spinning to knock the lead sword aside with one blade, her trailing blade slicing the bicep of the man holding it. He cried out, dropped his sword, and stumbled backward while the other two attacked.

Brandt circled to the side and kicked at a sword arm, redirecting a strike intended for Quinn's blindside. The soldier launched a backhand swing, and Brandt leaped backward to avoid it. Another swing forced him further back, and he scrambled around the barrel to get clear.

Brandt's attacker turned toward Quinn, who was fighting with the third soldier. Her swords flashed in a flurry as she blocked her opponent's strikes. Ducking and spinning, she sliced across her opponent's thigh, drawing a cry of pain. The other soldier thrust his sword toward her, which she narrowly dodged. With Quinn outnumbered, Brandt rushed back in to help.

He leaped, kicking the back of one man's head before the soldier could strike again. The man staggered, and Quinn's blade flashed, taking the guard's sword hand off. He stumbled backward, holding the bloody stump with horror etched on his face. Brandt spun with a high kick, striking the side of the wounded man's head and sending him stumbling to the floor. When Brandt turned around, the third soldier was lying in a pool of blood, his thighs bleeding, his throat slit. The guard with the missing hand lay beside him, either unconscious or dead. The third man, the one with the sliced arm, was nowhere in sight.

"Back to the barrel." Brandt's voice squeaked with an edge of panic. "We don't have much time."

He and Quinn shifted behind it, ready to push it further, but they were interrupted when more soldiers ran into the room – many more soldiers, fanning out with weapons drawn. Some held those odd metal tubes with wooden handles, the weapons pointed toward Brandt and Quinn. A boom and a flash of green blasted from one of the tubes, and something struck the metal band of the barrel, narrowly missing Brandt's hand. The impact created a spark as the projectile sailed past and hit the stack of iron ingots with a deep clang.

"Stop!" The portly man in white reappeared, emerging between the line of guards. The side of his face was bloody and swollen from

Quinn's roundhouse kick. "Don't fire the muskets! That barrel is filled with flash powder. You'll kill us all if it ignites!"

The guards, more than twenty in all, began to advance. With her short swords still drawn, Quinn put her boot against the barrel and gave it a hard shove, the barrel rolling toward the guards. She then knelt with her swords pointed toward the stone floor, the tips touching the trail of metallic powder.

"Come any closer and I'll create a spark. It will be the last thing you ever do."

The guards stopped dead in their tracks. The barrel slowed, its path curving until it came to rest against the furthest workbench, a few short strides in front of the guards.

"Jarlish!" A male guard with stripes on his tabard looked toward the man in the white smock – the same man Quinn had knocked out. "What do you suggest?"

Jarlish scowled at Quinn. "Don't attack. She's right."

The portly man shuffled beyond the line of guards and spread his hands out. "Surely, you don't want to die, young lady," he crooned. "Tell us what you want, and I'm sure we can come to an accommodation."

Quinn's steely gray eyes narrowed and she sneered. "I don't..."

Brandt's hand on her shoulder stopped her mid-sentence. She looked up at him as he shifted in front of her with his back turned to the enemy soldiers. Moving discreetly, he drew his coal out and traced a rune on the palm of his hand with her watching.

"What are you doing?" Anger was apparent in her voice, despite the hushed volume. "We must destroy this place, even if we go with it." She frowned, staring at his hand. "I don't know that rune."

"It's new. I'm going to try something...something dangerous. If it works, we may get out alive. If not...you know what to do." He took a deep breath, gathering his courage. "Whatever happens, I want you to know that you *have* stolen my heart. More importantly, I don't want it back."

He stared into her eyes and saw the steel of her spirit, a strength that inspired him. His pulse hammered in his ears, his breathing ragged as he allowed the tension of the moment to overcome him. With closed eyes, he sought Chaos, and it welcomed him with a heated embrace. The raw tumult of energy filled him, his veins on fire, his eyes bulging as he opened them and looked upon the Speed rune. As the energy poured from him, into the rune, exhaustion filled the vacuum. The rune pulsed, faded, and thunder struck.

The world flashed white. Brandt staggered to one knee. His vision cleared. Spittle flew from his lips, slowed, and stopped. No, it still fell, but at such a slow pace, the image held him captive. He gaped at it in wonder. He waved his hand beneath it, back and forth numerous times as it fell in a white trail, ever so slowly. His heart still hammered, a rapid beat matched by the surges of energy that ran throughout his body, causing his muscles to twitch as if they yearned to do something – anything.

He stood upright and turned toward the guards. They appeared frozen in place. Some even had their eyes closed. Frowning, he stared at them and wondered why everything had become so very silent. The eyes of one of the soldiers began to drift shut as if he were growing tired. In contrast, the guard beside him began to open his eyes at the same, drawn out pace. Like a fogged window wiped clean, the obscured view before Brandt became clear. *Those men are blinking*, he thought. *A blink for them is an eternity for me*. Realization of his advantage struck. He grinned, and he ran.

His steps were a blur, fluid and effortless. Rather than running toward his opponents, he ran back to the bin of coal and grabbed the shovel leaning against it. As quick as thought, he crossed the room and stopped before the enemy.

His attack began with a guard at one end, smashing the shovel into the man's hand. The sword arm moved during the contact and then froze, his grip loosening and the sword pointing toward the floor as it began to slip from his grip. Brandt moved to the next guard and drove the butt of the shovel handle into his stomach. The third received a blow to the head. The fourth had his legs swept out from beneath him. Brandt actually laughed aloud when he saw the man seemingly floating in the air, his body twisted in mid flop.

When Brandt came to a guard holding what Jarlish had called a musket, he saw a burst of green flame oozing from the barrel. From the flame, a black chunk of metal emerged, sailing toward Quinn. With a desperate upswing, he smacked the metal ball with the shovel blade, altering its path, the trajectory now toward the third-story balcony.

He spun and smacked the man with the musket in the head before continuing down the line. By the time he had dealt a blow to each of the armed guards, the sword tip of the first man was striking the floor. Brandt's grin resurfaced. *This is fun.*

The twenty-two guards were all in various states of succumbing to his attack – some doubled over as if about to vomit, others collapsing with their faces etched in pain, others hanging in the air, horizontal as they fell. *They are helpless against me.* He then remembered his mission, and the grin slid away. *We need to destroy this place and get out of here.*

Bolting toward the heart of the courtyard, Brandt stopped before a forge. He stuck his shovel into the coals, shying his face away in the process. The heat was intense. When he withdrew the shovel, orange glowing coals rested on the blade. He turned and walked back to where Quinn waited, still kneeling with her blades pressed against the floor. A glance toward the guards revealed some now striking the floor, joining weapons that already lay there.

Brandt lifted the shovel high over the trail of flash powder. With a prayer on his lips, he tilted it and released the hot coals. He tossed the shovel aside, turned toward Quinn, and lifted her up. It took some wrangling to get her over his shoulder without cutting himself on her swords. He then turned to find the coals, still falling, now four feet above the floor. *It's time to run.* So he ran.

He shot the gap between the falling guards, sped out the door, and flew into a hallway with a number of doors on each side, some of them open. Shop workers stood in one doorway, peering toward the courtyard he had just vacated. More guards were at the far end of the corridor, a man and a woman both frozen in mid stride as they ran into the building. He slowed and slid behind the running guards, through the open door, and found himself outside.

The portcullis was a quarter of the way lowered, and he panicked. *They are trying to seal the castle!*

With Quinn still on his shoulder, he ran toward the gate in a blur until the world lurched, coming back to life. The portcullis dropped a few feet, and a rush of noise arose. As quickly as it had begun, the noise stopped, replaced by hollow silence when the portcullis slowed and the world froze in place. He continued running, fearful that the augmentation was fading. Another lurch and the gate fell further, the clatter of the chains a roar. The guards turned toward him, alarm in their eyes as they, again, froze. The gate was mere strides away, and he ran harder, but experienced another lurch, this one more dramatic. As if waking from a dream, the world came back to life – a fast, furious, and noise-filled existence. The energy fled from Brandt and left him gasping, staggering as he stumbled through the gate.

The portcullis slammed down a step behind him, the force of it knocking a blade from Quinn's hand. A massive series of thumping explosions erupted from the castle. A blast of heat struck Brandt from behind, the concussion of the blast shaking his bones. He fell face-first, dumping Quinn to the road with an "Oof."

The world darkened, and the darkness called to him. Exhaustion held his body captive and left him unable to move. Quinn shifted beneath him and pushed him off her. He rolled to his back, opened his eyes, and blinked. Stars dotted the evening sky, beyond an orange glow from the castle ground. His thoughts were sluggish, his vision clouded, as if he were half-asleep. When he turned his head, he found the wall a short distance away, the sky above it churning with smoke lit by the raging inferno beneath it. To his other side, Quinn was rising to her feet, holding a sword in one hand, her head in the other. A section of the castle appeared in the sky, spinning as it fell and landed in the brush beside the road. The thump of it striking the ground was massive, reigniting the urgency within Brandt.

With a concerted effort, he rolled over and rose to his hands and knees. His breath was ragged, his muscles weak – shaking as if he had not eaten in days. Looking through the portcullis, he saw a tower of flames, hundreds of feet in the sky. The men on the wall began shouting. Brandt tried to stand and fell. Quinn's hand appeared. He gripped it, allowing her to help him to his feet.

"What happened? How'd we escape?" Quinn asked as he rose to his feet.

"I'll explain later." He placed his feet in a broad stance, wobbling. "We need to get out of here."

She turned toward the wall as the shouts resumed. Her eyes grew wide, and she scurried back to the downed portcullis to retrieve her fallen sword. She sheathed them both before turning toward him. A loud bang came from atop the wall and Quinn cried out, staggering as she held her arm. She hurried toward him, and he saw blood dripping from her shoulder.

"Run!" She said as she passed him.

Brandt hobbled forward, down the hillside road. He moved as fast as he could muster, but his strength was sapped, his energy a shadow of what was normal.

Quinn looked back at him, still holding her arm as she ran down the hill. Another shot echoed in the night, joined by the squeaking pulleys from the portcullis rising. After rounding a bend, they reached a point where the road branched.

"Which way?" Quinn slowed at the intersection.

"Let's try the left route," he shouted as he caught up to her.

She bolted left and continued down the hill with him trailing behind. Down and down, they went, him thankful to have gravity's assistance while also concentrating on keeping his feet under him, fearful of falling face-first. Doing so would likely be a death sentence.

Shouts arose behind them, growing louder. Brandt wanted nothing more than to lie down and rest. If Quinn hadn't been with him, he might have done just that. Since she needed him, he ran.

A few minutes later, the ground began to level and another sound emerged – a low rush. *Water*, he thought. *I hear water*. He was thirsty. So thirsty. Water sounded wonderful.

More shouts came from behind him, drawing even closer.

The sound grew louder as a river came into view, white rapids visible in the starlight. The river ran along the road, and Brandt kept looking toward it, his thirst demanding to be quenched. He noticed an oddly shaped silhouette resting along the bank. Slowing, he stared toward it until he realized what it was.

"Quinn," he gasped as he came to a stop. She stopped and turned around as he pointed toward the river. "There's a boat. Let's take it. I can't run any longer."

Without a word, she ran toward the boat with Brandt scrambling to reach it. He gripped one side of the bow, pushing while she pushed from the other side. It took a bit of rocking, but they freed it from the bank and slid the stern into the water.

"Get in," he said.

Quinn climbed in and sat as he pushed, stepping into the water before he jumped atop the bow, balancing with his stomach on the lip. Using his last tendrils of energy, he pulled himself forward and fell in.

The current swept them away. Shouts arose.

"They took the boat! Shoot them!"

A bang in the night was joined by a thud when a shot hit the boat. Quinn ducked, joining Brandt on the floor of the rowboat. More shots rang out, another hitting the side of the boat, more splashing into the river. The shouts soon faded and were replaced by the soothing rush of water. Exhaustion overcame Brandt's fear, and sleep welcomed him

30

COLOSSUS

R hythmic bursts of air puffed from the Chaos pump, the sound echoing off the walls of the barren stone chamber. Everson stared into the steaming bath waters, watching the trail of bubbles rising to the surface. A chain of interconnected bamboo ran from the pump, into the water, bending and flexing as Henrick repeatedly crossed the deep end of the pool.

After ten minutes below the water's surface, the metal and glass dome that encased Henrick's head popped up with water spilling from it. His shoulders and torso followed as he strode into the shallow end of the pool. When Henrick reached the water's edge, he unbuckled the straps that secured the oversized helmet to the harness he wore. He then gripped the helmet, twisted it a quarter turn, and lifted it off his head, the bamboo tubing connected to the rear of the helmet coming with it.

Henrick shook his head as he set the helmet on the floor beside the pool. "It worked wonderfully. Your Chaos-charged air pump is exactly what I needed. I never once struggled to breath."

Everson moved to the pump and flipped a lever, the pump falling quiet. "I'm glad to have helped. I was sure that compressing air into the tubes would alleviate the breathing problem you were facing."

Climbing the stairs, Henrick sat at the edge of the bath and began removing the harness. "Yes, before this, I'd find myself gasping after about a minute and was ready to faint after two minutes. That just wouldn't be enough time to explore a wreck."

Everson's gaze shifted to Henrick's odd boots, dangling in the water. "It appears that the added weight helped as well."

Henrick lifted a leg, grunting as the boot emerged from the water. The soles were four inches thick. "Yes. The buoyancy now appears balanced. The Increase Gravity Infusion was exactly what I needed. The boots aren't too heavy to walk with while under water, but they weigh enough to keep me on the ocean floor."

With the harness unstrapped, Henrick set it aside, his wet tunic now clinging to his overweight body. He then began loosening the straps on his weighted boots. While watching this, Everson pictured Henrick walking on the ocean floor, trailed by a length of Elastic infused bamboo tubing.

"You'll need more augmented bamboo to make the air lines long enough for deeper dives," Everson noted.

"That should be easy enough. I have the bamboo, I just need the augmentations applied." Henrick's face twisted in a grimace as he pulled on a boot, grunting. It popped free and he set it on the floor beside the harness. "My main concern is getting back to the surface when I'm eighty feet down."

Everson considered the idea and thought of the lifts he had installed in the Atrium. The same mechanism wouldn't work under water. However, the water's natural buoyancy might make it easier to lift the weight. His gaze fell on the air pump and an idea struck. "We could build a Chaos-powered winch. With a rope connected to your harness, someone above the water could engage the winch and lift you up."

With the second boot removed, Henrick stared at Everson, his eyes narrowed. Finally, he nodded. "Yes. That could work." A grin crossed Henrick's face. "It's happening, Ev. My dream of exploring the ocean depths is coming to fruition." He stood, his wet clothes dripping water on the stone floor. "Just think of what might be waiting down there. Reefs. Fish. Sea life we know nothing about. And, best of all, shipwrecks."

A chuckle arose from Everson, feeding off Henrick's excitement. "It does sound amazing. You're right about shipwrecks. I bet there are ships that sank a thousand or more years ago. Just imagine what we might learn from them." Everson removed the clamp that secured the air lines to the pump, handing the tubing to Henrick, who began to gather it in coils. "We know little of civilization's history from before the founding of the Empire. That event was little more than two hundred years ago." Excitement about the idea began to bubble inside him, capturing his imagination.

"Yes. You understand." A grin spread across Henrick's face, and he clapped Everson on the back. "Now you see it – why this has been my dream for years. Not only can we explore an entire new world under the sea, but we can also explore mankind's past."

"Well, it's a valid pursuit, Henrick. Despite the nasty events transpiring in the world, I am glad to see someone focused on advancing our knowledge of the world and of ourselves. I'm glad I could help, if even just for a bit."

Henrick nodded. "Thanks again, Everson." He turned and stored his diving gear into a crate. Bending down, he lifted the crate, grunting and staggering under the weight. "I'll come back later for the boots."

Everson scooped his hands beneath the air pump, held it with both arms, clutching it to his chest, and headed toward the exit. Opening the door, he held it while Henrick hurried past. The duo then walked along the basement corridor, past the interrogation rooms, and to the stairwell. Henrick led Everson down the main floor corridor. Stopping outside a storage room, Henrick set the crate down and unlocked the door.

The door swung open to reveal a small storage room. Shelves lined one wall, housing earlier attempts at underwater helmets and a few other odds and ends. A coil of bamboo tubing hung beside the shelves, above a workbench covered by various hand tools.

Henrick pushed the tools aside and gestured toward the bench. "You can leave the pump here."

Everson placed the pump on the bench, happy to be free of the weight. The pump wasn't big, but it was made of metal – cylinders, a flywheel, actuators, and housing – and that added to its load. A Chaos-charged chunk of stone also powered the pump, a chunk sizeable enough that Everson expected it could run for days before it needed a new charge.

"I had best head back to the Forge." Everson moved to the open doorway, glancing backward. "Ivy will have my hide if I make her work alone the whole day." A reflection on the floor drew his attention. "Don't slip on the puddle you just created."

Henrick looked down at his bare feet. "Yeah. I'll clean this up and change into some dry clothing."

Everson left Henrick's storage room and headed down the hall, his thoughts shifting toward his own project. It was still occupying his thoughts when he opened the door and entered the Forge.

Unoccupied work areas waited at the near end of the building. Everson paid them little attention, instead focusing on the massive machine that stood at the heart of it all. Other than Henrick, every gadgeteer at the Ward had been recruited to help finish the creation.

Ivy stood on a scaffold beside the invention, shouting out directions to an older gadgeteer named Julian. Short, scrawny, and petite, Julian had notably angular eyes and favored wearing an odd, cone-shaped hat with a wide brim, even when he was inside. Currently wearing said hat, the man stood at the controls of a steam-powered lift. When the customized catapult he was raising neared the pulley at the top, Julian stopped the motor and the object stopped rising. Two other engineers, a quiet woman named Frieda and a chunky man named Willard, pulled the guide rope and the pulley slid down the track, toward the scaffold where Ivy waited.

Everson stopped beside the scaffold and gazed upon the converted steam engine. The machine now appeared very different than it had before the project began. A second set of wheels now joined the first set, creating eight wheels in all. The outer band of each wheel had been modified, first with nubs that added traction, then with an Elastic augmentation that added grip and reduced road vibration.

His gaze rose to the massive metal plates covering the front of the contraption. That wedge, as Everson liked to call it, had been Ivy's idea. The Reduce Gravity and Elastic augmentations added to the wedge lightened the weight and made it almost indestructible.

"Easy, now." Ivy said in a loud, clear voice. "It's almost in position. And...stop!"

The two gadgeteers pulling the guide lines stopped. Ivy leaned in, checking the catapult's alignment. "Julian! Lower it carefully. Be ready to stop if I shout."

Julian flipped a lever, and the steam engine driving the lift squealed, sending puffs of white steam into the air. *And people wonder why the Forge is always so hot,* Everson thought.

The catapult lowered and suddenly dropped a foot.

"Easy!" Ivy shouted. "Only a few more inches." She pushed on it, straining as it moved sideways. "Stop!"

Ivy reached into the satchel at her hip and removed four thick bolts as she noticed Everson watching. "Everson, I didn't see you come in. Would you mind coming up here to help me bolt this in place?"

Ugh. I should have thought of that. "Yes. I'll be right up."

He circled to the stairs at the far end of the scaffold. Taking high steps that made his mechanical legs whirr and hiss, he climbed up and joined her.

Ivy gave him a sidelong look while she extended her hand with two bolts in her grip. "I thought you might miss this entire stage of the project."

Everson's gaze dropped to the floor as she set the bolts in his palm. "I'm sorry. It's not that I wanted to miss it." *I have let her down.* The thought left a lump in Everson's throat. "Henrick has been working so hard," he explained, but the words seemed hollow. "He just needed a little help to pull the last bit together."

Her hand touched his arm, rubbing it gently.

"Don't worry, Ev." Her voice had quieted so only he could hear her. He looked up and found her brown eyes looking into his. "I was only giving you a hard time. I'm proud that you would set aside your own project to help Henrick...despite the rivalry he has with you."

Everson frowned. "Rivalry? I have no rivalry with him."

Ivy smiled. "Oh, I know *you* feel that way. The rivalry only exists in Henrick's own head." She leaned close and kissed him on the cheek before whispering, "You are too good a person, too selfless to consider Henrick or anyone else a rival. Perhaps your assistance will help Henrick change his perspective as well."

He found himself nodding. "Yes. A bit of his own success might be just what he needs."

Ivy smiled and squeezed his arm. "Enough talk of Henrick. Let's get this catapult installed."

Nodding, he shifted to one side of the machine and found the eyelets at the base slightly misaligned from the mounting brackets. He pushed on the catapult, straining to move it. The suspended machine moved just enough that he was able to slide a bolt through the hole. With one bolt in place, the others fit easily. Ivy produced four huge nuts from her satchel, and they each took turns tightening them with a big wrench. When the machine was completely mounted, the couple stood upon the scaffold to admire their work. The two-arm catapult was specially crafted, including the gears installed beneath each launch arm. Teeth from those small gears locked into the teeth of two larger gears poking out of the machine.

"I've decided to use the name you suggested," Everson announced.

She eyed him, her gaze carrying a warning. "*You* decided?"

He knew the look and hastily backpedaled. "I mean, I agree with your idea. I think *Colossus* is a wonderful name for *our* creation. It's much better than *Battle Carriage*."

A smile crossed her face, bringing Everson relief. He had dodged an arrow. "Battle Carriage is not horrible, but Colossus sounds more impressive, regardless of whose idea it was."

"True."

Her grin widened. "Just don't forget, it *was* my idea."

He laughed and wrapped an arm about her, pulling her against him. "I'm glad you came up with it. You've had as much to do with the construction of this metal monster as I have. In addition, just about every one of your ideas has been amazing."

"Just about?"

Everson hunched his shoulders. "Well, I still don't see how adding a privy to it is feasible."

She laughed, hitting playfully on the chest. "That was a joke."

"So you say…"

She nudged him in the stomach and spun from his grip. "It's time to climb down and wash up. Dinner will be ready soon."

Following her, he carefully backed down the steep stairs to the shop floor. Julian, Frieda, and Willard were already heading toward the exit. Ivy grabbed Everson's hand and pulled him toward the door, following the others. Before they reached it, Benny Hedgewick appeared in the doorway and stared toward the machine at the core of the room.

"Hello, Benny," Everson said in greeting.

Hedgewick's attention remained directed toward Colossus. "Your construction appears to be coming along nicely."

"Thank you, Master Hedgewick," Everson glanced toward his latest creation – an imposing mass of metal and magic. "We have a few more modifications to add, and it will be ready to test again."

"I will be interested to see the results," Hedgewick said as he turned toward Everson. "However, that is not why I stopped by."

"Go on."

"The mining expedition just returned from Selbin. They were able to gather some flash powder after all. In fact, half a wagon full is now waiting in the stables.

A grin spread across Everson's face. "That's wonderful news. In anticipation of a new supply of flash powder, I have been working on some drawings for a new flash bomb design."

Hedgewick's eyebrows shot up, cocking his spectacles askew. "Where are these drawings?"

"They are in my room," Everson shrugged. "Why do you ask?"

"Because, Everson." Hedgewick's hand gripped Everson's shoulder. "I wish to help you produce these new weapons. War is coming, and it's time for ICON's leaders to engage rather than allowing you wardens to have all the fun."

War is coming. The words repeated in Everson's mind. While he appreciated Benny Hedgewick's help, the statement left him cold. His mind turned to Quinn, and he found himself praying that he might see his sister again someday. *Please, Quinn. Please be safe.*

31

THE JOLTED JACKAROO

Quinn stirred, groaning when she shifted. Her arm throbbed mightily. It was cold, but she was damp with sweat. She opened her eyes, blinking at the blur of light above. Lifting her head, she found herself lying atop Brandt, who was still asleep in the bottom of the boat. The upper half of her sleeve was thick with blood – wet and sticky. Quinn knew she needed to stop the bleeding or she would die. Wincing at the pain, she tried to get up. Spots appeared in her vision as the world tilted and twisted, her stomach twisting with it. She collapsed, her vision narrowing to blackness.

— ✚ —

A strike against the back of her head jolted Quinn awake. She squeezed her eyes to the pain, groaning. Her own voice sounded distant. She felt cold – so cold. Opening her eyes, she saw the blur of a face looking down at her.

"Sorry," Brandt said. "I tried to be gentle, but you were lying on top of me."

Quinn mumbled. "My arm…it hurts so much. I'm so cold." Her eyes drifted closed. Keeping them open was difficult.

His voice came from somewhere distant "You have lost a lot of blood. Your wound looks...nasty."

She felt him draw the knife from the sheath on her leg. He lifted her arm, and she gasped, her eyes bulging in pain. Her breath wheezed, each desperate gasp an effort.

"Again, sorry. You have a metal slug in your arm. I have to cut it out."

Brandt pulled her sleeve away from her arm, the cloth sticking to her wound for a moment before it pulled free. Again, she gasped. The world was a blur of black and red, obscured by a curtain of agony. He cut the sleeve away and pulled it down her arm. Every movement sent a sharp ache up into her shoulder and drove tears from her eyes. The darkness pulled at her, attempting to drag her down with it. His voice was an anchor that she focused on as she tried to remain awake.

"Hold still. This is going to hurt."

The knife bit into her flesh and Quinn cried out. Pain overwhelmed her. The knife dug deeper, twisting. It was as if he were cutting through her arm. Her breathing grew more ragged, her teeth clenched tightly as darkness closed in.

⸺ ♦ ⸺

A deep gasp caused Quinn's back to arch, a shiver wracking her body. She blinked her eyes open and found Brandt looking down at her, his eyes filled with concern. The pain was gone, now replaced by a powerful hunger.

Taking deep, labored breaths as if she had just run for miles, Quinn sat up, the motion rocking the small boat. She looked at her arm to find it bare from her shoulder to her wrist, still stained with blood around the now healed wound.

"Thank Issal," he said while gently caressing her cheek with his thumb. "It worked." A tear tracked down his face.

She nodded. "Thank you."

"I was so afraid. You had lost a fair amount of blood, and infection had already set in. Your body was trying to fight it, but there is no fighting a chunk of dirty metal buried in your flesh." He wiped his face dry with his knuckles and sat back on the seat, releasing a sigh of relief, the movement again rocking the boat. He turned and picked up a metal bucket, handing it to her. "Drink. You had a fever and must be dehydrated."

Suddenly aware of a powerful thirst, Quinn eagerly accepted the bucket. The water was cold – cold and amazing. It poured down her chin and spilled down the front of her coat, but she didn't care. After downing what seemed like a gallon, she lowered the bucket and handed it back to him as she caught her breath.

"Where did you get the bucket?" she asked between gasps.

"It was in the boat, likely in case of the leak becoming worse."

Quinn looked past him and saw an inch or two of water in the stern, beyond the seat. She then realized that she was sitting in a shallow pool, perhaps a half inch deep. With a concerted effort, she pulled her legs beneath her and pushed herself to a squat, causing the boat to rock until she turned and sat beside him on the bench.

The river had widened, now over a hundred feet across. They were in a valley, surrounded by hills that drifted past. Turning to look backward, Quinn found the sun high above the peaks of the Sol Mai Mountains.

"I'm sure you're starving," Brandt said. "It's too bad we had to leave our packs behind."

Quinn snorted. "You have no idea. I'm so hungry, I would eat the packs themselves if I could chew them."

He put his arm around her. "You know, I have been trying to perform healing for years. Every attempt was a dismal failure...until now."

She leaned into him and gave him a kiss. "I'm thankful you were here with me...and that you were able to make it work."

His arm squeezed her, as if he were afraid of letting go. "Me, too. I...I couldn't bear it if you died."

Quinn struggled with a response. Without knowing what to say, she simply rested her head against his shoulder and closed her eyes. A long moment later, she lifted her head to look at him. His hair was a mess, his face stained with soot, dirt, and streaks of blood. Yet, he looked wonderful to her. When Brandt turned toward her, she gave him a smile.

The boat rounded a bend, and the river grew even wider as the hills became fields. Scattered buildings appeared along the both banks, the fields partially plowed as farmers worked in them. In the distance, a city loomed over the north side of the river. A pale wall surrounded the city, and a dirt road ran along the river, heading toward it. Before the city was an ancient bridge spanning the river, supported by intermittent stone pillars built upon small islands.

"That must be Yarth," Brandt dug the oar from beneath the bench. "We need to get off the river before we reach the bridge. They are sure to post guards there, and we don't need anyone connecting us with what happened back at Corvichi." He stuck the oar in the water and began to paddle. "Besides, where there's a city, there's food."

A thought occurred to her – one that posed a problem. "How are we going to buy food? Our money is with our packs, left in the woods back there."

"True." He continued to paddle, guiding the ship toward the north riverbank. "At least we have other things of value. One quick stop, and we'll have more than enough coin to pay for food and shelter."

She frowned. "What do we have?"

"Your two swords. We can sell one and earn enough coin to survive for a while."

Her hands darted to the two hilts. "My swords?" She frowned. "Why not something of yours?"

"Like what?" He looked down at himself. "My handsome looks?" He shook his head. "Don't worry, Quinn. We'll just sell one of them. You can replace it in the future. You might be surprised at how much one of those swords is worth." He arched a brow. "Unless you would rather rob somebody of their hard-earned coin."

"No. Thievery is not a path I'd choose, not with what's at stake." Quinn sighed, "We can sell a sword. However," She crossed her arms over her chest. "I plan to be angry with you for a while."

"Me? What did I do?"

She glared at him. "You're making me sell one of my babies."

He laughed while paddling, the boat now approaching the north shore. "Fine. You can be angry with me. I'll figure out a way to make it up to you."

A few minutes later, the boat nosed into a shallow bank and

stopped with a lurch. Quinn jumped out and pulled it forward another stride before Brandt set the oar down and climbed out.

They scaled the steeper portion of the riverbank, trampled through the reeds that grew there, and joined the quiet road that led to Yarth.

For a while, it was quiet with just the distant sound of a farmer chopping at the ground with a hoe. That sound faded and other sounds arose from the city – familiar sounds that reminded Quinn of her childhood in Cinti Mor. While she had embraced her new life – a life of danger and excitement – part of her yearned for a quieter, more peaceful existence. She wondered if the world would ever again allow her to retreat and have such a life.

It turned out that Brandt had been correct. Quinn's short sword was worth far more than she had realized. When the couple left the weapons shop in search of an inn, Quinn found herself feeling self-conscious about carrying so much gold. She couldn't recall holding a single gold piece in her entire life, and now she held five gold Imperials, gripping them so hard that her hand began to cramp.

Brandt led her to an inn named The Jolted Jackaroo. The sign above the door made Quinn chuckle, depicting the image of a startled bird with an egg shooting out its backside.

Opening the door, Brandt held it for Quinn and followed her inside. The inn was quiet, dark, and smelled of roasted lamb. Quinn's stomach rumbled angrily after the long, stressful night and the healing Brandt had performed. Only three among the inn's two dozen tables were occupied. Brandt chose an empty table, pulled a chair out for Quinn, and sat across from her. She exhaled a sigh of relief as she settled into the chair.

A middle-aged woman with brown hair in a bun bustled past them, carrying a plate of steaming food in each hand. "I'll be right with you."

"That smells wonderful," Quinn muttered.

"Yes, it does. I'm starving after yesterday's trail rations and nothing to break my fast this morning. If I'm this hungry, you must be famished."

Quinn nodded. "You have no idea. Don't be shocked if I begin to hallucinate and bite the waitress, just from the aroma."

He chuckled. "That would be interesting." His laughter subsided and he became serious. "We will need to check in with the Ward. They will want to hear of what happened and what we learned last night."

Quinn knew he was correct but didn't wish to acknowledge it. The past few months had begun to catch up to her – the stressful situations, rulers scheming, people dying. It often seemed as if she were juggling flash bombs, any miscalculation resulting in death – her death or that of many others. It would be wonderful to pause a moment and just be.

The waitress approached and stopped by the table, eying them doubtfully. "What will it be?"

Noting waitress's expression, Quinn appraised Brandt's appearance, observing the soot on his cheek, his blood-stained hands, his torn sleeve. She looked down at herself, missing one sleeve, her skin covered in dried blood. Her breeches were torn, knees stained with mud. She reached for the tail of hair hanging over her shoulder. It was matted, snarled, and greasy. *She must think we just crawled out of a dungeon.*

Brandt paid no apparent attention to the woman's look or her tone. "We'll take whatever you're serving for lunch, along with two glasses of wine…if you have it."

"We…do."

"Great. We'll need a room for the night as well."

The woman put her hands on her ample hips and arched a brow. "You have coin to pay for all this?"

He looked at Quinn, who realized she still held the gold in her fist. With her thumb, she slid one coin out, picked it up, and held it toward the waitress.

"I'm sure this will cover it."

The waitress's expression transformed, her eyes glistening as she reached for the coin, picked it from Quinn's grip, and slid it through the loose laces of her neckline. "Yes. That will do just fine. I'll be right back with your food."

The woman walked toward the kitchen, and Quinn reached out to grip Brandt's hand. Her voice was quiet, almost timid as she leaned forward and whispered, "Let's hold off a day before you contact your sister."

He looked down at his hand in hers. "Why? What's wrong?"

"I...we should take a day for ourselves...spend some time together...without worrying about kingdoms or empires or who lives and who dies."

His brow furrowed as he appeared to contemplate her request. "That sounds awfully irresponsible." His lips drew up in a smirk. "Perhaps I can be swayed to wait a day...or two...maybe longer."

Quinn smiled and squeezed his hand. "Two days sounds wonderful." Her eyes flicked toward the kitchen. "We paid her enough to stay for a week or more."

"If two days sounds wonderful, a week sounds amazing," his smirk widened into a full smile. "We have more gold left. I could take you shopping for some new clothes as well."

"You don't like my clothes?" She looked down at herself and grinned. "Thank Issal they are black. Even then, I look dreadful."

"Well, *I* would never say you look dreadful. Dirty, yes. Perhaps a bit disheveled, sure. Yet, you're still beautiful to me." He waved his hand before his face, pinching his nose. "The smell, however... Let's just say we both could use a bath."

Quinn laughed. Somehow, despite everything happening around them, she found herself happy to be with Brandt. That bit of happiness was just what she needed – a light in the dark times to come. Despite what they had accomplished, war was coming to Issalia.

That was a problem for another day.

EPILOGUE

Prince Broland stared out the window, watching white flakes drift down and spin when captured by an eddy. Once again, the ground outside the Nor Torin citadel was turning white as the snow began to gather. Over the previous few weeks, snow had fallen several times only to melt days later. He recalled the first such event, his initial experience with snow. It had given him a thin slice of joy, the first since Kony's betrayal. Now, the snow meant nothing more than cold and miserable weather. It left the world outside seeming as bleak as Broland felt on the inside.

His gaze shifted beyond the citadel walls, toward the harbor that lay below the city. Through the shifting white haze of snow, he found ships clogging the bay. It seemed as if they, too, simply desired shelter from the winter weather. Unfortunately, that would not be the case.

He absently scratched his itching cheek and rubbed at the new beard growing there. It had come in nicely around his mouth but still appeared patchy on his cheeks. After never allowing more than a few day's stubble in the past, he longed to shave it off. His father had made it clear that wasn't an option.

"A beard can give a man a new look, altering his appearance. Only those who know your face well will be likely to recognize you," his father had said. "At this point, we need every advantage possible."

In contrast to Broland's beard-in-progress, his father's beard had grown in thick to the point that he had to already been forced to trim it.

The door opened behind him, drawing Broland from his musing.

"It's time," his father said as he entered the room. "Are you ready?"

"Do we really have to leave," Broland gestured toward the window, "in this weather?"

King Brock crossed the room, grabbed a thick wool cloak, and threw it over his shoulders. "Welcome to winter in Nor Torin. If anything, the weather will grow worse if we wait." He cinched the cloak so it covered his black coat and obscured the Chaos rune on his left breast. The man did not wear his crown, nor had there been any public announcement of his extended visit. "Don your cloak, Broland. It will help, especially once we're on the water."

As instructed, Broland gathered his cloak and trailed his father out the door. Two armed guards waited in the corridor, following when the king and prince headed toward the stairwell. A rapid descent brought them out a side door on the ground level.

A thin layer of white covered the courtyard, while footprints leading to the waiting carriage tainted the otherwise alabaster canvas. Eight mounted soldiers waited beside the carriage, half stationed ahead of it, the other half behind. Broland and his father headed straight for the open carriage door. Broland nodded to the driver who held the door as he climbed in. A man waited in the carriage, the same man who had been their host during their stay in Nor Torin.

"As I age," King Cassius said as Brock and Broland settled on the bench across from him, "I find that winter affects me more each year." The gray-haired man looked out the window at the drifting flakes. "Aches from injuries healed long ago return to haunt me. Perhaps Issal grants me pain as a reminder of the lives I have taken. Regardless, my...condition," he held a shaking hand before his face, "only exacerbates the issue."

"If you seek warmer weather, you could abdicate and put one of your boys on the throne," Brock suggested. "Cities in the south enjoy a warmer climate, and I'd be happy to have your wisdom among Kantarian royalty. In fact, Wayport will soon be in need of a new duke. I trust you, and I am confident you would be outstanding in that role."

Cassius shook his head as the carriage lurched into motion. "I appreciate the offer, Brock, but my place is here. My people are here." His gaze shifted to the window again as the carriage approached the citadel gate. "When I agreed to accept this crown, it was a life-long pact."

Brock reached over and gripped the man's arm. "I understand, old friend."

During his stay at Nor Torin, a visit that had lasted four weeks, Broland had discovered much about the king. Stories about Cassius DeSanus' exploits were common among the castle guards, despite the deeds behind those stories being decades old. As a captain in the Holy Army, an entity that no longer existed, Cassius had become a legend – a legend known as The Calm. Tall, strong, and athletic, his skill in wielding a sword had been unmatched while his demeanor during battle was consistently emotionless and calculating. The man's current condition might have made others doubtful of his legendary prowess, but Broland had grown up around General Budakis, a similar icon who had been subject to the same deadly poison that inflicted Cassius. The result left both men shells of the warriors they had once been.

Broland's thoughts turned sour as he recalled the general's murder – a murder at the hands of a trusted companion. *If I ever find you, Kony, you will discover the harsh reality of revenge.*

The carriage turned and began a downhill journey toward the harbor. Despite the weather, the city remained active and alive, unwilling to bend to nature's whims. It would require more than a few inches of snow to force the citizens of Nor Torin indoors.

"I want to thank you again for your help, Cassius," Brock said.

Cassius waved the comment aside. "Nonsense. This is not just your fight, Brock." He stared out the window, watching the snow drift past. "Left unchecked, the Empire will consume us all. We would then be right back to where we were twenty years ago. Regardless of what Varius and her ilk believe, it is wrong to condemn people simply because of an inherent ability. The ostracization of Unchosen during the Ministry's reign was wrong." He looked Brock in the eye. "What they plan now is…genocide. I find that downright evil."

"Regardless, I appreciate your support. Given the weapons we now face…"

Cassius nodded, his expression grim. "We dare not lose."

"Yes," Brock agreed. "But what price must we pay? I swore I would never again enlist civilians to fight a war for me, and yet I find myself recanting that oath. An oath is a promise backed by integrity. Without my integrity, what am I?"

"You are still a good man, Brock." There was an earnestness in Cassius' gaze as he stared at Broland's father. "Perhaps the best I have known."

The ground leveled and Broland looked out the window. The warehouses and docks of the harbor slid past. Empty wagons rolled down the docks, returning to the warehouses to reload. A cluster of armed guards, all dressed in the dark green and brown of Torinland, waited for them. The carriage drew to a stop, and a soldier marched forward to open the door.

Broland climbed out as a gust of wind struck, forcing him to blink away the snow and cinch his cloak tight. He yanked the hood over his head and turned his back on the wind.

Brock and Cassius were clasping forearms, leaning close as they spoke quietly. After a moment, Brock climbed out of the carriage and turned toward his fellow king.

"Issal willing, I'll see you in the spring."

Cassius nodded. "Until then, my friend, be well."

The carriage door closed, and the driver snapped the reins, the horses lurching into motion.

Brock turned and waved Broland forward. "Let's get on the ship and get out of this wind."

Turning, they headed toward the nearest pier, accompanied by an escort of twenty Torinland guards.

Four ships hugged the pier, two on each side, each vessel rocking gently as the water roiled. When he reached the first ship, Brock led Broland up the plank and on deck. Ten of the guards followed while the remainder continued on to the next vessel.

Two sailors unhooked the mooring lines, ran up the plank, and pulled it on board while others scurried about the ship, responding to the captain's commands. Broland looked up at the quarterdeck and found a familiar face – the same person shouting the commands. The ship's captain then turned toward a tall, rough-looking man and gave some direction before heading down to the main deck and walking purposefully toward Brock and Broland.

"Welcome aboard Razor, Your Majesty," Tenzi said with a shallow bow.

"Thank you, Captain." Brock replied in a loud voice before stepping closer, his volume dropping significantly. "I'm sorry we could not depart sooner, Tenzi. I know you are eager to free Parker and Dalwin, but...I must consider the bigger picture. There are far more than two lives at stake."

Tenzi pressed her lips together, her frustration apparent. "I just hope they are still..."

Brock put his hand on her shoulder. "As do I. Both men are my friends, but my crown does not allow me to place a higher value on their lives than that of thousands of subjects."

She looked away. "I know. I just feel so...helpless."

"We will recapture Wayport. And when we do, Chadwick and Illiri will pay for their betrayal."

"Oh, they will pay. If I have my way," she drew a knife and ran her finger along the blade. "It will be a very drawn out payment, one that might take days or weeks to complete."

"Tenzi...I cannot condone torture." Brock's tone was harder than steel.

"Fine," Tenzi sighed. She sheathed her dagger, and a gust of wind forced her to hold her hat down. "I have a ship to sail. Why don't you two rest in my cabin? It's warm in there now that I finally got the hole repaired. At least *that* came out of sitting here for eight days."

"Very well."

Tenzi turned and marched toward the quarterdeck with Brock and Broland trailing behind. When she climbed to the quarterdeck, the father and son duo ducked into the door beside the stairs.

The room was dark save for one window along the outer wall and a pale glowlamp on a wall sconce. Unlike the dark boards surrounding it, the far wall was constructed of fresh, pale planks. Broland rubbed his hands together and blew in them for warmth as he crossed the room and sat on the bed. In the meantime, Brock grabbed a chair, sat at the table, and withdrew a map from his coat. Broland watched as his father unfolded the map and spread it across the table.

"How long will it take to sail to Wayport?" Broland asked.

His father looked up at him, blinking in thought. "Remember, we have stops to make at Port Choya and Sunbleth. Even then, it depends on the weather. All things considered, I expect to land in Wayport ten days from now."

Broland had never been to Wayport. He had never been anywhere other than Kantar until now. The trip, their mission, led him to recall the day Tenzi had arrived in Nor Torin, a week earlier.

He and his father had been in Cassius' study, the two kings sharing conjecture as to what the Empire might do next. Cassius sat in the heart of the room, resting on a padded chair while Broland leaned against the wall and his father stared out the window beside him. The door opened, and a guard leaned in, drawing the attention of all three men.

"Excuse me, your Majesty. You have a visitor who…"

A short blond woman dressed in tight breeches and tall boots pushed past the guard, bursting into the room to address the Torinland king.

"Cassius, I need your help! Parker…" Tenzi stopped mid-sentence her mouth agape as she stared across the room. "Brock! You're alive!"

Broland's father shifted from his position beside the window, speaking as he crossed the room. "Yes. Very much so, I assure you."

"I heard you were assassinated." Tenzi's gaze flicked toward Broland. "Your son as well. And Ashland, she…"

"Ashland is fine." Brock stopped before Tenzi and put his hand on her shoulder. "She was in a coma, but awoke and has now recovered. She sits on the throne in my stead."

"Why are you here? Why does everyone believe you are dead?"

"They believe I am dead because that is what I wish them to believe." Brock clasped his hands behind his back as he paced. Broland had seen his father do it often, particularly when Brock was thinking aloud. "The Empire sent an assassin to kill me. I thought it best if they believed they had succeeded. By doing so, they will now focus else-where. While the Empire believes I am dead, I can move about freely and prepare a counter attack."

Brock stopped and looked at Broland. "As for my son's false death, it is for his protection. With me out of the way, he would be the

Empire's next target. Unfortunately, I fear Ashland has now become a target. It is a burden she has accepted, and Wharton will do what he must to protect her." Brock smiled. "Besides, our enemies will find my wife far from helpless."

Tenzi glanced toward Cassius and then looked back at Brock. "I need your help. Parker and Dalwin have been captured."

"Dalwin is alive?" Cassius said.

"Yes. But that may soon change." She pulled the black, wide-brimmed hat from her head and smoothed back her blond locks as she stared at Brock. "Your son and another warden freed Pretencia from the citadel dungeon in Sol Polis."

"Brandt?"

Tenzi nodded. "Yes, Brandt. Delvin put him on my ship and had me deliver him to Sol Polis. Two nights later, he returned to my ship with the king of Kalimar. We sailed off in the dark of night and made for Wayport. My ship required restocking, and I thought it best to notify Chadwick of the situation while I was in port…but Chadwick betrayed us. He has joined the Empire's cause, Brock. It sounds like they promised him all of Kantaria in return."

Brock's fists clenched tight, his knuckles turning white. "That slime. I'm sure it was Illiri who convinced him to switch sides. Chadwick bends to her will…or perhaps her beauty. Regardless, I wish he had never married that woman."

Tenzi nodded. "Illiri is a scheming wench for sure. While I was in the room, she forced Chadwick's betrayal after a young man with dark hair told him you were dead."

Broland's eyes narrowed. "A young man with black hair? Amber eyes?" He stood, holding his hand a few inches above his head. "About this tall?"

"Yeah. That sounds right."

"Kony," Broland growled.

"Yes. Kony." Tenzi nodded. "That was what Chadwick called him. After Kony informed Chadwick of your death, the duke called for our arrest. I made a run for it, barely escaping with my life. Parker and Dalwin were not so lucky. Both had been shackled and were headed to the dungeon." Tenzi's gaze shifted from Brock to Cassius and back to Brock. "I need your help to free them."

Brock stared at Tenzi for a long moment. Silence ruled the room, and Broland found himself holding his breath. Finally, Brock shifted closer to Tenzi, his hand on her arm.

"I will help them, but I cannot do it until we are ready." Brock's gaze locked on Cassius. "We are gathering forces, supplies, and ships. If we can use the Razor, it will make things go faster, but I cannot leave until I am ready."

Tenzi's fierce gaze softened, her eyes pleading. "Please, Brock. I don't want to lose him. I *can't* lose him."

Brock wrapped his arms about Tenzi, her head resting against his shoulder. "I know. He's my friend, too. However, this fight is bigger than just you and me. We fight for the freedom of thousands, and I cannot afford to be selfish. Just pray to Issal that he remains safe until we arrive. If he is in Wayport when we land, I will see him freed. I promise."

Broland saw the pain in his father's eyes as he said the words. For the first time, he thoroughly comprehended the difficult decisions one must make when ruling a country. His own desire for revenge suddenly seemed petty and selfish.

The ship rocked hard, the motion shaking Broland from the memory as he nearly fell off Tenzi's bed.

"We hit the breakers," his father said. "This might be an unpleasant journey with the storm over us."

The ship had cleared the relatively smooth waters of the harbor and the waves had grown tenfold. The room tilted and twisted as the ship rocked, seemingly bending Broland's vision as his stomach turned sour.

"I don't feel well." Broland's hand went to his stomach.

"Seasickness." Brock nodded, knowingly. "It's only your second voyage, and the last was quite tame. I suggest you go back outside and watch the shoreline until your stomach settles. It helps."

Without another word, Broland stood and stumbled toward the door.

As Broland closed the door behind him, a gust of wind struck and he raised his hood, holding it with one hand while the other pinched his cloak together. The deck tilted, and he staggered to the port-side rail, looking toward shore as the ship altered direction, gradually turning south. The shipyards along the coast appeared empty, dormant for the winter. The hull of a partially built ship, and the frames to hold another ship, appeared lonely and forgotten.

Seven other vessels trailed behind Tenzi's ship, all part of the armada Broland's father and King Cassius had gathered. Broland expected the fleet would double in size by the time they reached Wayport. Each was well stocked with food for the soldiers and the citizens who had been enlisted.

As the ships sailed farther from shore, the waves grew larger. When the Razor would rise, Broland's breakfast would rise with it. When the ship dipped, it only grew worse. Another rise and another dip caused his breakfast to find its way into the sea.

Once emptied, his stomach began to feel better. He wiped his mouth with the back of his hand and breathed in the fresh, cool air. The falling snow around him had turned to a cold mist, yet the tree-covered hillsides sliding past remained coated in white. Between him and the shoreline, waves struck black rocks jutting above the water, creating white sprays that fanned and fell in foam. He stared at the shoreline for a long while, hoping to stave off another wave of nausea. The scene was surreal, despite the cold.

The ship eased past a rocky point to reveal another sheltered bay, surrounded by the tall cliffs that defined most of the shoreline between Nor Torin and Kantar. In the bay, Broland spotted ships – a dozen or more. He frowned, wondering why ships might be moored in such an odd location. Sailors scurried about those ships, climbing the masts and unfurling the sails. Alarmed, Broland turned, hurried to the stairs, and climbed up to the quarterdeck.

Tenzi was at the helm, focused on the south horizon. Holding the rail beside her, Broland pointed and shouted.

"Why are those ships gathered in that bay?"

When she turned, Tenzi's eyes narrowed. "Those are Ri Starian vessels. It's rare to see them along this coast."

Broland's father had emerged from the cabin and was climbing to the quarterdeck. "Ri Star? What are they doing down here?"

The Ri Starian ships raised anchor and began drifting toward deeper water as the Razor and the trailing armada sailed past. Tenzi called for another sailor to take the helm while she dug out a tube with glass on each end. She pointed it toward the ships and looked through the tube, watching the Ri Starian ships sail out of the bay.

With shock, she gasped. "Flash cannons! They plan to attack!"

"What?" Broland mumbled as he turned toward the approaching fleet.

A flash of green fire and a puff of smoke billowed from the lead Ri Starian ship. A boom followed, and a projectile struck the trailing ship of the Torin armada, sending a blast of splinters into the air.

"This is bad," Brock's tone was grim. "Queen Olvaria has thrown her lot in with the Empire."

Broland cast his mind back to what his lore instructor taught him about Ri Star. Among the other notes, of which there were few, one thing had remained firmly entrenched in his memory. Ri Starian ships were the fastest in the world. In addition, they were now armed with flash cannons.

Another Ri Starian ship fired, its projectile also striking the trailing Torin ship, this time near the waterline. The wounded ship rocked, tilted to one side, and turned toward shore, but it was too late. The ship was slowing and sinking while sailors and passengers scrambled for the lifeboat.

Broland stared in transfixed horror as he watched the ship sink with the enemy fleet sailing past it. He suddenly realized the gravity of the situation. Enemy ships were in pursuit, armed with flash canons and gaining on them. The Razor might be their next target.

NOTE FROM THE AUTHOR

I hope you enjoyed An Imperial Gambit and that you look forward to book four in the Wardens of Issalia series, set to release in Spring, 2019.

For the inside scoop on my writing, notifications of new releases, and alerts about various fantasy book giveaways, sign up for my author newsletter at www.jeffreylkohanek.com.

Best Wishes,
Jeffrey L. Kohanek

BOOKS BY JEFFREY L. KOHANEK

Runes of Issalia
The Buried Symbol: Runes of Issalia Book 1
The Emblem Throne: Runes of Issalia Book 2
An Empire in Runes: Runes of Issalia Book 3
Runes of Issalia ebook Boxed Set
* * *
Heroes of Issalia: Runes Series+Rogue Legacy
* * *
Rogue Legacy: Runes of Issalia Prequel

Wardens of Issalia
A Warden's Purpose: Wardens of Issalia Book 1
The Arcane Ward: Wardens of Issalia Book 2
An Imperial Gambit: Wardens of Issalia Book 3
More coming in 2019…

Printed in Great Britain
by Amazon